THE SECRET SEVEN
COLLECTION

THE SECRET SEVEN COLLECTION

ENID BLYTON

Hodder
Children's
Books

a division of Hodder Headline Limited

This collection first published in Great Britain in 2004 by
Hodder Children's Books
Secret Seven first published in Great Britain in 1949
Secret Seven Adventure in Great Britain in 1950
Well Done, Secret Seven in Great Britain in 1951
Secret Seven on the Trail in Great Britain in 1952
Revised editions published in Great Britain in 1992

For further information on Enid Blyton please contact
www.blyton.com

2 4 6 8 10 9 7 5 3 1

A Catalogue record for this book is available
from the British Library

ISBN 0 340 89364 8

Typeset by Hewer Text Limited, Edinburgh
Printed and bound in Great Britain by
Clays Ltd, St Ives plc

The paper used in this book is a natural recyclable product
made from wood grown in sustainable forests.
The hard coverboard is recycled.

Hodder Children's Books
a division of Hodder Headline Limited
338 Euston Road
London NW1 3BH

CONTENTS

THE SECRET SEVEN

CONTENTS

CHAPTER ONE

Plans for an S.S. meeting

'WE'D BETTER have a meeting of the Secret Seven,' said Peter to Janet. 'We haven't had one for ages.'

'Oh, yes, let's!' said Janet, shutting her book with a bang. 'It isn't that we've forgotten about the Society, Peter – it's just that we've had such a lot of exciting things to do in the Christmas holidays we simply haven't had time to call a meeting.'

'But we must,' said Peter. 'It's no good having a Secret Society unless we use it. We'd better send out messages to the others.'

'Five notes to write,' groaned Janet. 'You're quicker at writing than I am, Peter – you write three and I'll write two.'

'Woof!' said Scamper, the golden spaniel.

'Yes, I know you'd love to write one, too, if you could,' said Janet, patting the silky golden head. 'You can carry one in your mouth to deliver. That can be *your* job, Scamper.'

'What shall we say?' said Peter, pulling a piece of paper towards him and chewing the end of his pen as he tried to think of words.

5

'Well – we'd better tell them to come here, I think,' said Janet. 'We could use the old shed at the bottom of the garden for a meeting-place, couldn't we? Mummy lets us play there in the winter because it's next to the boiler that heats the greenhouse, and it's quite warm.'

'Right,' said Peter, and he began to write. 'I'll do this message first, Janet, and you can copy it. Let's see – we want one for Pam, one for Colin, one for Jack, one for Barbara – who's the seventh of us? I've forgotten.'

'George, of course,' said Janet. 'Pam, Colin, Jack, Barbara, George, you and me – that's the seven – the Secret Seven. It sounds nice, doesn't it?'

The Seven Society was one that Peter and Janet had invented. They thought it was great fun to have a little band of boys and girls who knew the password, and who wore the badge – a button with S.S. on.

'There you are,' said Peter, passing his sheet of paper to Janet. 'You can copy that.'

'It doesn't need to be my *best* writing, does it?' said Janet. 'I'm so slow if I have to do my best writing.'

'Well – so long as it's readable,' said Peter. 'It hasn't got to go by post.'

Janet read what Peter had written: 'IMPORTANT. A meeting of the Secret Seven will be held tomorrow morning in the shed at the bottom of our garden at 10 o'clock. Please give PASSWORD.'

'Oh – what *was* the last password we had?' said Janet in alarm. 'It's so long since we had a meeting that I've forgotten.'

'Well, it's a good thing for you that you've got me to remind you,' said Peter. 'Our latest password was Wenceslas, because we wanted a Christmassy one. Fancy you forgetting that!'

'Oh, yes, of course. Good King Wenceslas,' said Janet. 'Oh, dear – now I've gone and made a mistake in this note already. I really mustn't talk while I'm doing it.'

There was a silence as the two of them wrote their notes. Janet always wrote with her tongue out, which made her look very funny. But she said she couldn't write properly unless her tongue *was* out, so out it had to come.

Peter finished first. He let Scamper lick the envelopes. He was good at that; he had such a nice big wet tongue.

'You're a very licky dog,' said Peter, 'so you must be pleased when you have things like this to lick. It's a pity we're not putting stamps on the letters, then you could lick those, too.'

'Now shall we go and deliver the secret messages?' said Janet. 'Mummy said we could go out; it's a nice sunny morning – even if it is cold!'

'Woof! woof!' said Scamper, running to the door when he heard the word 'out'. He pawed at the door impatiently.

Soon the three of them were out in the frost and snow. It was lovely. They went to Colin's first. He was out, so they left the note with his mother.

Then to George's. He was in, and was very excited when he heard about the meeting to be held in the shed.

Then to Pam's. Jack was there too, so Peter left two notes. Then there was only Barbara left. She was away!

'Bother!' said Peter. But when he heard she was coming back that night he was pleased. 'Will she be able to come and see us tomorrow morning?' he asked Barbara's mother, and she said yes, she thought so.

'Well, that's all five,' said Janet as they turned to go home. 'Come on, Scamper. We'll go for a run in the park.'

They had a lovely time in the park, throwing snowballs and making tracks in the crisp new snow. Scamper discovered a frozen pond. He stepped on to the ice but his legs slid out from under him. He struggled to stand up, but couldn't. In the end the laughing children had to haul him off the pond.

Scamper was cross. He turned and growled at the pond. He didn't understand it at all. He could drink it in the summer, and paddle in it – now look at it! Something strange had happened, and he didn't like it.

That afternoon the two children and Scamper went down to the old shed. It was warm, because the boiler was going well nearby to heat the big greenhouse. Peter looked round.

'It feels quite cosy. Let's arrange boxes for seats – and get the old garden cushions out. And we'll ask

Mummy if we can have some lemonade or something, and biscuits. We'll have a really proper meeting!'

They pulled out some boxes and fetched the old cushions. They laid sacks on the ground for a carpet, and Janet cleaned a little shelf to put the lemonade and biscuits on, if their mother let them have them.

'There are only five boxes that are sittable on,' said Peter. 'Someone will have to sit on the floor.'

'Oh, no – there are two enormous flowerpots in the

corner over there,' said Janet. 'Let's drag them out and turn them upside down. They'll be fine to sit on then.'

So, with the five boxes and the two flowerpots, there were seats for everyone.

The bell rang for tea. 'Well, we've just finished nicely,' said Peter. 'I know what I'm going to do tonight, Janet.'

'What?' asked Janet.

'I'm going to draw two big letter Ss,' said Peter, 'and colour them green – cut them out, mount them on cardboard, and then stick them to the door of the shed.'

'Oh, yes – S.S. – Secret Seven,' said Janet. 'That would be *grand*!'

CHAPTER TWO

The Secret Seven Society

THE NEXT MORNING five children made their way to Old Mill House, where Peter and Janet lived. It took its name from the ruined mill that stood up on the hill, some distance away, which had not been used for many years.

George came first. He walked down the garden and came to the shed. The first thing he saw was the sign on the door, S.S. There it was, bold and clear in bright green.

He knocked on the door. There was a silence. He knocked again. Still no reply, though he felt sure that Peter and Janet were there because he was certain he had seen Janet's face at the little window of the shed.

He heard a snuffling under the door. That must be Scamper! He knocked again, impatiently.

'Give the password, silly!' said Peter's voice.

'Oh, I forgot,' said George. 'Wenceslas!'

The door opened at once. George grinned and went in. He looked round. 'This is very cosy. Is it to be our meeting-place these hols?'

'Yes. It's nice and warm here,' said Peter. 'Where's your badge? Your button with S.S. on?'

'Bother – I forgot it,' said George. 'I hope I haven't lost it.'

'You're not a very good member,' said Janet sternly. 'Forgetting to say the password, and forgetting your badge as well.'

'Sorry,' said George. 'To tell you the truth I'd almost forgotten about the Secret Society too!'

'Well, you don't deserve to belong then,' said Peter.

'Just because we haven't met for some time! I do think—'

There was another knock at the door. It was Pam and Barbara. There was silence in the shed. Everyone was listening for the password.

'Wenceslas,' hissed Barbara, in such a peculiar voice that everyone jumped.

'Wenceslas,' whispered Pam. The door opened, and in they went.

'Good – you're both wearing your badges,' said Peter, pleased. 'Now where are Colin and Jack? They're late.'

Jack was waiting for Colin at the gate. He had forgotten the password! Oh dear, whatever could it be? He thought of all sorts of things – Nowell – Wise Men – what *could* it be? He felt sure it was something to do with Christmas carols.

He didn't like to go to the meeting-place without knowing the password. Peter could be very strict. Jack didn't like being ticked off in front of people, and he racked his brains to try to think of the word. He saw Colin away in the distance and decided to wait for him. Colin would be sure to know the word!

'Hallo!' said Colin, as he came up. 'Seen the others yet?'

'I saw Pam and Barbara going in,' said Jack. 'Do you know the password, Colin?'

'Of course I do,' said Colin.

'I bet you don't!' said Jack.

'Well, I do – it's Wenceslas!' said Colin. 'Aha – sucks to you, Jack – you thought I didn't know it!'

'Thanks for telling me,' grinned Jack. 'I'd forgotten it. Don't tell Peter. Come on down the path. Hey! Look at the S.S. for Secret Seven on the door.'

They knocked. 'WENCESLAS,' said Colin in a very loud voice.

The door opened quickly and Peter's indignant face looked out. 'Whatever are you shouting for? Do you want everyone in the village to know our password, you fool?'

'Sorry,' said Colin, going in. 'Anyway, there's nobody but us to hear.'

'Wenceslas,' said Jack, seeing that Peter was not going to let him in without the password. The door shut and the seven settled down. Peter and Janet took the flowerpots for themselves. Everyone else sat on the boxes.

'This is a great meeting-place,' said George. 'Warm and cosy, and right away from the house.'

'Yes. I must say you and Janet have made it very comfortable,' said Barbara. 'Even a little curtain at the window.'

Peter looked round at the little company. 'We'll

16

have our meeting first, and then we'll have the eats and drinks,' he said.

Everyone's eyes went to the neat little shelf behind Colin. On it were arranged seven mugs, a plate of oatmeal biscuits, and a bottle of some dark-looking liquid. Whatever could it be?

'First of all,' went on Peter, 'we must arrange a new password, because Wenceslas doesn't seem right for after Christmas – besides, Colin yelled it out at the

top of his voice, so everyone probably knows it now.'

'Don't be so—' began Colin, but Peter frowned at him sternly.

'Don't interrupt. I'm the head of this society, and I say we will choose a new password. Also I see that two of you are not wearing your badges. George and Colin.'

'I told you I forgot about mine,' said George. 'I'll find it when I get home.'

'And I think I must have *lost* mine,' said Colin. 'I didn't forget it. I hunted all over the place. My mother says she'll make me another tonight.'

'Right,' said Peter. 'Now what about a new password?'

'Hey-diddle-diddle,' said Pam, with a giggle.

'Be sensible,' said Peter. 'This society is a serious one, not a silly one.'

'I thought of one last night,' said Jack. 'Would "Weekdays" do?'

'What's the sense of that?' asked Peter.

'Well – there are seven days in a week, aren't there – and we're the Seven Society,' said Jack. 'I thought it was rather good.'

'Oh, I see. Yes – it *is* rather good,' said Peter. 'Though actually, there are only five *week*days! Hands up those who think it's good.'

Everybody's hand went up. Yes, 'Weekdays' was a

good idea for a password for the Seven! Jack looked pleased.

'Actually I forgot our password today,' he confessed. 'I got it out of Colin. So I'm glad I've thought of a new one for us.'

'Well, nobody must forget this one,' said Peter. 'It might be very important. Now what about some grub?'

'Delumptious,' said Barbara, and everyone laughed.

'Do you mean "delicious" or "scrumptious"?' asked Janet.

'Both, of course,' said Barbara. 'What's that peculiar-looking stuff in the bottle, Janet?'

Janet was shaking it vigorously. It was a dark purple and had little black things bobbing about in it.

'Mummy hadn't any lemonade to give us, and we didn't particularly want milk because we'd had lots for breakfast,' she said. 'So we suddenly thought of a pot of blackcurrant jam we had! This is blackcurrant tea!'

'We mixed it with boiling water and put some more sugar into it,' explained Peter. 'It's really good – in fact, it's scrumplicious!'

'Oh – *that's* a mixture of scrumptious and delicious, too!' said Barbara with a squeal of laughter. 'Delumptious and scrumplicious – that just describes everything nicely.'

The blackcurrant tea really was good, and went very well with the oatmeal biscuits. 'It's good for colds, too,' said Janet, crunching up the skinny blackcurrants from her mug. 'So if anyone's getting a cold they probably won't.'

Everyone understood this peculiar statement and nodded. They set down their mugs and smacked their lips.

'It's a pity there's no more,' said Janet. 'But there wasn't an awful lot of jam left in the pot, or else we could have made heaps to drink.'

'Now, we have a little more business to discuss,' said Peter, giving Scamper a few crumbs to lick. 'It's no good having a Society unless we have some plan to follow – something to *do*.'

'Like we did in the summer,' said Pam. 'You know

20

– when we collected money to send some disabled children to the seaside.'

'Yes. Well, has anyone any ideas?' said Peter.

Nobody had. 'It's not really a good time to try and help people after Christmas,' said Pam. 'I mean – everyone's had presents and been looked after, even the very poorest, oldest people in the village.'

'Can't we solve a mystery, or something like that?' suggested George. 'If we can't find something wrong to put right, we might be able to find a mystery to clear up.'

'What kind of a mystery do you mean?' asked Barbara, puzzled.

'I don't really know,' said George. 'We'd have to be on the lookout for one – you know, watch for something strange or peculiar – and solve it.'

'It sounds exciting,' said Colin. 'But I don't believe we'd find anything like that – and if we did the police would have found it first!'

'Oh, well,' said Peter, 'we'll just have to keep our eyes open and wait and see. If anyone hears of any good deed we can do, or of any mystery that wants solving, they must at once call a meeting of the Secret Seven. Is that understood?'

Everyone said yes. 'And if we have anything to report we can come here to this Secret Seven shed and leave a note, can't we?' said George.

'That would be the best thing to do,' agreed Peter. 'Janet and I will be here each morning, and we'll look and see if any of you have left a note. I hope somebody does!'

'So do I. It's not much fun having a Secret Society that doesn't *do* anything,' said Colin. 'I'll keep a really good lookout. You never know when something might turn up.'

'Let's go and build snowmen in the field opposite the old house down by the stream,' said George, getting up. 'The snow's thick there. It would be fun. We could build quite an army of snowmen. They'd look funny standing in the field by themselves.'

'Oh, yes. Let's do that,' said Janet, who was tired of sitting still. 'I'll take this old shabby cap to put on one of the snowmen! It's been hanging in this shed for ages.'

'And I'll take this coat!' said Peter, dragging down a dirty, ragged coat from a nail. 'Goodness knows who it ever belonged to!'

And off they all went to the field by the stream to build an army of snowmen!

CHAPTER THREE

The cross old man

THEY DIDN'T build an army, of course! They only had time to build four snowmen. The snow was thick and soft in the field, and it was easy to roll it into big balls and use them for the snowmen. Scamper had a lovely time helping them all.

Janet put the cap on one of the snowmen, and Peter put the old coat round his snowy shoulders. They found stones for his eyes and nose, and a piece of wood for his mouth. They gave him a stick under his arm. He looked the best of the lot.

'I suppose it's time to go home now,' said Colin at last. 'My dinner's at half-past twelve, worse luck.'

'We'd better all go home,' said Pam. 'We'll all have to wash and change our things and put our gloves to dry. Mine are soaking and oooh, my hands are cold!'

'So are mine. I know they'll hurt awfully as soon as they begin to get a bit warm,' said Barbara, shaking her wet hands up and down. 'They're beginning now.'

They left the snowmen in the field and went out of the nearby gate. Opposite was an old house. It was empty except for one room at the bottom, where dirty curtains hung across the window.

'Who lives there?' asked Pam.

'Only a caretaker,' said Janet. 'He's very old and very deaf – and awfully bad-tempered.'

They hung over the gate and looked at the desolate old house.

'It's quite big,' said Colin. 'I wonder who it belongs to, and why they don't live in it.'

'Isn't the path up to the house lovely and smooth with snow?' said Janet. 'Not even the caretaker has trodden on it. I suppose he uses the back gate. Oh, Scamper – you naughty dog, come back!'

Scamper had squeezed under the gate and gone bounding up the smooth, snowy path. The marks of his feet were clearly to be seen. He barked joyfully.

The curtains at the ground-floor window moved and a cross, wrinkled old face looked out. Then the window was thrown up.

'You get out of here! Take your dog away! I won't have children or dogs here, pestering little varmints!'

Scamper stood and barked boldly at the old caretaker. He disappeared. Then a door opened at the side of the house and the old man appeared, with a big stick. He shook it at the alarmed children.

'I'll whack your dog till he's black and blue!' shouted the man.

'Scamper, Scamper, come here!' shouted Peter. But Scamper seemed to have gone completely deaf. The caretaker advanced on him grimly, holding the stick up to hit the spaniel.

Peter pushed open the gate and tore up the path to Scamper, afraid he would be hurt.

'I'll take him, I'll take him!' he shouted to the old man.

'What's that you say?' said the cross old fellow, lowering his stick. 'What do you want to go and send your dog in here for?'

'I didn't. He came in himself!' called Peter, slipping his fingers into Scamper's collar.

'Speak up, I can't hear you,' bellowed the old man, as if it was Peter who was deaf and not himself. Peter bellowed back:

'I DIDN'T SEND MY DOG IN!'

'All right, all right, don't shout,' grumbled the caretaker. 'Don't you come back here again, that's all, or I'll send the police after you.'

He disappeared into the side door again. Peter marched Scamper down the drive and out of the gate.

'What a bad-tempered man,' he said to the others. 'He might have hurt Scamper awfully if he'd hit him with that great stick.'

Janet shut the gate. 'Now you and Scamper have spoilt the lovely smooth path,' she said. 'Goodness, there's the church clock striking a quarter to one. We'll really have to hurry!'

'We'll let you all know when the next meeting is!' shouted Peter, as they parted at the corner. 'And don't forget the password and your badges.'

They all went home. Jack was the first in because he

lived very close. He rushed into the bathroom to wash his hands. Then he went to brush his hair.

'I'd better put my badge away,' he thought, and put up his hand to feel for it. But it wasn't there. He frowned and went into the bathroom. He must have dropped it.

He couldn't find it anywhere. He must have dropped it in the field when he was making the snowmen with the others. Bother! Blow!

'Mother's away, so she can't make me a new one,' he thought. 'And I'm sure Miss Ely wouldn't.'

Miss Ely was his sister's nanny. She liked Susie, Jack's sister, but she thought Jack was dirty, noisy and bad-mannered. He wasn't really, but somehow he never did behave very well with Miss Ely.

'I'll ask her if she *will* make one,' he decided. 'After all, I've been very good the last two days.'

Miss Ely might perhaps have said she would make him his badge if things hadn't suddenly gone wrong at dinner-time.

'*I* know where you've been this morning,' said Susie, slyly, when the three of them were at the table. 'Ha, ha. You've been to your silly Secret Society. You think I don't know anything about it. Well, I do!'

Jack glared at her. 'Shut up! You ought to know better than to talk about other people's secrets in public. You just hold that horrid, interfering tongue of yours.'

'Don't talk like that, Jack,' said Miss Ely at once.

'What's the password?' went on the annoying Susie. 'I know what the last one was because you wrote it down in your notebook so as not to forget and I saw it! It was—'

Jack kicked out hard under the table, meaning to get Susie on the shin. But most unfortunately Miss

Ely's long legs were in the way. Jack's boot hit her hard on the ankle.

She gave a loud cry of pain. 'Oh! My ankle! How dare you, Jack! Leave the table and go without your dinner. I shall not speak another word to you all day long, if that is how you behave.'

'I'm awfully sorry, Miss Ely,' muttered Jack, scarlet with shame. 'I didn't mean to kick *you*.'

'It's the kicking that matters, not the person,' said Miss Ely, coldly. 'It doesn't make it any better knowing that you meant to kick Susie, not me. Leave the room, please.'

Jack went out. He didn't dare to slam the door, though he felt like it. He wasn't cross with Susie any more. He had caught sight of her face as he went out of the room, and had seen that she was alarmed and upset. She had meant to tease him, but she hadn't meant him to lose his dinner.

He kicked his toes against each step as he went upstairs. It was a pity he'd been sent out before the jam tarts were served. He liked those so much. Blow Miss Ely! Now she certainly wouldn't make a new badge for him, and probably he would be turned out of the Society for losing it. Peter had threatened to do that to anyone who turned up more than once without a badge.

'I seem to remember something falling off me when

I was making that last snowman,' thought Jack. 'I think I'll go out and look this afternoon. I'd better go before it snows again, or I'll never find it.'

But Miss Ely caught him as he was going out and stopped him. 'No, Jack. You are to stay in today, after that extraordinary behaviour of yours at the dinner-table,' she said sternly. 'You will not go out to play any more today.'

'But I want to go and find something I lost, Miss Ely,' argued Jack, trying to edge out.

'Did you hear what I said?' said Miss Ely, raising her voice, and poor Jack slid indoors again.

All right! He would simply go out that night then, and look with his torch. Miss Ely should *not* stop him from doing what he wanted to do!

CHAPTER FOUR

What happened to Jack

JACK WAS as good as his word. He went up to bed at his usual time, after saying a polite good night to Miss Ely, but he didn't get undressed. He put on his coat and cap instead! He wondered whether he dared go downstairs and out of the garden door yet.

'Perhaps I'd better wait and see if Miss Ely goes to bed early,' he thought. 'She sometimes goes up to read in bed. I don't want to be caught. She'd only go and tell tales when Mother comes home.'

So he took a book and sat down. Miss Ely waited for the nine o'clock news on the radio and then she locked up the house and came upstairs. Jack heard her shut the door of her room.

Good! Now he could go. He slipped his torch into his pocket, because it really was a very dark night. The moon was not yet up.

He crept downstairs quietly and went to the garden door. He undid it gently. The bolt gave a little squeak but that was all. He stepped into the garden. His feet sank quietly into the snow.

He made his way to the lane and went down it to

the field, flashing his little torch as he went. The snow glimmered up, and there was a dim whitish light all round from it. He soon came to the field where they had built the snowmen, and he climbed over the gate.

The snowmen stood silently in a group together, almost as if they were watching and waiting for him. Jack didn't altogether like it. He thought one moved, and he drew his breath in sharply. But, of course, it hadn't. It was just his imagination.

'Don't be silly,' he told himself, sternly. 'You know they're only made of snow! Be sensible and look for your dropped button!'

He switched on his torch and the snowmen gleamed whiter than ever. The one with eyes and nose and mouth, with the cap and the coat on, seemed to look at him gravely as he hunted here and there. Jack turned his back on him.

'You may only have stone eyes, but you seem to be able to *look* with them, all the same,' he said to the silent snowman. 'Now don't go tapping me on the shoulder and make me jump!'

Then he suddenly gave an exclamation. He had found his badge! There lay the button in the snow, with S.S. embroidered on it, for Secret Seven. Hurrah! He must have dropped it here after all then.

He picked it up. It was wet with snow. He pinned it carefully on his coat. That really *was* a bit of luck to find it so easily. Now he could go home and get into bed. He was cold and sleepy.

His torch suddenly flickered, and then went out. 'Bother!' said Jack. 'The battery's gone. It *could* have lasted till I got home, really it could! Well, it's a good thing I know my way.'

He suddenly heard a noise down the lane, and saw the headlights of a car. It was coming very slowly. Jack was surprised. The lane led nowhere at all. Was the car lost? He'd better go and put the driver on the right road, if so. People often got lost when the roads were snowbound.

He went to the gate. The car came slowly by and then Jack saw that it was towing something – something rather big. What could it possibly be?

The boy strained his eyes to see. It wasn't big enough for a removal van, and yet it looked rather like the shape of one. It wasn't a caravan either, because there were no wide windows at the side. *Were* there any windows at all? Jack couldn't see any. Well, whatever *was* this curious van?

And where was it going? The driver simply *must* have made a mistake! The boy began to climb over the gate. Then he suddenly sat still.

The car's headlights had gone out. The car itself had stopped, and so had the thing it was towing. Jack could make out the dark shapes of the car and the van behind, standing quite still. What was it all about?

Somebody spoke to somebody else in a low voice. Jack could see that one or two men had got out of the car, but he could not hear their footsteps because of the snow.

How he wished the moon was up, then he could hide behind the hedge and see what was happening! He heard a man's voice speaking more loudly.

'Nobody about, is there?'

'Only that deaf fellow,' said another voice.

'Have a look, will you?' said the first voice. 'Just in case.'

Jack slipped quickly down from the gate, as he saw a powerful torch flash out. He crouched behind the snowy hedge, scraping snow over himself. There came the soft crunch of footsteps walking over frosty snow by the hedge. The flashlight shone over the gate and the man gave an exclamation.

'Who's there? Who are you?'

Jack's heart beat so hard against him that it hurt. He was just about to get up and show himself, and say who he was, when the man at the gate began to laugh.

'My word – look here, Nibs – a whole lot of snowmen standing out here! I thought they were alive at first, watching for us! I got a scare all right.'

Another man came softly to the first and he laughed too. 'Kids' work, I suppose,' he said. 'Yes, they look real all right, in this light. There's nobody about here at this time of night, Mac. Come on – let's get down to business.'

They went back towards the car. Jack sat up, trembling. What in the world could the men be doing down here in the snowy darkness, outside an old empty house? Should he try to see what they were up to? He didn't want to in the least. He wanted to go home as quickly as he could!

He crept to the gate again. He heard strange sounds from where the men were – as if they were unbolting something – opening the van perhaps.

And then there came a sound that sent Jack helter-skelter over the gate and up the lane as fast as his legs would take him! An angry, snorting sound, and then a curious high squeal – and then a noise of a terrific struggle, with the two men panting and grunting ferociously.

Jack couldn't think for the life of him what the noise was, and he didn't care, either. All he wanted was to get home before anything happened to *him*. Something was happening to somebody, that was certain, out there in the snowy lane. It would need a very, very brave person to go and interfere – and Jack wasn't brave at all, that night!

He came to his house, panting painfully. He crept in at the garden door and locked and bolted it. He went upstairs, not even caring if the stairs creaked under his feet! He switched on the light in his bedroom. Ah – that was better. He didn't feel so scared once he had the light on.

He looked at himself in the glass. He was very pale, and his coat was covered with snow. That was through lying in the snowy ditch below the hedge. He caught sight of his badge, still pinned on to his coat. Well, anyhow, he had *that*.

'I went out to find my badge – and goodness knows what else I've found,' thought the boy. 'Gosh – I must tell the others. We must have a meeting tomorrow. This is something for the Secret Seven! Wow! What a thrill for them!'

He couldn't wait to tell them the next day. He must slip out again – and go to the shed at the bottom of Peter's garden. He must leave a note there, demanding a meeting at once!

'It's important. Very, very important,' said Jack to himself, as he scribbled a note on a bit of paper. 'It really is something for the Society to solve.'

He slipped down the stairs again, and out of the garden door. He wasn't frightened any more. He ran all the way up the lane and round to Peter's house. The farmhouse stood dark and silent. Everyone was in bed; they did not stay up late at the farm.

Jack went down to the old shed. He fumbled at the door. It was locked. His hands felt the big letters, S.S., on the door itself. He bent down and slid his note under the crack at the bottom. Peter would find it the next day.

Then home he went again to bed – but not to sleep. Who had made that noise? What was that strange high van? Who were the men? It really was enough to keep anybody awake for hours!

CHAPTER FIVE

Exciting plans

NEXT MORNING Janet went down to the shed by herself. Peter was brushing Scamper. He was well and truly brushed every single morning, so it was no wonder his coat shone so beautifully.

'Just open the shed and give it an airing,' ordered Peter. 'We shan't be using it today. There won't be any meeting yet.'

Janet skipped down the path, humming. She took the key from its hiding-place – a little ledge beneath the roof of the shed – and slipped it into the lock. She opened the door.

The shed smelt rather stuffy. She left the door open and went to open the little window too. When she turned round she saw Jack's note on the floor.

At first she thought it was an odd piece of waste paper, and she picked it up and crumpled it, meaning to throw it away. Then she caught sight of a word on the outside of the folded paper.

'URGENT. VERY IMPORTANT INDEED.'

She was astonished. She opened the paper out and

glanced down it. Her mouth fell open in amazement. She raced out of the shed at top speed, yelling for Peter.

'Peter! PETER! Where are you? Something's happened, quick!'

Her mother heard her and called to her. 'Janet, Janet, what's the matter, dear? What's happened?'

'Oh – nothing, Mummy,' called back Janet, suddenly remembering that this was Secret Society business.

'Well, why are you screeching for Peter like that?' said her mother. 'You made me jump.'

Janet flew up the stairs to where Peter was still brushing Scamper. 'Peter! Didn't you hear me calling? I tell you, something's happened!'

'What is it?' asked Peter, surprised.

'Look – I found this paper when I went to the shed this morning,' said Janet, and she gave him Jack's note. 'It's marked "Urgent. Very Important Indeed". Look what it says inside.'

Peter read out loud what Jack had written:

Peter, call a meeting of the Secret Seven at once. Very important Mystery to solve. It happened to me last night about half-past nine. Get the others together at ten if you can. I'll be there.

Jack

'What on *earth* does he mean?' said Peter, in wonder. 'Something happened to *him* last night? Well, why is it such a mystery then? I expect he's exaggerating.'

'He's not, he's not. I'm sure he's not,' cried Janet, dancing from one foot to another in her excitement. 'Jack doesn't exaggerate, you know he doesn't. Shall I go and tell the others to come at ten if they can? Peter, it's exciting. It's a mystery!'

'You wait and see what the mystery is before you

get all worked up,' said Peter, who, however, was beginning to feel rather thrilled himself. 'I'll go and tell Colin and George – you can tell the girls.'

Janet sped off in one direction and Peter in another. How lovely to have to call a meeting already – and about something so exciting too.

It was about half-past nine when the two came back. Everyone had promised to come. They were all very anxious to know what Jack had got to say.

'Remember your badges,' Janet said to the two girls. 'You won't be admitted to an important meeting like this unless you know the password and have your badge.'

Everyone turned up early, eager to hear the news. Everyone remembered the password, too.

'Weekdays!' and the door was opened and shut.

'Weekdays,' and once more the door was opened and shut. Member after member passed in, wearing the badge and murmuring the password. Both Colin and George had their badges this morning. George had found his and Colin's mother had already made him one.

Jack was the last of all to arrive, which was most annoying because everyone was dying to hear what he had to say. But he came at last.

'Weekdays,' said his voice softly, outside the shed

door. It opened and he went in. Everybody looked at him expectantly.

'We got your note, and warned all the members to attend this meeting,' said Peter. 'What's up, Jack? Is it really important?'

'Well, you listen and see,' said Jack, and he sat down on the box left empty for him. 'It happened last night.'

He began to tell his story – how he had missed his badge and felt certain he had dropped it in the field where the snowmen were – how he had slipped out with his torch to find it, and what he had heard and seen from the field.

'That frightful noise – the snorting and the horrid squeal!' he said. 'It nearly made my hair stand on end. Why did those men come down that lane late at night? It doesn't lead anywhere. It stops a little further on just by a large holly hedge. And what could that thing be that they were towing behind?'

'Was it a cage, or something – or was it a closed van where somebody was being kept prisoner?' said Barbara, in a half-whisper.

'It wasn't a cage as far as I could see,' said Jack. 'I couldn't even see any windows to it. It was more like a small removal van than anything – but whatever was inside wasn't furniture. I tell you it snorted and squealed and struggled.'

'Was it a man inside, do you think?' asked Pam, her eyes wide with interest and excitement.

'No. I don't think so. It might have been, of course,' said Jack. 'But a man doesn't snort like that. Unless he had a gag over his mouth, perhaps.'

This was a new thought and rather an alarming one. Nobody spoke for a minute.

'Well,' said Jack, at last, 'it certainly is something for the Secret Seven to look into. There's no doubt about that. It's all very mysterious – very mysterious indeed.'

'How are we going to tackle it?' said George.

They all sat and thought. 'We had better find out if

we can tell anything by the tracks in the snow,' said Peter. 'We'll find out too if there are car-tracks up the drive to that old house.'

'Yes. And we could ask the old caretaker if he heard anything last night,' said Colin.

'Bags I don't do that,' said Pam at once. 'I'd hate to go and ask him questions.'

'Well, somebody's got to,' said George. 'It might be important.'

'And we might try and find out who owns the old empty house,' said Colin.

'Yes,' said Peter. 'Well, let's split up the inquiries. Pam, you go with George and see if you can find out who owns the house.'

'How do we find out?' asked Pam.

'You will have to use your common sense,' said Peter. 'I can't decide *every*thing. Janet, you and Barbara can go down the lane and examine it for car-tracks and anything else you can think of.'

'Right,' said Janet, glad that she hadn't got to question the caretaker.

'Colin, Jack and I will go into the drive of the old house and see if we can get the caretaker to tell us anything,' said Peter, feeling rather important as he made all these arrangements.

'What's Scamper to do?' asked Janet.

'He's going to come with *us*,' said Peter. 'In case the

caretaker turns nasty! Old Scamper can turn nasty too, if he has to!'

'Oh, yes – that's a good idea, to take Scamper,' agreed Jack, relieved at the thought of having the dog with him. 'Well – shall we set off?'

'Yes. Meet and report here this afternoon,' said Peter. 'You've discovered a most exciting mystery, Jack, and it's up to the Secret Seven to solve it as soon as they can!'

CHAPTER SIX

Finding out a few things

ALL THE Secret Seven set off at once, feeling extremely important. Scamper went with Peter, Colin and Jack, his tail well up, and he also felt very important. He was mixed up in a Mystery with the Society! No wonder he turned up his nose at every dog he met.

They left Pam and George at the corner, looking rather worried. The two looked at one another. '*How* are we going to find out who owns the house?' said Pam.

'Ask at the post office!' said George, feeling that he really had got a very bright idea. 'Surely if the house is owned by someone who has put in a caretaker, there must be letters going there.'

'Good idea!' said Pam, and they went off to the post office. They were lucky enough to see a postman emptying the letters from the letter-box outside. George nudged Pam.

'Come on. We must start somewhere. We'll ask him!'

They went up to the man. 'Excuse me,' said George. 'Could you tell us who lives at the old house down by the stream – you know, the empty house there?'

'How can anyone live in an empty house?' said the postman. 'Don't ask silly questions and waste my time! You children – you think you're so funny, don't you?'

'We didn't mean to be funny, or cheeky either,' said Pam in a hurry. 'What George means is – who owns the house? There's a caretaker there, we know. We just wondered who the house belongs to.'

'Why? Thinking of buying it?' said the postman, and laughed at his own joke. The children laughed too, wishing the man would answer their question.

'How would I know who owns the place?' he said, emptying the last of the letters into his sack. 'I never take letters there except to old Dan the caretaker, and he only gets one once in a month – his wages, maybe. Better ask at the estate agent's over there. They deal with houses, and they might know the owner – seeing as you're so anxious to find him!'

'Oh, *thank* you,' said Pam, joyfully, and the two of them hurried across to the estate agent's. 'We might have thought of this ourselves,' said Pam. 'But hold on – what shall we say if the man here asks why we want to know? You only go to an estate agent's if you want to buy or sell a house, don't you?'

They peeped in at the door. A boy of about sixteen

sat at a table there, addressing some envelopes. He didn't look very frightening. Perhaps *he* would know – and wouldn't ask them why they wanted the name of the owner.

They went boldly in. The boy looked up. 'What do you want?' he said.

'We've been told to ask who owns the old house down by the stream,' said George, hoping the boy might think that some grown-up had sent him to find out. Actually it was only Peter, of course, but he didn't see why he should say so.

'I don't think the house is on the market,' said the boy, turning over the pages of a big book. 'Do your parents want to buy it, or something? I didn't know it was to be sold.'

The two children said nothing, because they didn't really know what to say. The boy went on turning over the pages.

'Ah – here we are,' he said. 'No – it's not for sale – it was sold to a Mr J. Holikoff some time ago. Don't know why he doesn't live in it, I'm sure!'

'Does Mr Holikoff live anywhere here?' asked Pam.

'No – his address is 64, Heycom Street, Covelty,' said the boy, reading it out. ' 'Course, I don't know if he lives there now. Do your people want to get in touch with him? I can find out if this is his address now, if you like – he's on the telephone at this address.'

'Oh, no, thank you,' said George hastily. 'We don't want to know anything more, as the house is – er – not for sale. Thank you very much. Good morning.'

They went out, rather red in the face, but very pleased with themselves. 'Mr Holikoff,' said Pam to George. 'It's a peculiar name, isn't it? Do you remember his address, George?'

'Yes,' said George. He took out his notebook and wrote in it: 'Mr J. Holikoff, 64, Heycom Street, Covelty. Well, we've done our part of the job! I wonder how the others are getting on.'

They were getting on quite well. Janet and Barbara were busy examining the tracks down the lane that led to the stream. They felt quite like detectives.

'See – the car with the van behind, or whatever it was, turned into the lane from the direction of Templeton; it didn't come from our village,' said Janet. 'You can see quite clearly where the wheels almost wènt into the ditch.'

'Yes,' said Barbara, staring at them. 'The tracks of the van wheels are narrower than the wheels of the car that towed it, Janet. And look – just here in the snow you can see *exactly* what the pattern was on the wheels of the van. Not of the car, though – they're all blurred.'

'Don't you think it would be a good idea to take a note of the pattern of the tyre?' said Janet. 'I mean – it just *might* come in useful. And we could measure the width of the tyre print too.'

'I don't see how those things can possibly matter,' said Barbara, who wanted to go down the lane and join the three boys.

'Well, I'm going to try and copy the pattern,' said Janet firmly. 'I'd like to have *some*thing to show the boys!'

So, very carefully, she drew the pattern in her notebook. It was a funny pattern, with lines and circles and V-shaped marks. It didn't really look very good when she had done it. She had measured the print as best she could. She had no tape-measure with her, so she had placed a sheet from her notebook over the track, and had marked on it the exact size. She felt rather pleased with herself, but she did wish she had drawn the pattern better. Barbara laughed when she saw it. 'Goodness! What a mess!' she said.

Janet looked cross and shut her notebook up. 'Let's follow the tracks down the lane now,' she said. 'We'll see exactly where they go. Not many vans come down here – we ought to be able to follow the tracks easily.'

She was quite right. It was very easy to follow them. They went on and on down the lane – and then stopped outside the old house. There were such a lot of different marks there that it was difficult to see exactly what they were – footprints, tyre-marks, places where the snow had been kicked and ruffled up – it was hard to tell anything except that this was where people had got out and perhaps had had some kind of struggle.

'Look – the tyre-marks leave all this mess and go

on down the lane,' said Janet. She looked over the gate. Were the boys in the old house with the caretaker?

'Let's go and see if we can find the boys,' said Barbara.

'No. We haven't quite finished our job yet,' said Janet. 'We ought to follow the tracks as far as they go. Come on – we'll see if they go as far as the stream. There are *two* lots of tracks all down the lane, as we saw – so it's clear that the car and trailer went down, and then up again. We'll find out where they turned.'

That was easy. The tracks went down to a field-gate, almost to the stream. Someone had opened the gate, and the car had gone in with the trailer, and had made a circle there, come out of the gate again, and returned up the lane. It was all written clearly in the tyre-tracks.

'Well, that's the story of last night,' said Janet, pleased at their discoveries. 'The car and the thing it was pulling came from the direction of Templeton, turned down into this lane, stopped outside the old house, where people got out and messed around – and then went down to the field, someone opened the gate, the car and trailer went in and turned, and came out again and went up the lane – and disappeared into the night. Who or what it brought in the trailer-van goodness knows!'

'Funny thing to do at that time of night,' said Barbara.

'Very odd,' agreed Janet. 'Now let's go back to the old house and wait for the boys.'

'It's almost one o'clock,' said Barbara. 'Do you think they're still there?'

They hung over the gate and watched and listened. To their horror the old caretaker came rushing out as soon as he saw them, his big stick in his hand.

'More of you!' he cried. 'You wait till I get you. You'll feel my stick all right. Pestering, interfering children! You just wait!'

But Barbara and Janet didn't wait! They fled up the lane in fright, as fast as they could possibly go in the soft thick snow.

CHAPTER SEVEN

A talk with the caretaker

THE THREE boys and Scamper had had an exciting time. They had gone down the lane, noting the car-tracks as they passed. They came to the old house. They saw that the gate was shut. They leaned over the top and saw tracks going up the drive.

'There's my footprints that I made yesterday morning,' said Peter, pointing to them. 'And look, you can see Scamper's paw-marks here and there too – but our tracks are all overlaid with others – bigger footmarks – and other marks too, look – rather strange.'

'A bit like prints that would be made by someone wearing great flat, roundish slippers,' said Jack, puzzled. 'Who would wear slippers like that? Look, you can see them again and again, all over the place. Whoever wore them was prancing about a bit! Probably being dragged in.'

The boys leaned over the gate and considered all the marks carefully. They traced them with their eyes as far as they could see. 'Can any of you make out if the tracks go up the front door steps?' said Colin. 'I can't from here – but it rather looks to me as if the snow is smooth up the steps – not trampled at all.'

'I can't make out from here,' said Peter. 'Let's go up the drive. After all, we've got to interview the caretaker and find out if he heard anything last night. So we've got to go in.'

'What shall we say if he asks us why we want to know?' said Colin. 'I mean – if he's in this mystery, whatever it is, he may be frightfully angry if he thinks we know anything about it.'

'Yes, he might,' said Peter. 'We'll have to be rather clever over this. Let's think.'

They thought. 'I can't think of anything except to sort of lead him on a bit – ask him if he isn't afraid of burglars and things like that,' said Peter at last. 'See if we can make him talk.'

'All right,' said Colin. 'But it seems a bit feeble. Let's go in.'

Scamper ran ahead down the drive. He disappeared round a corner. The boys followed the footprints carefully, noting how the slipper-like ones appeared everywhere, as if the owner had gone from side to side and hopped about like mad!

'They *don't* go up the front door steps,' said Colin. 'I thought they didn't! They go round the side of the house – look here – right past the side door where the caretaker came out yesterday – and down this path – and round to the kitchen door!'

'Well – how strange!' said Peter, puzzled. 'Why did everyone go prancing round to the kitchen door when there's a front door and a side door? Yes – all three

tracks are here – two sets of shoe-prints – and those funny round slipper-prints too. It beats me!'

They tried the kitchen door, but it was locked. They peered in at the window. The kitchen was completely bare and empty. But they saw a gas-stove, a sink piled with plates, and a bucket nearby when they looked through the scullery window.

'I suppose the caretaker has the use of the scullery and that front room in the house,' said Jack.

'Look out – here he is!' said Peter suddenly.

The old man was shuffling into the empty kitchen. He saw the three boys through the window and went to fling it open in a rage.

'If you want that dog of yours, he's round in the front garden!' he shouted. 'You clear out. I won't have kids round here. You'll be breaking windows before I know where I am!'

'No, we shan't,' shouted Jack, determined to make the deaf old man hear. 'We'll just collect our dog and go. Sorry he came in here.'

'Aren't you rather lonely here?' shouted Colin. 'Aren't you afraid of burglars?'

'No. I'm not afraid, ' said the old fellow, scornfully. 'I've got my big stick – and there's nothing to steal here.'

'Somebody's been round to the back door, all the same,' shouted Peter, seeing a chance to discuss this bit of mystery with the caretaker and see if he knew anything about it. He pointed to all the tracks leading to the back door. The old man leaned out of the window and looked at them.

'They're no more than the tracks you've made yourself, tramping about where you've no business to be!' he said angrily.

'They're not. I bet it was burglars or something last night,' said Peter, and all three boys looked closely at the caretaker to see if his face changed in any way.

'Pah!' he said. 'Trying to frighten me, are you, with your silly boys' nonsense!'

'No. I'm not,' said Peter. 'Didn't you hear anything at all last night? If burglars *were* trying to get in, wouldn't you hear them?'

'I'm deaf,' said the old man. 'I wouldn't hear nothing at all – but wait now – yes, I did think I heard something last night. I'd forgotten it. Ah – that's odd, that is.'

The boys almost forgot to breathe in their excitement. 'What did you hear?' said Jack, forgetting to shout. The old man took no notice. He frowned, and his wrinkled face became even more wrinkled.

'Seems like I heard some squealing or some such noise,' he said slowly. 'I thought it was maybe some noise in my ears – I get noises often, you know – and I didn't go to see if anything was up. But, there now, nobody took nothing nor did any damage – so what's the use of bothering? If people want to squeal, let 'em, I say!'

'Was the squealing in the house?' shouted Peter.

'Well, I guess I wouldn't hear any squealing *out-side*,' said the old man. 'I'm deaf as a post, usually. Ah, you're just making fun of me, you are – trying to frighten an old man. You ought to be ashamed of yourselves!'

'Can we come in and look round?' shouted Colin, and the others looked eagerly at the caretaker. If only he would say yes! But he didn't, of course.

'What are you thinking of, asking to come in!' he cried. 'I know you kids – pestering creatures – wasting my time like this. You clear out and don't you come here again with your tale of burglars and such. You keep away. Kids like you are always up to mischief.'

Just at that moment Scamper came bounding up. He saw the old caretaker at the window and leapt up at him, in a friendly manner. The man jumped in alarm. He thought Scamper was trying to snap at him. He leaned forward and aimed a blow at him through the window with his stick. Scamper dodged and barked.

'I'm going to teach that dog a lesson!' cried the old man, in a fury. 'Yes, and you too – standing out there being cheeky! I'll teach you to make fun of me, you and your dog!'

He disappeared. 'He's going to dart out of the side door,' said Peter. 'Come on – we've learnt all we want to know. We'll go!'

CHAPTER EIGHT

Another meeting

THE MEETING that afternoon was very interesting and full of excitement. Everyone had something to report. They came punctually to the old shed, giving the password without a pause.

'Weekdays!'

'Weekdays!'

'Weekdays!' One after another the Seven passed in, and soon they were sitting round the shed. They all looked very important. Scamper sat by Peter and Janet, his long ears drooping down like a judge's wig, making him look very wise.

'Pam and George – you report first,' said Peter.

So they reported, telling how they had found out that the old house had been sold to a Mr J. Holikoff some time back, although he had never lived in it.

'Did you get his address?' asked Peter. 'It might be important.'

'Yes,' said George, and produced his notebook. He read the address.

'Good. We might have to get in touch with him if

we find that he ought to know something strange is going on in his empty house,' said Peter.

Pam and George felt very proud of themselves. Then the two girls reported. They told how they had discovered that the tracks came from the direction of the town of Templeton, and had gone down to the gates of the old house, where it was plain that they had stopped, as Jack had noticed the night before, when he heard the car. Then they told how the tracks had gone into the field, circled round and come out again – and had clearly gone up the lane and back the way they came.

'Good work,' said Peter. Janet took out her notebook and went rather red in the face.

'I've just got this to report, too,' she said, showing the page of the notebook on which she had tried to draw the tyre pattern. 'I don't expect it's much use, really – it's the pattern on the tyres of the van or trailer or lorry, or whatever it was that was pulled behind the car. And I measured the width, too.'

Everyone looked at the scribbled pattern. It didn't look anything much, but Peter seemed pleased.

'Even if it's no use, it was a good idea to do it,' he said. 'Just suppose it *was* some use – and the snow melted – your drawing would be the only pattern we had to track down the tyres.'

'Yes,' said Colin, warmly. 'I think that was good, Janet.'

Janet glowed with pride. She put away her note-book. 'Now you three boys report,' she said, though she herself had already heard part of it from Peter while they were waiting for the others to come that afternoon.

Peter made the report for the three of them. Every-one listened in silence, looking very thrilled.

'So, you see,' finished Peter, '*some*body went to the old house last night, got in through the kitchen door,

because the footsteps went right to there – and I think
they left a prisoner behind!'

Pam gasped. 'A prisoner! What do you mean?'

'Well, isn't it clear that there was a prisoner in that
big window-less van – a prisoner who was not to be
seen or heard – someone who was dragged round to
the kitchen and forced inside – and hidden somewhere in that house? Somebody who was hurt and
who squealed loudly enough for even the old deaf
caretaker to hear?' said Peter.

Everyone looked upset and uncomfortable.

'I don't like it,' said Colin. Nobody liked it. It was
horrid to think of a poor, squealing prisoner locked
up somewhere in that old, empty house.

'What about his food?' said Colin, at last.

'Yes – and water to drink,' said Janet. 'And *why* is he locked up there?'

'Kidnapped, perhaps,' said Jack. 'You know – this is really very serious, if we're right.'

There was a silence. 'Ought we to tell our parents?' asked Pam.

'Or the police?' said Jack.

'Well – not till we know a little bit more,' said Peter. 'There might be some quite simple explanation of all this – a car losing its way or something.'

'I've just thought of something!' said Jack. 'That van – could it have been some sort of ambulance, do you think! You know, the van that ill people are taken to hospitals in? Maybe it was, and the car took the wrong turning, and stopped when it found it had gone wrong. And the ill person cried out with pain, or something.'

'But the caretaker said he heard squealing too, inside the house,' said Peter. 'Still, that might have been some noises in his head, of course, like those he says he sometimes has. Well – it's an idea, Jack – it *might* have been an ambulance, pulled by a car, though I can't say I've ever seen one like the one you describe.'

'Anyway, we'd better not tell anyone till we've *proved* there's something odd going on,' said Colin. 'We should feel so silly if we reported all this to the police and then they found it was just something perfectly ordinary!'

'Right. We'll keep the whole thing secret,' said Peter. 'But, of course, we've got to do something about it ourselves. We can't leave it.'

'Of *course* we've got to do something,' said George. 'But what?'

'We'll think,' said Peter. So they all thought again. What would be the best move to make next?

'I've thought of something,' said Jack at last. 'It's a bit frightening, though.'

'Whatever is it?' chorused the others.

'Well – it seems to me that if there *is* a prisoner

locked up in one of the rooms of the old house, he will have to be fed and given water,' said Jack. 'And whoever does that would have to visit him at night. See? So what about us taking it in turn at night to go and watch outside the old house to see who goes in – then we might even follow them and see where they go, and who they've got there!'

'It seems a very good idea,' said Peter. 'But we'd have to watch two at a time. I wouldn't want to go and hide somewhere there all by myself!'

'*I* think that probably someone will be along to-night,' said George. 'Why shouldn't all four of us boys go and wait in hiding?'

'It would be difficult for four of us to hide and not be seen,' said Colin.

'Well – let's drape ourselves in white sheets or something and go and join the snowmen in the field!' said Peter, jokingly. To his surprise the other three boys pounced on his idea eagerly.

'Oh, *yes*, Peter – that's fine! Nobody would ever guess we weren't snowmen if we had something white round us!' said Colin.

'We get a good view of the lane, and could see and hear anyone coming along,' said George.

'Two could follow anyone into the house and two remain on guard outside, as snowmen, to give warning in case the other two got into trouble,' said Jack.

'I'd love to stand there with the snowmen! We'd have to wrap up jolly warmly, though.'

'Can't we girls come too?' asked Pam.

'I don't want to!' said Barbara.

'No,' said Peter. 'I am sorry but seven is too many. We'll have more chance of success if there are only four of us.'

'What about Scamper?' asked Jack, his eyes gleaming with excitement. 'Shall we take him?'

'We'd better, I think,' said Peter. 'He'll be absolutely quiet if I tell him.'

'I'll make him a little white coat,' said Janet. 'Then he won't be seen either. He'll look like a big lump of snow or something!'

They all began to feel very excited. 'What time shall we go?' said Colin.

'Well, it was about half-past nine, wasn't it, when the men arrived last night,' said Jack. 'We'll make it the same time then. Meet here at about nine tonight. My goodness – this *is* a bit of excitement, isn't it?'

CHAPTER NINE

Out into the night

JANET SPENT the whole of the afternoon making Scamper a white coat. Peter borrowed a ragged old sheet, and found an old white macintosh. He thought he could cut up the sheet and make it do for the other three, it was so big.

Janet helped him to cut it up and make arm-holes and neck-holes. She giggled when he put one on to see if it was all right.

'You do look peculiar,' she said. 'What about your head – how are you going to hide your dark hair? It will be moonlight tonight, you know.'

'We'll have to try and make white caps or something,' said Peter. 'And we'll paint our faces white!'

'There's some whitewash in the shed,' said Janet, with another giggle. 'Oh, dear – you *will* all look strange. Can I come to the shed at nine, Peter, and just see you all before you go?'

'All right – if you can creep down without anyone seeing you,' said Peter. 'I think Mummy's going out tonight, so it should be all right. If she's not, you mustn't come in case you make a noise and spoil the whole thing.'

Mummy *was* going out that night. Good! Now it would be easy to slip down to the shed. Peter told Janet she must wrap up very warmly indeed – and if she had fallen asleep she was not to wake up!

'I *shan't* fall asleep,' said Janet, indignantly. 'You know I couldn't possibly. Mind *you* don't.'

'Don't be silly,' said Peter. 'As if the leader in an important plan like this could fall asleep! My word, Janet – the Secret Seven are in for an adventure this time!'

At half-past eight the children's lights were out, and didn't go on again. But torches lit up their rooms, and Janet was very, very busy dressing up Scamper in his new white coat. He didn't like it at all, and kept biting at it.

'Oh, Scamper – you won't be allowed to go unless you look like a snow-dog!' said Janet, almost in despair. And whether or not Scamper understood what she said she didn't know – but from that moment he let her dress him up without any more trouble. He looked peculiar and very mournful.

'Come on, if you're coming – it's almost nine,' said a whispering voice. It was Peter's. Together the two children and Scamper crept down the stairs. They were very warmly wrapped up indeed – but as soon as they got out into the air they found that it was not nearly as cold as they expected.

'The snow's melting! There's no frost tonight,' whispered Janet.

'Gosh, I hope those snowmen won't have melted,' said Peter, in alarm.

'Oh, they won't *yet*,' said Janet. 'Come on – I can see one of the others.'

The passwords were whispered softly at the door of the shed, and soon there were five of the Secret Seven there. Peter lit a candle, and they all looked at one another in excitement.

'We've got to paint our faces white and put on our white things,' said Peter. 'Then we're ready.'

Jack giggled. 'Look at Scamper! He's in white too! Scamper, you look ridiculous.'

'Woof,' said Scamper, miserably. He *felt* ridiculous, too! Poor Scamper.

With squeals and gurgles of laughter the four boys painted their faces white. They had carefully put on their white things first so as not to mess up their overcoats. Janet fitted the little white skull caps she had roughly made, over each boy's head.

'Well! I shouldn't like to meet you walking down the lane tonight!' she said. 'You look terrifying!'

'Time we went,' said Peter. 'Goodbye, Janet. Go to

bed now and sleep tight. I'll tell you our adventures in the morning! I shan't wake you when I come in.'

'I shall stay awake till you come!' said Janet.

She watched them go off down the moonlit path, a row of weird white figures with horrid white faces. They really did look like walking snowmen, as they trod softly over the soft, melting snow.

They made their way quietly out of the gate and walked in the direction of the lane that led to the old house, keeping a sharp lookout for any passers-by.

They met no one except a big boy who came so quietly round a corner in the snow that not one of the four heard him. They stopped at once when they saw him.

He stopped too. He gazed at the four white snowmen in horror.

'Ooooh!' he said. 'Ow! What's this? Who are you?'

Peter gave a dreadful groan, and the boy yelled in alarm. 'Help! Four live snowmen! Help!'

He tore off down the road, shouting. The four boys collapsed in helpless giggles against the fence behind.

'Oh, dear!' said Jack. 'I nearly burst with laughter when you did that groan, Peter.'

'Come on – we'd better get away quickly before the boy brings somebody back here,' and they went chuckling on their way. They came to the lane where the old house stood and went down it. They soon came to the old house. It stood silent and dark, with its roof white in the moonlight.

'Nobody's here yet,' said Peter. 'There's no light anywhere in the house, and not a sound to be heard.'

'Let's go and join the merry gang of snowmen then,' said Jack. 'And I wish you'd tell Scamper not to get between my feet so much, Peter. He'll trip me up in this sheet thing I'm wearing.'

They climbed over the gate and went into the field. The snowmen still stood there, but alas! they were melting and were already smaller than they had been in the morning. Scamper went and sniffed at each one solemnly. Peter called him.

'Come here! You've got to stand as still as we do – and remember, not a bark, not a growl, not a whine!'

Scamper understood. He stood as still as a statue beside Peter. The boys looked for all the world like neat snowmen as they stood there in the snowy field.

They waited and they waited. Nobody came. They waited for half an hour and then they began to feel cold. 'The snow is melting round my feet,' complained Jack. 'How much longer do you think we've got to stand here?'

The others felt tired of it too. Gone were their ideas of staying half the night standing quietly with the snowmen! Half an hour was more than enough.

'Can't we go for a little walk, or something?' said Colin, impatiently. 'Just to get us warm.'

Peter was about to answer when he stopped and stiffened. He had heard something. What was it?

Colin began to speak again. 'Sh!' said Peter. Colin stopped at once. They all listened. A far-away sound came to their straining ears.

'It's that squealing noise,' said Jack, suddenly. 'I know it is! Only very faint and far away. It's coming from the old house. There is somebody there!'

Shivers went down their backs. They listened again, and once more the strange, far-away sound came on the night air.

'I don't like it,' said Peter. 'I'm going to the old house to see if I can hear it there. I think we ought to tell someone.'

'Let's all go,' said Colin. But Peter was quite firm about that.

'No. Two to go and two to remain on guard. That's what we said. Jack, you come with me. Colin and George, stay here and watch.'

Peter and Jack, two weird white figures with

strange white faces, went to the field gate, climbed it, and went to the gate of the old house. They opened it and shut it behind them. There was no noise at all to be heard now.

They went quietly up the drive, keeping to the shadows in case the old caretaker might possibly be looking out. They went to the front door and looked through the letter-box. Nothing was to be seen through there at all. All was dark inside.

They went to the side door. It was fastened, of course. Then they went to the back door and tried that. That was locked, too. Then they heard a strange thudding, thundering noise from somewhere in the house. They clutched at one another. What *was* going on in this old empty house?

'Look! That old man has left this window a bit open – the one he spoke to us out of this morning,' whispered Jack, suddenly.

'Goodness – has he, really? Then what about getting in and seeing if we can find the prisoner?' whispered Peter, in excitement.

It only took a minute or two to climb up and get inside. They stood in the dark kitchen, listening. There was no noise to be heard at all. Where could the prisoner be?

'Dare we search the whole house from top to bottom?' said Peter. 'I've got my torch.'

'Yes, we dare, because we must,' answered Jack. So, as quietly as they could they tiptoed into first the scullery and then an outhouse. Nobody there at all.

'Now into the hall and we'll peep into the rooms there,' said Peter.

The front rooms were bright with moonlight but the back rooms were dark. The boys pushed open each door and flashed the torch round the room beyond. Each one was silent and empty.

They came to a shut door. Sounds came from behind it. Peter clutched Jack. 'Somebody's in here. I expect the door's locked, but I'll try it. Stand ready to run if we're chased!'

CHAPTER TEN

In the old empty house

THE DOOR wasn't locked. It opened quietly. The sounds became loud at once. Somebody was in there, snoring!

The same thought came to both boys at once. It must be the caretaker! Quietly Peter looked in.

Moonlight filled the room. On a low, untidy bed lay the old caretaker, not even undressed! He looked dirty and shabby, and he was snoring as he slept. Peter turned to go – and his torch suddenly knocked against the door and fell with a crash to the floor.

He stood petrified, but the old man didn't stir. Then Peter remembered how deaf he was! Thank goodness – he hadn't even *heard* the noise! He shut the door quietly and the two boys stood out in the hall. Peter tried his torch to see if he had broken it. No, it was all right. Good.

'Now we'll go upstairs,' he whispered. 'You're not afraid, are you, Jack?'

'Not very,' said Jack. 'Just a *bit*. Come on.'

They went up the stairs that creaked and cracked in

a very tiresome manner. Up to the first floor with five or six rooms to peep into – all as empty as one another. Then up to the top floor.

'We'll have to be careful now,' said Jack. He spoke in such a whisper that Peter could hardly hear him. 'These are the only rooms we haven't been into. The prisoner must be here somewhere.'

IN THE OLD EMPTY HOUSE

All the doors were ajar! Well, then, how could there be a prisoner – unless he was tied up? The two boys looked into each room, half-scared in case they saw something horrid.

But there was absolutely nothing there at all. The rooms were either dark and empty, or full of moonlight and nothing else.

'It's strange, isn't it?' whispered Jack. 'Honestly I don't understand it. Surely those noises *did* come from the house somewhere? Yet there's nothing and no one here except the old caretaker!'

They stood there, wondered what to do next – and once more that far-away, muffled squealing came on the night air, a kind of whinnying noise, followed by a series of curious thuds and crashes.

'There *is* a prisoner here somewhere – and he's knocking for help – and squealing too,' said Peter, forgetting to whisper. 'Somewhere downstairs. But we've looked everywhere.'

Jack was making for the stairs. 'Come on – we must have missed a cupboard or something!' he called.

Down they went, not caring now about the noise they made. They came to the kitchen. The noises had stopped again. Then the thudding began once more. Jack clutched Peter.

'I know where it's coming from – under our feet! There's a cellar there. *That's* where the prisoner is!'

'Look for the cellar door then,' said Peter. They found it at last, in a dark corner of the passage between kitchen and scullery. They turned the handle – and what a surprise – the door opened!

'It's not locked!' whispered Jack. 'Why doesn't the prisoner escape then?'

Stone steps led downwards into the darkness. Peter flashed his torch down them. He called, in rather a shaky voice:

'Who's there? Who is it down there?'

There was no answer at all. The boys listened with straining ears. They could distinctly hear the sound of very heavy breathing, loud and harsh.

'We can hear you breathing!' called Jack. 'Do tell us who you are. We've come to rescue you.'

Still no reply. This was dreadful. Both boys were really scared. They didn't dare to go down the steps. Their legs simply refused to move downwards. Yet it seemed very cowardly to go back into the passage again.

And then another sound came to them – the sound of low voices somewhere! Then came the sound of a key being turned in a lock – and a door being opened!

Jack clutched Peter in a panic. 'It's those men I heard last night. They're back again. Quick – we must hide before they find us here.'

The two boys, strange little figures in white, stood for a moment, not knowing where to go. Then Peter stripped off his white sheet and cap. 'Take yours off, too,' he whispered to Jack. 'We shan't be so easily seen in our dark overcoats, if we slip into the shadows somewhere.'

They threw their things into a corner and then slipped into the hall. They crouched there in a corner, hoping that the men would go straight down into the cellar.

But they didn't. 'Better see if that old caretaker is asleep,' said a voice, and two men came into the hall to open the caretaker's door.

And then one of them caught sight of Peter's white-washed face, which gleamed eerily out of the middle of the dark shadows. Peter had forgotten his face was white!

'Good gracious – look there – in that corner! Whatever is it?' cried one of the men. 'Look – over there, Mac.'

The men looked towards the corner where the two boys were crouching. 'Faces! White faces!' said the other man. 'I don't like it. Here, switch on your torch. It's just a trick of the moonlight or something.'

A powerful torch was switched on, and the two boys were discovered at once! With a few strides the man called Mac went over to them. He picked up both boys at once, gave them a rough shake and set them on their feet.

'Now then – what's the meaning of this – hiding here with your faces all painted up like that! What are you doing?'

'Let go of my arm. You're hurting,' said Jack, angrily. 'The thing is – what are *you* up to?'

'What do you mean?' said the man roughly.

The thudding noise began again, and the two boys looked at the men.

'That's what I mean,' said Jack. 'Who's down there? Who are you keeping prisoner?'

Jack got a clout on the head that made him see stars. Then he and Peter were dragged to a nearby cupboard and locked in. The men seemed furiously angry for some reason or other.

Peter put his ear to the crack and tried to hear what they were saying.

'What are we going to do now? If those kids get anyone here, we're done.'

'Right. Keep the kids here too, then. Put them down with Kerry Blue! We'll fetch him tomorrow night and clear off, and nobody will know anything. The job will be done by then.'

'What about the kids?'

'We'll leave them locked up here – and send a card to the old caretaker to tell him to look down in his cellar the day after tomorrow. He'll get a shock when he finds the kids prisoners there! Serve them right, little pests.'

Peter listened. Who was Kerry Blue? What a peculiar name! He trembled when he heard the men coming to the door. But they didn't unlock it. One of them called through the crack.

'You can stay there for a while. Teach you to come poking your noses into what's no business of yours!'

Then began various curious noises. Something seemed to be brought into the scullery. The boys heard the crackling of wood as if a fire was being lit. Then a nasty smell came drifting through the cracks of the door.

'Oooh! They're boiling something. Whatever is it?' said Peter. 'Horrible smell!'

They couldn't think what it was. They heard a lot of squealing again, and some snorting, and a thundering noise like muffled hooves thudding on stone. It was all very, very extraordinary.

The cupboard, made to take a few coats, was small and cold and airless. The two boys were very uncomfortable. They were glad when one of the men unlocked the door and told them to come out.

'Now, you let us go,' began Peter, and got a rough blow on his shoulder at once.

'No cheek from you,' said one of the men and hustled the boys to the cellar door. He thrust both of them through it, and they half-fell down the top steps. The door shut behind them. They could hear it being locked. Blow, bother! Bother! Now *they* were prisoners too!

A noise came from below them. Oh dear – was Kerry Blue down there, whoever he was? 'Switch your torch on,' whispered Jack. 'For goodness sake let's have a look at the prisoner and see what he's like!'

CHAPTER ELEVEN

The prisoner

PETER SWITCHED on his torch, his hand trembling as he did so. What were they going to see?

What they saw was so surprising that both boys gave a gasp of amazement. They were looking down on a beautiful horse, whose pricked ears and rolling eyes showed that he was as scared as they were!

'A *horse*!' said Jack, feebly. 'It's a *horse*!'

'Yes – that squealing was its frightened whinny – and thudding was its hooves on the stone floor when it rushed about in panic,' said Peter. 'Oh, Jack – poor, poor thing! How *wicked* to keep a horse down here like this! Why do they do it!'

'It's such a beauty. It looks like a racehorse,' said Jack. 'Do you suppose they've stolen it? Do you think they're hiding it here till they can change it to another colour, or something – horse thieves do do that, you know – and then sell it somewhere under a different name?'

'I don't know. You may be right,' said Peter. 'I'm going down to him.'

'Aren't you afraid?' said Jack. 'Look at his rolling eyes!'

'No, I'm not afraid,' said Peter, who was quite used to the horses on his father's farm, and had been brought up with them since he was a baby. 'Poor thing – it wants talking to and calming.'

Peter went down the steps, talking as he went. 'So

you're Kerry Blue, are you? And a beautiful name it is, too, for a beautiful horse! Don't be frightened, beauty. I'm your friend. Just let me stroke that velvety nose of yours and you'll be all right!'

The horse squealed and shied away. Peter took no notice. He went right up to the frightened creature and rubbed his hand fearlessly down its soft nose. The horse stood absolutely still. Then it suddenly nuzzled against the boy and made funny little snorting sounds.

'Jack, come on. The horse is friendly now,' called Peter. 'He's such a beauty. What brutes those men are to keep a horse down in a dark cellar like this. It's enough to make it go mad!'

Jack came down the steps. He stroked the horse's back and then gave an exclamation. 'Ugh! He feels sticky and wet!'

Peter shone his torch on to the horse's coat. It gleamed wetly. 'Jack! You were right! Those men *have* been dyeing him!' cried Peter. 'His coat's still wet with the dye.'

'And that's the horrid smell we smelt – the dye being boiled up ready to use,' said Jack. 'Poor old Kerry Blue! What have they been doing to you?'

The horse had a mass of straw in one corner and a rough manger of hay in another. Oats were in a heavy pail. Water was in another pail.

'Well, if *we* want a bed, we'll have to use the straw,' said Peter. 'And have oats for a feed!'

'We shan't need to,' said Jack. 'I bet old Colin and George will come and look for us soon. We'll shout the place down as soon as we hear them!'

They settled down on the straw to wait. Kerry Blue decided to lie down on the straw too. The boys leaned against his warm body, wishing he didn't smell so strongly of dye.

Up in the field, where the snow was now rapidly melting, Colin and George had been waiting impatiently for a long time. They had seen Jack and Peter disappear over the gate, and had had a difficult time holding Scamper back, because he wanted to follow them. They had stood there quietly for about half an hour, wondering whenever Peter and Jack were coming back, when Scamper began to growl.

'He can hear something,' said Colin. 'Yes – a car – coming down the lane. I do hope it's not those men again. Jack and Peter will be caught, if so!'

The car had no trailer-van behind it this time. It stopped at the gate of the old house and two men got out. Scamper suddenly barked loud, and was at once cuffed by Colin. 'Idiot!' hissed Colin. 'Now you've given us away!'

One of the men came to the field gate at once. He gazed at the six snowmen. 'Come and look here!' he called to the other man, who went to stand beside him. How Colin and George trembled and quaked!

'What? Oh, we saw the snowmen there last night. Don't you remember?' he said. 'Some kids have been messing about again today and built a few more. Come on. That dog we heard barking must be a stray one about somewhere.'

The men left the gate and went up the drive to the house. Colin and George breathed freely again. That was a narrow escape! Thank goodness for their white faces, caps and sheets! Thank goodness Scamper was in white, too.

For a long time there was no sound at all. Colin and George got colder and colder and more and more impatient. WHAT was happening? They wished they knew. Were Jack and Peter caught?

At last, just as they thought they really must give up and go and scout round the house themselves to see what was happening, they heard sounds again. Voices! Ah, the men were back again. There was the sound of a car door being shut quietly. The engine started up. The car moved down the lane to turn in at the field gate again, go round in a circle and come out facing up the lane. It went by quickly, squelching in the soft, melting snow.

'They're gone,' said Colin. 'And we were real idiots not to have stolen up to the gate and taken the car's number! Now it's too late.'

'Yes. We *could* have done that,' said George. 'What shall we do now? Wait to see if Peter and Jack come out?'

'Yes, but not for too long,' said Colin. 'My feet are really frozen.'

They waited for about five minutes, and still no Peter or Jack came. So, sloshing through the fast-melting snow, the two boys went to the gate. They climbed over. Soon they were in the drive of the old house, hurrying up to the front door, with Scamper at their heels.

But, of course, they couldn't get in there, nor in the other doors either. And then, like Jack and Peter, they discovered the open window! In they went. They stood on the kitchen floor and listened. They could hear nothing at all.

They called softly. 'Jack! Peter! Are you here?'

Nobody answered. Not a sound was to be heard in the house. Then Scamper gave a loud bark and ran into the passage between the scullery and the kitchen. He scraped madly at a door there.

The boys followed at once, and no sooner had they got there than they heard Peter's voice.

'Who's there? That you, Colin and George? Say the password if it's you!'

'Weekdays! Where are you?' called George.

'Down here, in the cellar. We'll come up,' said Peter's voice. 'We're all right. Can you unlock the door – or has the key been taken?'

'No, it's here,' said Colin. 'Left in the door.'

He turned the key and unlocked the door. He pushed it open just as Jack and Peter came up to the top of the cellar steps!

And behind them came somebody else – somebody whose feet made a thudding sound on the stone steps – Kerry Blue! He wasn't going to be left behind in the dark cellar, all alone! He was going to stay with these nice kind boys.

Colin and George gaped in astonishment. They stared at Kerry Blue as if they had never seen a horse

in their lives before. A horse – down in the cellar –
locked up with Peter and Jack. How extraordinary!

'Have the men gone?' asked Peter, and Colin
nodded.

'Yes. Away in their car. That's why we came to
look for you. They saw us in the field because
Scamper barked – but they thought we were just
snowmen! What happened here?'

'Let's get out of the house,' said Peter. 'I just can't
bear being here any longer.'

He led Kerry Blue behind him, and Colin was
surprised that the horse made so little noise on the
wooden floor of the kitchen. He looked down at the
horse's hooves and gave an exclamation.

'Look! What's he's got on his feet?'

'Felt slippers, made to fit his great hooves,' said Peter, with a grin. 'That explains the curious prints we saw in the snow. I guess he had those on so that he wouldn't make too much noise down in the cellar! My word, he *was* scared when we found him. Come on – I'm going home!'

CHAPTER TWELVE

The end of the adventure

SIX FIGURES went up the snowy lane – two boys in dark anoraks, two in curious white garments and caps, a dog in a draggled white coat, and a proud and beautiful horse. All the boys had gleaming white faces and looked extremely weird, but as they didn't meet anyone it didn't matter.

Peter talked hard as he went, telling of all that had happened to him and Jack. Colin and George listened in astonishment, half-jealous that they, too, had not shared in the whole of the night's adventure.

'I'm going to put Kerry Blue into one of the stables at our farmhouse,' said Peter. 'He'll be all right now. What a shock for the men to find him gone! And tomorrow we'll tell the police. Meet at half-past nine – and collect Pam and Barbara on the way, will you? This really has been a wonderful mystery, and I do think the Secret Seven have done well! Goodness, I'm tired. I shall be asleep as soon as my head hits the pillow!'

They were all in bed and asleep in under half an

hour. Janet was fast asleep when Peter got in. He had carefully stabled Kerry Blue who was now quite docile and friendly.

In the morning, what an excitement! Peter told his father and mother what had happened and his father, in amazement, went to examine Kerry Blue.

'He's a very fine racehorse,' he said. 'And he's been dyed with some kind of brown stuff, as you can see. I expect those fellows meant to sell him and race him under another name. Well, you've stopped that, you and your Society, Peter!'

'What about getting on to the police now?' said the children's mother, anxiously. 'It does seem to me they ought to be after these men at once.'

'There's a meeting of the Secret Seven down in the shed at half-past nine,' said Peter. 'Perhaps the police could come to it.'

'Oh, no – I hardly think the police would want to sit on your flowerpots and boxes,' said Mummy. 'You must all meet in Daddy's study. That's the proper place.'

So, at half-past nine, when the Seven were all waiting in great excitement, and Scamper was going quite mad, biting a corner of the rug, the bell rang, and in walked two big policemen. They looked most astonished to see so many children sitting round in a ring.

'Good morning,' said the Inspector. 'Er – what is all this about? You didn't say much on the phone, sir.'

'No. I wanted you to hear the story from the children,' said Peter's father. He unfolded the morning paper and laid it out flat on the table. The children crowded round.

On the front page was a big photograph of a lovely

horse. Underneath it were a few sentences in big black letters.

KERRY BLUE STOLEN.
FAMOUS RACEHORSE DISAPPEARS.
NO SIGN OF HIS HIDING-PLACE.

'I expect you saw that this morning,' said Peter's father. 'Peter, tell him where Kerry Blue is.'

'In our stables!' said Peter, and thoroughly enjoyed the look of utter amazement that came over the faces of the two policemen.

They got out notebooks. 'This is important, sir,' said the Inspector to Peter's father. 'Can you vouch for the fact that you've got the horse?'

'Oh, yes – there's no doubt about it,' said Peter's father. 'You can see him whenever you like. Peter, tell your story.'

'We're going to take it in turns to tell bits,' said Peter. He began. He told about how they had made snowmen in the field. Then Jack went on to tell how he had gone to look for his Secret Seven badge in the field, and how he had seen the car and its trailer-van.

'Of course I know now it was a horse-box,' he said. 'But I didn't know then. I couldn't think what it was – it looked like a small removal van, or something. I couldn't see any proper windows either.'

So the story went on – how they had interviewed the caretaker and what he had said – how they had tracked the car down to the field gate and up the lane again. Then how four boys had dressed up as snowmen with Scamper and gone to watch.

Then came the exciting bit about Peter and Jack creeping into the house to find the prisoner – and being caught themselves. And then Colin and George took up the tale and told how they in their turn went into the old house to find Jack and Peter.

'Adventurous kids, aren't they?' said the Inspector, with a twinkle in his eye, turning to Peter's mother.

'Very,' she said. 'But I don't at all approve of this night-wandering business, Inspector. They should all have been in bed and asleep.'

'Quite,' said the Inspector, 'I agree with you. They should have told the police, no doubt about that, and left *them* to solve the mystery. Wandering about at night dressed up as snowmen – I never heard anything like it!'

He spoke in such a severe voice that the children felt quite alarmed. Then he smiled and they saw that actually he was very pleased with them.

'I'll have to find out the name of the owner of the
old house,' he said, 'and see if he knows anything
about these goings-on.'

'It's a Mr Holikoff, 64, Heycom Street, Covelty,'
said George at once. 'We – Pam and I – found that
out.'

'Good work!' said the Inspector, and the other
policeman wrote the address down at once. 'Very
good work indeed.'

'I suppose they don't know the number of the car,
do they?' asked the second policeman. 'That would be
a help.'

'No,' said Colin, regretfully. 'But the other two

girls here know something about the horse-box, sir.
They took the measurements of the tyres and even
drew a copy of the pattern on them – it showed in the
snow, you see.'

'Janet did that,' said Barbara, honestly, wishing she
hadn't laughed at Janet for doing it. Janet produced
the paper on which she had drawn the pattern and
taken the measurements. The Inspector took it at
once, looking very pleased.

'Splendid. Couldn't be better! It's no good looking for tracks today, of course, because the snow's
all melted. This is a very, very valuable bit of

evidence. Dear me, what bright ideas you children have!'

Janet was scarlet with pleasure. Peter looked at her and smiled proudly. She was a fine sister to have – a really good member of the Secret Seven!

'Well, these children seem to have done most of the work for us,' said the Inspector, shutting his note-book. 'They've got the address of the owner – and if he happens to have a horse-box in his possession, whose tyres match these measurements and this pattern, then he'll have to answer some very awkward questions.'

The police went to see Kerry Blue. The children crowded into the stable too, and Kerry Blue put his ears back in alarm. But Peter soon soothed him.

'Yes. He's been partly dyed already,' said the Inspector, feeling his coat. 'If he'd had one more coat of colour he'd be completely disguised! I suppose those fellows meant to come along and do that tonight – and then take him off to some other stable. But, of course, they had to hide him somewhere safe while they changed the colour of his coat – and so they chose the cellars of the old empty house – belonging to Mr J. Holikoff. Well, well, well – I wonder what *he* knows about it!'

The children could hardly wait to hear the end of

the adventure. They heard about it at the very next meeting of the Secret Seven – which was called, not by the members themselves, but by Peter's father and mother.

It was held in the shed, and the two grown-ups had the biggest boxes as seats. Janet and Peter sat on the floor.

'Well,' said Peter's father. 'Mr Holikoff *is* the owner of the horse-box – and of the car as well. The police waited in the old house for the two men last night – and they came! They are now safely under lock and key. They were so surprised when they found Kerry Blue gone that they hardly struggled at all!'

'Who does Kerry Blue belong to, Daddy?' said Peter. 'The papers said he was owned by Colonel James Healey. Is he sending someone to fetch him?'

'Yes,' said his father. 'He's sending off a horse-box for him today. And he has also sent something for the Secret Seven. Perhaps you'd like to see what it is, Peter.'

Peter took an envelope from his father and opened it. Out fell a shower of tickets. Janet grabbed one.

'Oooh – a circus ticket – and a pantomime ticket too! Are there seven of each?'

There were! Two lovely treats for everyone – except Scamper.

'But he can have a great big delumptious, scrumplicious bone, can't he, Mummy?' cried Janet, hugging him.

'Whatever are you talking about? Is that some foreign language?' asked her mother in astonishment, and everyone laughed.

On the envelope was written, 'For the Secret Seven Society, with my thanks and best wishes, J. H.'

'How very kind of him,' said Peter. 'We didn't want any reward at all. The adventure was enough reward – it was brilliant!'

'Well, we'll leave you to talk about it,' said his mother, getting up. 'Or else we shall find that *we* belong to your Society too, and that it's the Secret Nine, instead of the Secret Seven!'

'No – it's the Secret *Seven*,' said Peter, firmly. 'The best Society in the world. Hurrah for the Secret Seven!'

SECRET SEVEN ADVENTURE

CONTENTS

CHAPTER ONE

A Secret Seven meeting

THE SECRET SEVEN SOCIETY was having its usual weekly meeting. Its meeting place was down in the old shed at the bottom of the garden belonging to Peter and Janet. On the door were the letters S.S. painted in green.

Peter and Janet were in the shed, waiting. Janet was squeezing lemons into a big jug, making lemonade for the meeting. On a plate lay seven ginger biscuits and one big dog biscuit.

That was for Scamper, their golden spaniel. He sat with his eyes on the plate, as if he was afraid his biscuit might jump off and disappear!

'Here come the others,' said Peter, looking out of the window. 'Yes – Colin – George – Barbara – Pam and Jack. And you and I make the Seven.'

'Woof,' said Scamper, feeling left out.

'Sorry, Scamper,' said Peter. 'But you're not a member – just a hanger-on – but a very *nice* one!'

Bang! Somebody knocked at the door.

'Password, please,' called Peter. He never unlocked the door until the person outside said the password.

119

'Rabbits!' said Colin, and Peter unlocked the door. 'Rabbits!' said Jack, and 'Rabbits,' said the others in turn. That was the very latest password. The Secret Seven altered the word every week, just in *case* anyone should get to hear of it.

Peter looked at everyone keenly as they came in and sat down. 'Where's your badge, Jack?' he asked.

Jack looked uncomfortable. 'I'm awfully sorry,' he said, 'but I think Susie's got it. I hid it in my drawer, and it was gone when I looked for it this morning. Susie's an awful pest sometimes.'

Susie was Jack's sister. She badly wanted to belong to the Society, but as Jack kept patiently pointing out, as long as there were Seven in the Secret Seven, there couldn't possibly be any more.

'Susie wants a telling off,' said Peter. 'You'll have to get back the badge somehow, Jack, and then in future don't hide it in a drawer or anywhere, but pin it on to your pyjamas at night and wear it. Then Susie can't get it.'

'Right,' said Jack. He looked round to see if everyone else was wearing a badge. Yes – each member had a little round button with the letters S.S. neatly worked on it. He felt very annoyed with Susie.

'Has anyone anything exciting to report?' asked Peter, handing round the seven ginger biscuits. He tossed Scamper the big dog biscuit, and the spaniel caught it deftly in his mouth. Soon everyone was crunching and munching.

Nobody had anything to report at all. Barbara looked at Peter.

'This is the fourth week we've had nothing to report, and nothing has happened,' she said. 'It's very dull. I don't see much point in having a Secret Society if it doesn't *do* something – solve some mystery or have an adventure.'

'Well, think one up, then,' said Peter, promptly. 'You seem to think mysteries and adventures grow on trees, Barbara.'

Janet poured out the lemonade. '*I* wish something exciting would happen, too,' she said. 'Can't we make up some kind of adventure, just to go on with?'

'What sort?' asked Colin. 'Oooh, this lemonade's sour!'

'I'll put some more honey in,' said Janet. 'Well, I mean, couldn't we dress up as Red Indians or something, and go somewhere and stalk people without their knowing it? We've got some lovely American Indian clothes, Peter and I.'

They talked about it for a while. They discovered that between them they had six sets of American Indian clothes.

'Well, I know what we'll do, then,' said George. 'We'll dress up, and go off to Little Thicket. We'll split into two parties, one at each end of the thicket – and we'll see which party can stalk and catch Colin – he's the only one without Indian dress. That'll be fun.'

'I don't much want to be stalked by all six of you,' said Colin. 'I hate being jumped on all at once.'

'It's only a game!' said Janet. 'Don't be silly.'

'Listen – there's somebody coming!' said Peter. Footsteps came up the path right to the shed. There was a tremendously loud bang at the door, which made everyone jump.

'Password!' said Peter, forgetting that all the Secret Seven were there.

'Rabbits!' was the answer.

'It's *Susie!*' said Jack in a rage. He flung open the door, and there, sure enough, was his cheeky sister, wearing the S.S. button, too!

'I'm a member!' she cried. 'I know the password and I've got the badge!'

Everyone got up in anger, and Susie fled, giggling as she went. Jack was scarlet with rage.

'I'm going after her,' he said. 'And now we'll have to think of a new password, too!'

'The password can be Indians!' Peter called after him. 'Meet here at half-past two!'

CHAPTER TWO

An American Indian afternoon

AT HALF-PAST two the Secret Seven Society arrived by ones and twos. Jack arrived first, wearing his badge again. He had chased and caught Susie, and taken it from her.

'I'll come and bang at the door again and shout the password,' threatened Susie.

'That won't be any good,' said Jack. 'We've got a new one!'

Everyone said the new password cautiously, just in *case* that tiresome Susie was anywhere about.

'Indians!'

'Indians!' The password was whispered time after time till all seven were gathered together. Everyone had brought American Indian suits and head-dresses. Soon they were all dressing, except Colin, who hadn't one.

'Now off we go to Little Thicket,' said Peter, prancing about with a most terrifying-looking hatchet. Fortunately, it was only made of wood. 'I'll take Janet and Jack for my two men, and George can have Barbara and Pam. Colin's to be the one we both try to stalk and capture.'

125

'No tying me to trees and shooting off arrows at me,' said Colin, firmly. 'That's fun for you, but not for me. OK?'

They had all painted their faces in weird patterns, except Colin. Jack had a rubber knife which he kept pretending to plunge into Scamper. They really did look a very fierce collection of Indians indeed.

They set off for Little Thicket, which was about half a mile away, across the fields. It lay beside a big mansion called Milton Manor, which had high walls all round it.

'Now, what we'll do is to start out at opposite ends of Little Thicket,' said Peter. 'My three can take this end, and you three can take the other end, George. Colin can go to the middle. We'll all shut our eyes and count one hundred – and then we'll begin to hunt for Colin and stalk him.'

'And if I spot any of you and call your name, you have to get up and show yourselves,' said Colin. 'You'll be out of the game then.'

'And if any one of us manages to get right up to you and pounce on you, then you're his prisoner,' said Peter. 'Little Thicket is just the right kind of place for this!'

It certainly was. It was a mixture of heather and bushes and trees. Big, heathery tufts grew there, and patches of wiry grass, small bushes, and big and little

126

trees. There were plenty of places to hide, and anyone could stalk a person from one end of the thicket to the other without being seen, if he crawled carefully along on his tummy.

The two parties separated, and went to each end of Little Thicket. A fence bounded one side and on the other the walls of Milton Manor grounds rose strong and high. If Colin could manage to get out of either end of Little Thicket uncaptured, he would be clever!

He went to stand in the middle, waiting for the others to count their hundred with their eyes shut. As soon as Peter waved a handkerchief to show that the counting had begun, Colin ran to a tree. He climbed quickly up into the thick branches, and sat himself on a broad bough. He grinned.

'They can stalk me all they like, from one end of the thicket to the other, but they won't find me!' he thought. 'And when they're all tired of looking and give up, I'll shin down and stroll up to them!'

The counting was up. Six American Indians began to spread out and worm their way silently through heather and thick undergrowth and long grass.

Colin could see where some of them were by the movement of the undergrowth. He kept peeping between the boughs of his tree, chuckling to himself. This was fun!

And then something very surprising caught his eye. He glanced over to the high wall that surrounded the grounds of Milton Manor, and saw that somebody was astride the top! Even as he looked the man jumped down and disappeared from view, and Colin heard the crackling of undergrowth. Then everything was still. Colin couldn't see him at all. He was most astonished. What had the man been doing, climbing over the wall?

Colin couldn't for the life of him think what was the best thing to do. He couldn't start yelling to the others from the tree. Then he suddenly saw that Peter, or one of the others, was very near where the man had gone to ground!

It was Peter. He had thought he had heard somebody not far from him, and he had felt sure it was Colin, squirming his way along. So he squirmed in that direction too.

Ah! He was sure there was somebody hiding in the middle of that bush! It was a great gorse bush, in full bloom. It must be Colin hiding there.

Cautiously Peter wriggled on his tummy right up to the bush. He parted the brown stems, and gazed in amazement at the man there. It wasn't Colin, after all!

As for the man, he was horrified. He suddenly saw a dreadful, painted face looking at him through the bush, and saw what he thought was a real hatchet aimed at him. He had no idea it was only wood!

He got up at once and fled – and for a moment Peter was so amazed that he didn't even follow!

CHAPTER THREE

A shock for Colin

BY THE TIME Peter had stood up to see where the horrified man had gone, he had completely disappeared. There wasn't a sign of him anywhere.

'Bother!' said Peter, vexed. 'Fat lot of good I am as an American Indian. Can't even stalk somebody right under my nose. Where in the world has the man gone?'

He began to hunt here and there, and soon the others, seeing him standing up, knew that something had happened. They called to him.

'Peter – what is it? Why are you showing yourself?'

'There was a man hiding under one of the bushes,' said Peter. 'I just wondered why. But he got up and shot away. Anyone see where he went?'

No one had seen him at all. They clustered round Peter, puzzled. 'Fancy – seven of us crawling hidden in this field – and not one saw the man run off,' said Pam. 'We haven't even seen Colin!'

'The game's finished for this afternoon,' said Peter. He didn't want anyone to come suddenly on the man in hiding – it might be dangerous. 'We'll call Colin.'

So they yelled for him. 'Colin! Come out, wherever you are! The game's finished.'

They waited for him suddenly to stand up and appear. But he didn't. There was no answer to their call, and no Colin suddenly appeared.

'Colin!' yelled everyone. 'Come on out.'

Still he didn't come. He didn't even shout back. It was strange.

'Don't be funny!' shouted George. 'The game's over! Where are you?'

Colin was where he had been all the time – hidden up in his tree. Why didn't he shout back? Why didn't he shin down the tree and race over to the others, pleased that he hadn't been caught?

He didn't show himself for a very good reason. He was much too frightened to!

He had had a shock when he saw the man drop down from the wall, and run to the thicket and hide – and he had an even greater shock when he saw him suddenly appear from a nearby bush, and run to the foot of the tree that he himself was hiding in.

Then he heard the sounds of someone clambering up at top speed – good gracious, the man was climbing the very tree that Colin himself had chosen for a hiding place!

Colin's heart beat fast. He didn't like this at all.

What would the man say if he suddenly climbed up on top of him? He would certainly be very annoyed.

The man came steadily up. But when he was almost up to the branch on which Colin sat, he stopped. The branch wasn't strong enough to hold a man, though it was quite strong enough for a boy.

The man curled himself up in a fork of the tree just below Colin. He was panting hard, but trying to keep his breathing as quiet as possible. Peter was not so very far away and might hear it.

Colin sat as if he was turned to stone. Who was this man? Why had he come over the wall? Why had he hidden in Little Thicket? He would never have done that if he had known it was full of the Secret Seven playing Indians!

And now here he was up Colin's tree, still in hiding – and at any moment he might look up and see Colin. It was very unpleasant indeed.

Then Colin heard the others shouting for him. 'Colin! Come out, wherever you are – the game's finished!'

But poor Colin didn't dare to come out, and certainly didn't dare to shout back. He hardly dared to breathe, and hoped desperately that he wouldn't have to sneeze or cough. He sat there as still as a mouse, waiting to see what would happen.

The man also sat there as still as a mouse, watching the six children below, peering at them through the leaves of the tree. Colin wished they had brought old Scamper with them. He would have sniffed the man's tracks and gone to the foot of the tree!

But Scamper had been left behind. He always got much too excited when they were playing Indians, and by his barking gave away where everyone was hiding!

After the others had hunted for Colin and called him, they began to walk off. 'He must have escaped us and gone home,' said Peter. 'Well, we'll go too. We can't find that man, and I don't know that I want to, either. He looked a nasty bit of work to me.'

In despair, Colin watched them leave Little Thicket and disappear down the field-path. The man saw them go too. He gave a little grunt and slid down the tree.

Colin had been able to see nothing of him except the top of his head and his ears. He could still see nothing of the man as he made his way cautiously out of the thicket. He was a far, far better American Indian than any of the Secret Seven, that was certain!

And now – was it safe for Colin to get down? He certainly couldn't stay up in the tree all night!

CHAPTER FOUR

Is it an adventure?

COLIN SLID down the tree. He stood at the foot, looking warily round. Nobody was in sight. The man had completely vanished.

'I'll run at top speed and hope for the best,' thought Colin, and off he went. Nobody stopped him! Nobody yelled at him. He felt rather ashamed of himself when he came to the field-path and saw the cows staring at him in surprise.

He went back to the farmhouse where Peter and Janet lived. Maybe the Secret Seven were still down in the shed, stripped of their American Indian things and wiping the paint off their faces.

He ran down the path to the shed. The door was shut as usual. The S.S. showed up well with the two letters painted so boldly. There was the sound of voices from inside the shed.

Colin knocked. 'Let me in!' he cried. 'I'm back too.'

There was a silence. The door didn't open. Colin banged again impatiently. 'You know it's only me. Open the door!'

Still it didn't open. And then Colin remembered.

He must give the password, of course! What in the world was it? Thankfully he remembered it, as he caught a glimpse of brilliant American Indian feathers through the shed-window.

'Indians!' he shouted.

The door opened. 'And now *every*body in the district knows our latest password,' said Peter's voice in disgust. 'We'll have to choose another. Come in. Wherever have you been? We yelled and yelled for you at Little Thicket.'

'I know. I heard you,' said Colin, stepping inside. 'I'm sorry I shouted out the password like that. I wasn't thinking. But I've got some news – most peculiar news!'

'What?' asked everyone, and stopped rubbing the paint from their faces.

'You know when Peter stood up and shouted out that he'd found a man in hiding, don't you?' said Colin. 'Well, I was quite nearby – as a matter of fact, I was up a tree!'

'Cheat!' said George. 'That's not playing Red Indians!'

'Who said it wasn't?' demanded Colin. 'I bet Red Indians climbed trees as well as wriggling on their tummies. Anyway, I was up that tree – and, guess what – the man that Peter found came running up to my tree, and climbed it too!'

'Gosh!' said George. 'What did you do?'

'Nothing,' said Colin. 'He didn't come up quite as far as I was – so I just sat tight, and didn't make a sound. I saw him before Peter did, actually. I saw him on the top of the wall that surrounds Milton Manor – then he dropped down, ran to the thicket and disappeared.'

'What happened in the end?' asked Janet, excited.

'After you'd all gone, he slid down the tree and went,' said Colin. 'I didn't see him any more. I slid down too, and ran for home. I felt a bit scared, actually.'

'Whatever was he doing, behaving like that?' wondered Jack. 'What was he like?'

'Well, I only saw the top of his head and his ears,' said Colin. 'Did *you* see him closely, Peter?'

'Yes, fairly,' said Peter. 'But he wasn't anything out of the ordinary really – clean-shaven, dark-haired – nothing much to remember him by.'

'Well, I suppose that's the last we'll hear of him,' said Barbara. 'The adventure that passed us by! We shall never know exactly what he was doing, and why.'

'He spoilt our afternoon, anyway,' said Pam. 'Not that we'd have caught Colin – hiding up a tree like that. We'll have to make a rule that trees are not to be climbed when we're playing at stalking.'

140

IS IT AN ADVENTURE?

'When's our next meeting – and are we going to have a new password?' asked Janet.

'We'll meet on Wednesday evening,' said Peter. 'Keep your eyes and ears open for anything exciting or mysterious or adventurous, as usual. It *is* a pity we didn't capture that man – or find out more about him. I'm sure he was up to no good.'

'What about a password?' asked Janet again.

'Well – we'll have "Adventure", I think,' said Peter. 'Seeing we've just missed one!'

They all went their several ways home – and, except for Colin, nobody thought much more of the peculiar man at Little Thicket. But the radio that evening suddenly made all the Secret Seven think of him again!

'Lady Lucy Thomas's magnificent and unique pearl necklace was stolen from her bedroom at Milton Manor this afternoon,' said the announcer. 'Nobody saw the thief, or heard him, and he got away in safety.' Peter and Janet sprang up at once. 'That's the man we saw!' yelled Peter. 'Would you believe it! Call a meeting of the Secret Seven for tomorrow, Janet – this is an adventure again!'

CHAPTER FIVE

An important meeting

THAT NIGHT the Secret Seven were very excited. Janet and Peter had slipped notes into everyone's letterbox. 'Meeting at half-past nine. IMPORTANT! S.S.S.'

Colin and George had no idea at all what was up, because they hadn't listened to the radio. But the others had all heard of the theft of Lady Lucy Thomas's necklace, and, knowing that she lived by Little Thicket, they guessed that the meeting was to be about finding the thief!

At half-past nine the Society met. Janet and Peter were ready for them in the shed. Raps at the door came steadily. 'Password!' called Peter, sternly, each time.

'Adventure!' said everyone in a low voice. 'Adventure!' 'Adventure!' One after another the members were admitted to the shed.

'Where's that awful sister of yours – Susie?' Peter asked Jack. 'I hope she's not about anywhere. This is a really important meeting today. Got your badge?'

'Yes,' said Jack. 'Susie's gone out for the day. Anyway, she doesn't know our latest password.'

'What's the meeting about?' asked Colin. 'I know something's up by the look on Janet's face. She looks as if she's going to burst!'

'*You'll* feel like bursting when you know,' said Janet. 'Because you're going to be rather important, seeing that you and Peter are the only ones who saw the thief we're going after.'

Colin and George looked blank. They didn't know what Janet was talking about, of course. Peter soon explained.

'You know the man that Colin saw yesterday, climbing over the wall that runs round Milton Manor?' said Peter. 'The one *I* saw hiding in the bush – and then he went and climbed up into the very tree Colin was hiding in? Well, it said on the radio last night that a thief had got into Lady Lucy Thomas's bedroom and taken her magnificent pearl necklace.'

'Gracious!' said Pam with a squeal. 'And that was the man you and Colin saw!'

'Yes,' said Peter. 'It must have been. And now the thing is – what do we do about it? This is an adventure – if only we can find that man – and if *only* we could find the necklace too – that would be a fine feather in the cap of the Secret Seven.'

There was a short silence. Everyone was thinking hard. 'But how can we find him?' asked Barbara at last. 'I mean – only you and Colin saw him, Peter – and then just for a moment.'

'And don't forget that I only saw the top of his head and tips of his ears,' said Colin. 'I'd like to know how I could possibly know anyone from those things. Anyway, I can't go about looking at the tops of people's heads!'

Janet laughed. 'You'd have to carry a stepladder about with you!' she said, and that made everyone else laugh too.

'Oughtn't we to tell the police?' asked George.

'I suppose so,' said Peter, considering the matter carefully. 'Not that we can give them any help at all, really. Still – that's the first thing to be done. Then maybe we could help the police, and, anyway, we could snoop round and see if we can find out anything on our own.'

'Let's go down to the police station now,' said George. 'That would be an exciting thing to do! Won't the inspector be surprised when we march in, all seven of us!'

They left the shed and went down to the town. They trooped up the steps of the police station, much to the astonishment of the young policeman inside.

'Can we see the inspector?' asked Peter. 'We've got some news for him – about the thief that stole Lady Lucy's necklace.'

The inspector had heard the clatter of so many feet and he looked out of his room. 'Hallo, *hallo*!' he said, pleased. 'The Secret Seven again! And what's the password this time?'

Nobody told him, of course. Peter grinned.

'We just came to say we saw the thief climb over the wall of Milton Manor yesterday,' he said. 'He hid in a bush first and then in a tree where Colin was hiding. But that's about all we know!'

The inspector soon got every single detail from the Seven, and he looked very pleased. 'What beats me is how the thief climbed that enormous wall!' he said. 'He must be able to climb like a cat. There was no ladder used. Well, Secret Seven, there's nothing much you can do, I'm afraid, except keep your eyes open in case you see this man again.'

'The only thing is – Colin only saw the top of his head, and I only caught a quick glimpse of him, and he looked so very, *very* ordinary,' said Peter. 'Still you may be sure we'll do our best!'

Off they all went again down the steps into the street. 'And *now*,' said Peter, 'we'll go to the place where Colin saw the man getting over the wall. We just *might* find something there – you never know!'

CHAPTER SIX

Some peculiar finds

THE SEVEN made their way to Little Thicket, where they had played their game of American Indians the day before.

'Now, where exactly did you say that the man climbed over?' Peter asked Colin. Colin considered. Then he pointed to a holly tree.

'See that holly? Well – he came over the wall between that tree and the little oak. I'm pretty certain that was exactly the place.'

'Come on, then – we'll go and see,' said Peter. Feeling really rather important, the Seven walked across Little Thicket and came to the place between the holly tree and the little oak. They stood and gazed up at the wall.

It was at least ten or eleven feet high. How could anyone climb a sheer wall like that without even a ladder?

'Look – here's where he leapt down,' said Pam, suddenly, and she pointed to a deep mark in the ground near the holly tree. They all looked.

'Yes – that must have been where his feet landed,'

said George. 'Pity we can't tell anything from the mark – I mean, if it had been footprints, for instance, it would have helped a lot. But it's only just a deep mark – probably made by his heels.'

'I wish we could go to the other side of the wall,' said Peter, suddenly. 'We might perhaps find a footprint or two there. Let's go and ask the gardener if we can go into the grounds. He's a friend of the cow-man who works on our farm, and he knows me.'

'Good idea,' said George, so off they all went again. The gardener was working inside the front garden, beyond the great iron gates. The children called to him, and he looked up.

'Hey John!' shouted Peter. 'Could we come in and look round? About that thief, you know. We saw him climb over the wall, and the inspector of police has asked us to keep our eyes open. So we're looking round.'

John grinned. He opened the gates. 'Well, if I come with you, I don't reckon you can do much harm,' he said. 'Beats me how that thief climbed those walls. I was working here in the front garden all yesterday afternoon, and if he'd come in at the gates I'd have seen him. But he didn't.'

The seven children went round the walls with John. Colin saw the top of the holly tree and the top of the little nearby oak jutting above the wall. He stopped.

'This is where he climbed up,' he said. 'Now let's look for footprints.'

There were certainly marks in the earth – but no footprints.

The Seven bent over the marks.

'Funny, aren't they?' said Peter, puzzled. 'Quite round and regular – and about three inches across – as if someone had been pounding about with a large-sized broom handle – hammering the end of it into the ground. What could have made these marks, John?'

'Beats me,' said John, also puzzled. 'Maybe the police will make something of them, now they know you saw the thief climb over the wall just here.'

Everyone studied the round, regular marks again. There seemed no rhyme or reason for them at all. They looked for all the world as if someone had been stabbing the ground with the tip of a broom handle or something – and why should anyone do that? And anyway, if they did, how would it help them to climb over a wall?

'There's been no ladder used, that I *can* say,' said John. 'All mine are locked up in a shed – and there they all are still – and the key's in my pocket. How that fellow climbed this steep wall, I can't think.'

'He must have been an acrobat, that's all,' said Janet, looking up to the top of the wall. Then she spotted something, and pointed to it in excitement.

'Look – what's that – caught on that sharp bit of brick there – half-way up?'

Everybody stared. 'It looks like a bit of wool,' said Pam at last. 'Perhaps, when the thief climbed up, that

152

sharp bit caught his clothes, and a bit of wool was pulled out.'

'Help me up, George,' ordered Peter. 'I'll get it. It might be a very valuable clue.'

George hoisted him up, and Peter made a wild grab at the piece of wool. He got it, and George let him down to the ground again. They all gathered round to look at it.

It was really rather ordinary – just a bit of blue wool thread with a tiny red strand in it. Everyone looked at it earnestly.

'Well – it *might* have been pulled out of the thief's jersey,' said Janet at last. 'We can all look out for somebody wearing a blue wool pullover with a tiny thread of red in it!'

And then they found something else – something *much* more exciting!

CHAPTER SEVEN

Scamper finds a clue

IT WAS really Scamper the spaniel who found the biggest clue of all. He was with them, of course, sniffing round eagerly, very interested in the curious round marks. Then he suddenly began to bark loudly.

Everyone looked at him. 'What's up, Scamper?' said Peter.

Scamper went on barking. The seven felt a bit scared, and looked hastily round, half afraid that there might be somebody hidden in the bushes!

Scamper had his head up, and was barking quite madly. 'Stop it,' said Peter, exasperated. 'Tell us what you're barking at, Scamper! Stop it, I say.'

Scamper stopped. He gave Peter a reproachful look and then gazed up above the children's heads. He began to bark again.

Everyone looked up, to see what in the world the spaniel was barking at. And there, caught neatly on the twig of a tree, was a cap!

'Look at that!' said Peter, astonished. 'A cap! Could it belong to the thief?'

'Well, if it does, why in the world did he throw his cap up there?' said Janet. 'It's not a thing that thieves usually do – throw their caps up into trees and leave them!'

The cap was far too high to reach. It was almost as high up as the top of the wall! John the gardener went to get a stick to knock it down.

'It could only have got up there by being thrown,' said George. 'So it doesn't really seem as if it could have belonged to the thief. He really wouldn't go throwing his cap about like that, leaving such a very fine clue!'

'No. You're right, I'm afraid,' said Peter. 'It can't be his cap. It must be one that some tramp threw over the wall some time or other.'

John came back with a bamboo stick. He jerked the cap off the twig and Scamper pounced on it at once.

'Drop it, Scamper; drop it!' ordered Peter, and Scamper dropped it, looking hurt. Hadn't he spotted the cap himself? Then at least he might be allowed to throw it up into the air and catch it!

The Seven looked at the dirty old cap. It was made of tweed, and at one time must have showed a rather startling check pattern – but now it was so faded that it was difficult even to see the pattern. Janet looked at it in disgust.

156

'Ugh! What a tatty old cap! I'm sure that some tramp had finished with it and threw it over the wall – and it just stuck up there on that tree branch. I'm sure it isn't a clue at all.'

'I think you're right,' said Colin, turning the cap over and over in his hands. 'We might as well chuck it over into Little Thicket. It's no use to us. Bad luck, Scamper – you thought you'd found a thumping big clue!'

He made as if to throw the cap up over the wall, but Peter stopped him. 'No, don't! We'd better keep it. You never know. We'd kick ourselves if we threw away something that might prove to be a clue of some kind – though I do agree with you, it probably isn't.'

'Well, *you* can carry the smelly thing then,' said Colin, giving it to Peter. 'No wonder somebody threw it away. It smells like anything!'

Peter stuffed it into his pocket. Then he took the tiny piece of blue wool thread, and put that carefully into the pages of his notebook. He looked down at the ground where the curious marks were.

'I almost think we'd better make a note of these too,' he said. 'Got a measure, Janet?'

She hadn't, of course. But George had some string, and he carefully measured across the round marks, and then snipped the string to the right size. 'That's the size of the marks,' he said, and gave his bit of string to Peter. It went carefully into his notebook too.

'I can't help thinking those funny marks all over the place are some kind of clue,' he said, putting his notebook away. 'But what, I simply can't imagine!'

They said good-bye to John, and made their way home across the fields. Nobody could make much of the clues. Peter did hope the adventure wasn't going to fizzle out, after all!

'I still say that only an acrobat could have scaled that high wall,' said Janet. 'I don't see how any ordinary person could have done it!'

Just as she said this, they came out into the lane. A big poster had been put up on a wall nearby. The children glanced at it idly. And then Colin gave a shout that made them all jump!

'Look at that – it's a poster advertising a circus! And see what it says – Lion-tamers, Daring Horse-riders, Performing Bears – Clowns – and Acrobats! Acrobats! Look at that! Supposing – just supposing . . .'

They all stared at one another in excitement. Janet might be right. This must be looked into at once!

CHAPTER EIGHT

A visit to the circus

PETER LOOKED at his watch. 'Bother!' he said in dismay. 'It's nearly dinner-time. We must all get back home as fast as we can. Meet at half-past two again, Secret Seven.'

'We can't!' said Pam and Barbara. 'We're going to a party.'

'*Don't* have a meeting without us,' begged Pam.

'I can't come either,' said George. 'So we'd better make it tomorrow. Anyway, if the thief *is* one of the acrobats at the circus, he won't be leaving this afternoon! He'll stay there till the circus goes.'

'Well – it's only just a *chance* he might be an acrobat,' said Janet. 'I only just *said* it could only be an acrobat that scaled that high wall. I didn't really mean it!'

'It's worth looking into, anyhow,' said Peter. 'Well – meet tomorrow at half-past nine, then. And will everybody please think hard, and have some kind of plan to suggest? I'm sure we shall think of something good!'

Everyone thought hard that day – even Pam and Barbara whispered together in the middle of their party! 'I vote we go and see the circus,' whispered Pam. 'Don't you think it would be a good idea? Then we can see if Peter recognises any of the acrobats as the thief he saw hiding under that bush!'

When the Secret Seven met the next day, muttering the password as they went through the door of the shed, everyone seemed to have exactly the same idea!

162

'We should visit the circus,' began George.

'That's just what Pam and I thought!' said Barbara.

'I thought so too,' said Colin. 'In fact, it's the only sensible thing to do. Don't you think so, Peter?'

'Yes. Janet and I looked in the local paper, and we found that the circus opens this afternoon,' said Peter. 'What about us all going to see it? I don't know if I would recognise any of the acrobats as the thief – I really only caught just a glimpse of him, you know – but it's worth trying.'

'You said he was dark and clean-shaven,' said Colin. 'And I saw that his hair was black, anyway. He had a little thin patch on the top. But it isn't much to go on, is it?'

'Has anyone got any money?' asked Pam. 'To buy circus tickets, I mean? I haven't any at all, because I had to buy a birthday present to take to the party yesterday.'

Everyone turned out their pockets. The money was put in a pile in the middle and counted.

'The tickets are three pounds for children,' said Peter with a groan. 'Three pounds! They must think that children are *made* of money. We've got just twelve pounds here, that's all. Only four of us can go.'

'I've got five pounds in my money-box,' said Janet.

'And I've got three pounds at home,' said Colin. 'Anyone got one more pound to spare?'

'Oh yes – I'll borrow it from Susie,' said Jack.

'Well, don't go and tell her the password in return for the pound!' said Colin, and got a kick from Jack and an angry snort.

'Right. That looks as if we can all go, after all,' said Peter, pleased. 'Meet at the circus field ten minutes before the circus begins. Don't be late, anyone! And keep your eyes peeled for anyone wearing a dark blue pullover with a tiny thread of red in it – because it's pretty certain the thief must have worn a jersey or pullover made of that wool.'

Everyone was very punctual. All but Pam had money with them, so Peter gave her enough for her ticket. They went to the ticketbox and bought seven tickets, feeling really rather excited. A circus was always fun – but to go to a circus and keep a look out for a thief was even more exciting than usual!

Soon they were all sitting in their seats, looking down intently on the sawdust-strewn ring in the middle of the great tent. The band struck up a lively tune and a drum boomed out. The children sat up, thrilled.

In came the horses, walking proudly, their feathery plumes nodding. In came the clowns, somersaulting and yelling; in came the bears; in came all the performers, one after another, greeting the audience with smiles.

The children watched out for the acrobats, but they were all mixed up with the other performers – five clowns and conjurers, two clever stilt-walkers, and five men on ridiculous bicycles. It was impossible to tell which were the acrobats.

'They are third on the programme,' said Peter. 'First come the horses – then the clowns – and then the acrobats.'

So they waited, clapping the beautiful dancing horses, and laughing at the ridiculous clowns until their sides ached.

'Now for the acrobats!' said Peter, excitedly. 'Watch, Colin, watch!'

CHAPTER NINE

A good idea – and a disappointment

THE ACROBATS came in, turning cart-wheels and springing high into the air. One came in with his body bent so far over backwards that he was able to put his head between his legs. He looked very peculiar indeed.

Peter nudged Colin. 'Colin! See that fellow with his head between his legs – he's clean-shaven like the man I saw hidden in the bush – and he's got black hair!'

Colin nodded. 'Yes – he may be the one! All the others have moustaches. Let's watch him carefully and see if he could really leap up a high wall, and over the top.'

All the Secret Seven kept their eyes glued on this one acrobat. They had seen that the others had moustaches, so that ruled them out – but this one fitted the bill – he was dark-haired and had no moustache!

Could he leap high? Would he show them that he could easily leap up a steep wall to the top? They watched eagerly. The clean-shaven acrobat was easily the best of them all. He was as light as a feather.

When he sprang across the ring it almost seemed as if his feet did not even touch the ground.

He was a very clever tight-rope walker too. A long ladder was put up, and was fixed to a wire high up in the roof of the tent. The children watched the acrobat spring lightly up the ladder, and they turned to look at one another – yes – if he could leap up a ladder like that, hardly touching the rungs with feet or hands, he could most certainly leap up a twelve-foot wall to the top!

'I'm sure that one's the thief,' whispered Janet to Peter. He nodded. He was sure, too. He was so sure, that he settled down to enjoy the circus properly, not bothering to look out for a thief any longer, now that he had made up his mind this was the one.

It was quite a good circus. The performing bears came on, and really seemed to enjoy themselves boxing with each other and with their trainer. One little bear was so fond of its trainer that it kept hugging his legs, and wouldn't let him go!

Janet wished she had a little bear like that for a pet. 'He's just like a big teddy,' she said to Pam, and Pam nodded.

The clowns came in again – and then the two stilt-walkers, with three of the clowns. The stilt-walkers were ridiculous. They wore long skirts over their stilts, so that they looked like tremendously tall people, and they walked stiffly about with the little clowns teasing them and jeering at them.

Then a strong cage was put up, and the lions were brought in, snarling. Janet shrank back. 'I don't like this,' she said. 'Lions aren't meant to act about. They only look silly. Oh dear – look at that one – he won't get up on his stool. I know he's going to pounce on his keeper.'

But he didn't, of course. He knew his performance and went through it very haughtily with the others. They ambled away afterwards, still snarling.

Then a big elephant came in and began to play cricket with his trainer. He really enjoyed that, and when he hit the ball into the audience six times running, everyone clapped like mad.

Altogether, the children enjoyed themselves enormously. They were sorry when they found themselves going out into the big field again.

'If we could only hunt for thieves in circuses every time, it would be very enjoyable,' said Janet. 'Peter – what do you think? Is that dark-haired, clean-shaven acrobat the thief? He's the only likely one of the acrobats, really.'

'Yes – all the others have moustaches,' said Peter. 'I wonder what we ought to do next? It would be a good thing, perhaps, to go and find him and talk to him. He might let something slip that would help us.'

'But what excuse can we give for going to find him?' said George.

'Oh – ask him for his autograph!' said Peter. 'He'll think that quite natural!'

The others stared at him in admiration. What a brainwave! Nobody had thought of half such a good idea.

A GOOD IDEA – AND A DISAPPOINTMENT

'Look,' whispered Barbara. 'Isn't that him over there, talking to the bear-trainer? Yes, it is. Does he look like the thief to you, Peter, now that you can see him close?'

Peter nodded. 'Yes, he does. Come on – we'll all go boldly up and ask him for an autograph. Keep your eyes and ears open.'

They marched up to the acrobat. He turned round in surprise. 'Well – what do you want?' he asked with a grin. 'Want a lesson on how to walk the tight-rope?'

'No – your autograph, please,' said Peter. He stared at the man. He suddenly seemed much older then he had looked in the ring. The acrobat laughed. He mopped his forehead with a big red handkerchief.

'It was hot in the tent,' he said. 'Yes, you can have my autograph – but just let me take off my wig first. It makes my head so hot!'

And, to the children's enormous surprise, he loosened his black hair – and lifted it off completely! It was a wig – and under it, the acrobat was completely bald. Well – *what* a disappointment!

CHAPTER TEN

Trinculo the acrobat

THE SEVEN stared at him in dismay. Why – his head was completely bald except for a few grey hairs right on the very top. He couldn't possibly be the thief. Colin had distinctly seen the top of the thief's head when he had sat above him in the tree – and he had said that his hair was black, except for a little round bald patch in the centre.

Colin took the wig in his hand. He looked at it carefully, wondering if perhaps the thief had worn the wig when he had stolen the necklace. But there was no little round bald patch in the centre! It was a thick black wig with no bare patches at all.

'You seem to be very interested in my wig,' said the acrobat, and he laughed. 'No acrobat can afford to be bald, you know. We have to look as young and beautiful as possible. Now, I'll give you each my autograph, then you must be off.'

'Thank you,' said Peter, and handed the man a piece of paper and a pencil.

The little bear came ambling by, all by itself, snorting a little.

'Oh, *look*!' said Janet in delight. 'Oh, will it come to us, do you think? Come here, little bear.'

The bear sidled up and rubbed against Janet. She put her arms round it and tried to lift it – but it was unexpectedly heavy. A strange, sulky-looking youth came after it, and caught it roughly by the fur at its neck.

'Ah, bad boy!' he said, and shook the little creature. The bear whimpered.

'Oh, don't!' said Janet in distress. 'He's so sweet. He only came over to see us.'

The youth was dressed rather peculiarly. He had on a woman's bodice, spangled with sequins, a bonnet with flowers in – and dirty flannel trousers!

Peter glanced at him curiously as he led the little bear away. 'Was he in the circus?' he asked. 'I don't remember him.'

'Yes – he was one of the stilt-walkers,' said the acrobat, still busily writing autographs. 'His name's Louis. He helps with all the animals. Do you want to come and see the bears in their cage some time? – they're very tame – and old Jumbo would love to have a bun or two if you like to bring him some. He's as gentle as a big dog.'

'Oh yes – we'd *love* to!' said Janet, at once thinking how much she would love to make friends with the dear little bear. 'Can we come tomorrow?'

'Yes – come tomorrow morning,' said the acrobat. 'Ask for Trinculo – that's me. I'll be about somewhere.'

The children thanked him and left the field. They said nothing till they were well out of hearing of any of the circus people.

'I'm glad it wasn't that acrobat,' said Janet. 'He's

nice. I like his funny face, too. I did get a shock when he took off his black hair!'

'So did I,' said Peter. 'I felt an idiot, too. I thought I had remembered how the thief had looked – when I saw Trinculo's face, I really did think he looked like the thief. But he doesn't, of course. For one thing, the man I saw was much younger.'

'We'd better not go by faces, it seems to me,' said Colin. 'Better try to find someone who wears a blue pullover with a red thread running through it!'

'We can't go all over the district looking for *that*,' said Pam. 'Honestly, that's silly.'

'Well, have you got a better idea?' asked Colin.

She hadn't, of course. Nor had anyone else. 'We're stuck,' said Peter, gloomily. 'This is a silly sort of mystery. We keep thinking we've got somewhere – and then we find we haven't.'

'Shall we go to the circus field tomorrow?' asked Pam. 'Not to try to find the thief, of course, because we know now that he isn't any of the acrobats. But should we go just to see the animals?'

'Yes. I did like that little bear,' said Janet. 'And I'd like to see old Jumbo close to, as well. I love elephants.'

'I don't think I'll come,' said Barbara. 'I'm a bit scared of elephants, they're so enormous.'

'I won't come, either,' said Jack. 'What about you,

George? We said we'd swop stamps tomorrow, you know.'

'Yes – well, we won't go either,' said George. 'You don't mind, do you, Peter? I mean, it's nothing to do with the Society, going to make friends with bears and elephants.'

'Well, Janet and Pam and Colin and I will go,' said Peter. 'And mind – everyone is to watch out for a blue pullover with a little red line running through it. You *never* know what you'll see if you keep your eyes open!'

Peter was right – but he would have been surprised to know what he and Janet were going to spot the very next day!

CHAPTER ELEVEN

Pam's discovery

NEXT MORNING Janet, Peter, Colin and Pam met to go to the circus field. They didn't take Scamper, because they didn't think Jumbo the elephant would like him sniffing round his ankles.

He was very angry at being left, and they could hear his miserable howls all the way up the lane. 'Poor Scamper!' said Janet. 'I wish we could have taken him – but he might get into the lions' cage or something. He's so very inquisitive.'

They soon came to the field. They walked across it, eyeing the circus people curiously. How different they looked in their ordinary clothes – not *nearly* so interesting, thought Janet. But then, how exciting and magnificent they looked in the ring.

One or two of them had built little fires in the field and were cooking something in black pots over the flames. Whatever it was that was cooking smelt most delicious. It made Peter feel very hungry.

They found Trinculo, and he was as good as his word. He took them to make friends with Jumbo, who trumpeted gently at them, and then, with one

swing of his strong trunk, he set Janet high up on his
great head. She squealed with surprise and delight.

They went to find the little bear. He was delighted
to see them, and put his paws through the bars to
reach their hands. Trinculo unlocked the cage and let
him out. He lumbered over to them and clasped his
arms round Trinculo's leg, peeping at the rest of them
with a roguish look on his funny bear-face.

180

'If only he wasn't so *heavy*,' said Janet, who always loved to pick up any animal she liked and hug it. 'I wish I could buy him.'

'Goodness – whatever would Scamper say if we took him home?' said Peter.

Trinculo took them to see the great lions in their cages. The sulky youth called Louis was there with someone else, cleaning out the cages. The other man in the cage grinned at the staring children. One of the lions growled.

Janet backed away. 'It's all right,' said the trainer. 'They're all harmless so long as they are well fed, and don't get quarrelsome. But don't come too near, Missy, just in case. Here you, Louis. Fill the water-trough again – the water's filthy.'

Louis did as he was told. The children watched him tip up the big water-trough and empty out the dirty water. Then he filled it again. He didn't seem in the least afraid of the lions. Janet didn't like him, but she couldn't help thinking how brave he was!

They were all sorry when it was time to go. They said good-bye to Trinculo, went to pat the little bear once more, and then wandered across the field to Jumbo. They patted as far as they could reach up his pillar-like leg, and then went along by the row of colourful caravans to the gate at the end of the field.

Some of the caravanners had been doing their

washing. They had spread a good deal of it out on the grass to dry. Others had rigged up a rough clothes-line, and had pegged up all kinds of things to flap in the wind.

The children wandered by, idly looking at everything they passed. And then Pam suddenly stopped short. She gazed closely at something hanging on one of the lines. When she turned her face towards them, she looked so excited that the others hurried over to her.

'What is it?' asked Peter. 'You look quite red! What's up?'

'Is anybody looking at us?' asked Pam in a low voice. 'Well, Peter – hurry up and look at these socks hanging on this line. What do they remind you of?'

The others looked at the things on the line – torn handkerchiefs, little frocks belonging to children, stockings and socks. For a moment Peter felt sure that Pam had spotted a blue pullover!

But there was no pullover flapping in the wind. He wondered what had attracted Pam's attention. Then he saw what she was gazing at.

She was looking very hard indeed at a pair of blue wool socks – and down each side of them ran a pattern in red! Peter's mind at once flew to the scrap of wool he had in his pocket-book – did it match?

In a trice he had it out and was comparing it with the sock. The blue was the same. The red was the same. The wool appeared to be exactly the same too.

'And see here,' whispered Pam, urgently. 'There's a little snag in this sock – just here – a tiny hole where a bit of the wool has gone. I'm pretty certain, Peter, that that's where your bit of blue wool came from – this sock!'

Peter was sure of it, too. An old woman came up and shooed them away. 'Don't you dare touch those clothes!' she said.

Peter didn't dare to ask who the socks belonged to. But if only, only he could find out, he would know who the thief was at once!

CHAPTER TWELVE

One-leg William

THE OLD circus woman gave Pam a little push. 'Didn't you hear me say go away!' she scolded. They all decided to go at once. Pam thought the old woman looked really rather like a witch!

They walked quickly out of the field, silent but very excited. Once they were in the lane they all talked at once.

'We never *thought* of socks! We thought we had to look for a pullover!'

'But it's socks all right – that pair is made of exactly the same wool as this bit we found caught on to that wall!'

'Gracious! To think we didn't dare to ask whose socks they were!'

'If only we had, we'd know who the thief was.'

They raced back to the farmhouse, longing to discuss what to do next. And down in the shed, patiently waiting for them, were Jack, George and Barbara! They didn't give the others a chance to tell about the socks – they immediately began to relate something of their own.

185

'Peter! Janet! You know those strange round marks we saw on the inside of the wall! Well, we've found some more, exactly like them!' said Jack.

'Where?' asked Peter.

'In a muddy patch near old Chimney Cottage,' said Jack. 'George and I saw them and went to fetch Barbara. Then we came to tell you. And what's more, Barbara knows what made the marks!'

'You'll never guess!' said Barbara.

'Go on – tell us!' said Janet, forgetting all about the socks.

'Well, when I saw the marks – round and regular, just like the ones we saw – I couldn't think what they were at first,' said Barbara. 'But then, when I remembered who lived in the nearby cottage, I knew.'

'What were they?' asked Peter, eagerly.

'Do you know who lives at Chimney Cottage?' asked Barbara. 'You don't. Well, I'll tell you – it's One-leg William! He had a leg bitten off once by a shark, and he's got a wooden leg – and when he walks in the mud with it, it leaves round marks – *just* like the marks we saw on the other side of the wall. It must be One-leg William who was the thief.'

The others sat and thought about this for a few moments. Then Peter shook his head.

'No. One-leg William couldn't possibly be the thief. He couldn't have climbed over the wall with one

leg – and besides – the thief wore a pair of socks – and that means *two* legs!'

'How do you know he wore socks?' asked Barbara, astonished.

They told her about the socks on the line away in the circus field. Barbara thought hard.

'Well – I expect the thief *was* a two-legged man with socks – but I don't see why One-leg William couldn't have been with him to help in some way – give him a leg-up, or something. The marks are *exactly* the same! What was One-leg William doing there, anyway?'

'That's what we must find out,' said Peter, getting up. 'Come on – we'll go and ask him a few questions – and see those marks. Fancy them being made by a one-legged man – I never, never thought of that!'

They made their way to Chimney Cottage. Just outside was a very muddy patch – and sure enough, it was studded with the same round, regular marks that the children had seen over Milton Manor wall. Peter bent down to study them.

He got out his notebook and took from it the bit of string that George had cut when he measured the width of the other round marks. He looked up in surprise.

'No – these marks *aren't* the same – they're nearly an inch smaller – you look!' He set the string over one of the marks, and the others saw at once that it was longer than the width of the marks.

'Well! Isn't that odd!' said George. 'It *couldn't* have been One-leg William, then. Is there another man with a wooden leg in the district? One whose leg might be a bit wider and fit the marks?'

Everyone thought hard – but nobody could think of a man with a wooden leg. It was really exasperating! 'We keep *on* thinking we're solving things, and we aren't,' said Peter. 'There's no doubt in my mind that a man with a wooden leg was there with the thief, though goodness knows why – but it wasn't One-leg William. And we do know that the *thief* can't have only one leg because he definitely wears two socks!'

'We know his socks – but we don't know *him*!' said Janet. 'This mystery is getting more mysterious than ever. We keep finding out things that lead us nowhere!'

'We shall have to go back to the circus field tomorrow and try to trace those socks,' said Peter. 'We can't ask straight out whose they are – but we could watch and see who's wearing them!'

'Right,' said Colin. 'Meet there again at ten – and we'll have a look at every sock on every foot in that field!'

CHAPTER THIRTEEN

A coat to match the cap

AT TEN o'clock all the Secret Seven were in the circus field. They decided to go and see Trinculo the acrobat again, as an excuse for being there. But he was nowhere to be found.

'He's gone off to the town,' said one of the other acrobats. 'What do you want him for?'

'Oh – just to ask him if we can mess around a bit,' said Jack. 'You know – have a look at the animals and so on.'

'Carry on,' said the acrobat, and went off to his caravan, turning cart-wheels all the way. The children watched him in admiration. 'How *do* they turn themselves over and over their hands and feet like that?' asked Pam. 'Just exactly like wheels turning round and round!'

'Have a shot at it,' said George, with a grin. But when Pam tried to fling herself over on her hands, she crumpled up at once, and lay stretched out on the ground, laughing.

A small circus-girl came by and laughed at Pam. Then she immediately cart-wheeled round the field,

191

turning over and over on her hands and feet just as cleverly as the acrobat.

'Look at that,' said George, enviously. 'Even the kids can do it. We shall have to practise at home.'

They went to look at the little bear, who, however, was fast asleep. Then they wandered cautiously over to the clothes line. The socks were gone! Aha! Now perhaps someone was wearing them. Whoever it was would be the thief.

The children strolled round the field again, looking at the ankles of every man they saw. But to their great annoyance all they could see had bare ankles! Nobody seemed to wear any socks at all. How maddening!

Louis came up to the lions' cage and unlocked it. He went inside and began to do the usual cleaning. He took no notice of the lions at all, and they took no notice of him. Janet thought it must be marvellous to go and sweep all round the feet of lions and not mind at all!

He had his flannel trousers rolled up to his knees. His legs were quite bare. On his feet were dirty old rubber shoes.

The children watched him for a little while, and then turned to go. Another man came up as they left, and they glanced casually down at his ankles, to see what kind of socks he wore, if any. He was bare-legged, too, of course!

But something caught Jack's eyes, and he stopped and stared at the man intently. The fellow frowned. 'Anything wrong with me?' he said, annoyed. 'Stare away!'

Jack turned to the others, his face red with excitement. He pushed them on a little, till he was out of the man's hearing.

'Did you see that coat he was wearing?' he asked. 'It's like that cap we found up in the tree – only not quite so filthy dirty! I'm sure it is!'

All seven turned to look round at the man, who was by now painting the outside of the lions' cage, making it look a little smarter than before. He had taken off his coat and hung it on the handle of the lions' cage. How the Seven longed to go and compare the cap with the coat!

'Have you got the cap with you?' asked Pam in a whisper. Peter nodded, and patted his coat pocket. He had all the 'clues' with him, of course!

Their chance suddenly came. The man was called away by someone yelling for him, and went off, leaving his paint-pot, brush and coat. Immediately the children went over to the coat.

'Pretend to be peering into the lions' cage while I compare the cap with the coat,' said Peter in a low voice. They all began to look into the cage and talk about the lions, while Peter pulled the cap out of his pocket and quickly put it against the coat.

He replaced the cap at once. There was no doubt about it – the cap and coat matched perfectly. Then was this fellow who was painting the lions' cage the thief? But why had he thrown his cap high up in a tree? Why did he leave it behind? It just didn't make sense.

The man came back, whistling. He stooped down to pick up his paint-brush, and Colin got a splendid view of the top of his head. He gazed at it.

Then all the children moved off in a body longing to ask Peter about the cap. Once they were out of hearing, he nodded to them. 'Yes,' he said. 'They match. That man *may* be the thief, then. We'll have to watch him.'

'No good,' said Colin, unexpectedly. 'I just caught sight of the top of his head. He's got black hair – but no round bare patch at the crown, like the man had who sat below me in that tree. *He's* not the thief!'

CHAPTER FOURTEEN

The peculiar marks again

THE SEVEN went to sit on the rails of the fence that ran round the circus field.

They felt disheartened.

'To think we find somebody wearing a coat that *exactly* matches the cap we found – and yet he can't possibly be the thief because the top of his head is wrong!' groaned Peter. 'I must say this is a most aggravating adventure. We keep finding out exciting things – and each time they lead us nowhere at all!'

'And if we find anyone wearing those socks that we are sure belong to the thief, it won't be him at all either,' said Janet. 'It will probably be his aunt, or something!'

That made everyone laugh. 'Anyway,' said Peter, 'we're not absolutely *certain* that the cap has anything to do with the theft of the necklace. We only found it flung high up in a tree, you know, near where the thief climbed over the wall.'

'It has got something to do with the mystery,' said George. 'I'm sure of it – though I can't for the life of me think how.'

They all sat on the fence and gazed solemnly over the field. What an annoying adventure this was! And then Janet gave a little squeal.

'What is it? Have you thought of something?' asked Peter.

'No. But I'm seeing something,' said Janet, and she pointed over to the right. The others looked where she pointed, and how they stared!

The field was rather wet just there, and in the damp part were round, regular marks just like those they had seen by the wall – and very like the smaller marks made by the one-legged man near his cottage!

'I think *these* marks are the right size,' said Peter, jumping down in excitement. 'They look bigger than the marks made by the one-legged man's wooden leg. I'll measure them.'

He got out his bit of string and laid it carefully across one of the marks. Then across another and another. He looked up joyfully.

'See that. Exactly the same size! Every one of these round marks is the same as those we saw in the ground below the wall the thief climbed!'

'Then – there must be another one-legged man here, in the circus – a man with a wooden leg that measures the same as those round marks,' said Colin, excitedly. 'He's not the thief, because a one-legged man couldn't climb the wall, but he must have been *with* the thief!'

'We must find him,' said George. 'If we can find who his friend is, or who he shares a caravan with, we shall know his friend is the thief – and I expect we'll find that the thief is wearing those socks, too! We're getting warmer!'

Peter beckoned to the small circus girl who had turned cart-wheels some time before. 'Excuse me!' he called. 'We want to talk to the one-legged man here. Which is his caravan?'

'Don't be daft,' said the small girl. 'There isn't a one-legged man here. What'd he be doing in a circus? All of us here have got our two legs – and we need them! You're daft!'

'Come on now,' said Peter firmly. 'We know there *is* a one-legged man here and we mean to see him. Here's some chocolate if you'll tell us where he is.'

The little girl snatched the chocolate at once. Then she laughed rudely. 'Chocolate for nothing!' she said. 'You're nuts! I tell you, there isn't a one-legged man here!'

And before they could ask her anything else, she was gone, turning over on hands and feet as fast as any clown in the circus!

'You run after her,' called a woman from a nearby

caravan. 'But she won't tell you no different. We haven't got any one-legged man here!'

She went into her caravan and shut the door. The Seven felt quite taken aback. 'First we find marks outside Chimney Cottage and are certain they belong to the thief,' groaned Peter, 'but they belong to a one-legged man who is nothing to do with this adventure – and then we find the *right* marks, right size and all – and we're told there isn't a one-legged man here at all! It's really very puzzling!'

'Let's follow the marks,' said Janet. 'We shall find them difficult to see in the longer grass – but maybe we can spot enough to follow them up.'

They did manage to follow them. They followed them to a small caravan parked not far off the lions' cage, next to a caravan where Louis was sitting on the steps. He watched them in surprise.

They went up the steps of the small caravan and peered inside. It seemed to be full of odds and ends of circus properties. Nobody appeared to live there.

A stone skidded near to them and made them jump. 'You clear off, peeping and prying where you've no business to be!' shouted Louis, and picked up another stone. 'Do you hear me? Clear off!'

CHAPTER FIFTEEN

A shock for Peter and Colin!

THE SEVEN went hurriedly out of the circus field and into the lane. George rubbed his ankle where one of Louis's stones had struck him.

'Beast!' he said. 'Why didn't he want us to peep in that little old caravan? It's only used for storing things, anyway.'

'Maybe the thief has hidden the pearls there!' said Janet with a laugh.

Peter stared at her and thought hard. 'Do you know – you might be right!' he said, slowly. 'We are certain the thief belongs to the circus – we're certain the pearls must be there – and why should Louis be so upset when we just peeped into that caravan?'

'I wish we could search it and see,' said Colin, longingly. 'But I don't see how we can.'

'Well, *I* do!' said Peter. 'You and I will go to *tonight's* performance of the circus, Colin – but we'll slip out at half-time, when all the performers are in the ring, or behind it – and we'll see if those pearls *are* hidden there!'

203

'But surely they won't be?' asked Pam. 'It seems such a silly place.'

'I've got a sort of a hunch about it,' said Peter, obstinately. 'I just can't explain it. Those strange round marks seemed to lead there, didn't they? Well, that's peculiar enough, to begin with.'

'It certainly is,' said Barbara. 'Marks made by a one-legged man who doesn't exist! This is a silly adventure, I think.'

'It isn't really,' said George. 'It's a bit like a jigsaw puzzle – the bits look quite odd and hopeless when they're all higgledy-piggledy – but as soon as you fit them together properly, they make a clear picture.'

'Yes – and what we've got so far is a lot of odd bits that really belong to one another – but we don't know how they fit,' said Pam. 'A bit of blue wool belonging to socks we saw on the line – a tweed cap that matches a coat worn by someone we know isn't the thief! Strange marks that turn up everywhere and don't tell us anything.'

'Come on – let's get home,' said Jack, looking at his watch. 'It's almost dinner-time. We've spent all the morning snooping about for nothing. Actually I'm beginning to feel quite muddled over this adventure. We keep following up trails that aren't any use at all.'

'No more meetings today,' said Peter, as they walked down the lane. 'Colin and I will meet tonight by ourselves and go to the circus. Bring a torch, Colin. Gosh – suppose we found the pearls hidden in that old caravan!'

'We shan't,' said Colin. 'I can't think why you're so set on searching it. All right – meet you at the circus gate tonight!'

He was there first. Peter came running up a little later. They went in together, groaning at having to pay out another six pounds, 'Just for half the show, too,' whispered Peter.

The two boys went into the big tent and found seats near the back, so that they could easily slip out unnoticed. They sat down and waited for the show to begin.

It really was very good, and the clowns, stilt-walkers and acrobats seemed better than ever. The boys were quite sorry to slip out before the show was over.

It was dark in the circus field now. They stopped to get their direction. 'Over there,' said Peter, taking Colin's arm. 'See – that's the caravan, I'm sure.'

They made their way cautiously towards the caravan. They didn't dare to put on their torches in case someone saw them and challenged them. Peter fell over the bottom step of the caravan, and then began to climb up carefully.

'Come on,' he whispered to Colin. 'It's all clear! The door isn't locked, either. We'll creep in, and begin our search immediately!'

The two boys crept into the caravan. They bumped into something in the darkness. 'Dare we put on our torches yet?' whispered Colin.

'Yes. I can't hear anyone near,' whispered back Peter. So, very cautiously, shading the beam with their hands, they switched on their torches.

A SHOCK FOR PETER AND COLIN!

They got a dreadful shock at once. They were in the wrong caravan! This wasn't the little caravan in which all kinds of things from the circus were stored – this was a caravan people lived in. Good gracious! Suppose they were caught, what a row they would get into.

'Get out, quickly!' said Peter. But even as he spoke Colin clutched his arm. He had heard voices outside! Then someone came up the step. Whatever *were* they going to do now!

CHAPTER SIXTEEN

Prisoners

'QUICK! HIDE under that bunk thing – and I'll hide under this,' whispered Peter in a panic. He and Colin crawled underneath, and pulled the hangings over them. They waited there, trembling.

Two men came into the caravan, and one of them lit a lamp. Each sat down on a bunk. Peter could see nothing of them but their feet and ankles.

He stiffened suddenly. The man on the bunk opposite had pulled up his trouser legs, and there, on his feet, were the blue socks with the faint red lines running down each side!

To think he was sitting opposite the man who must be the thief – and he couldn't even see his face to know who it was! Who could it be?

'I'm clearing out tonight,' said one man. 'I'm fed up with this show. Nothing but grousing and quarrelling all the time. And I'm scared the police'll come along sooner or later about that last job.'

'You're always scared,' said the man with the socks. 'Let me know when it's safe to bring you the pearls. They can stay put for months, if necessary.'

'Sure they'll be all right?' asked the other man. The man with the socks laughed, and said a most peculiar thing.

'The lions will see to that,' he said.

Peter and Colin listened, frightened and puzzled. It was plain that the thief was there – the man with the socks, whose face they couldn't see – and it was also quite plain that he had hidden the pearls away for the time being – and that the first man had got scared and was leaving.

'You can say I'm feeling too sick to go on again in the ring tonight,' said the first man, after a pause.

'I'll go now, I think, while everyone's in the ring. Get the horse, will you?'

The man with the socks uncrossed his ankles and went down the steps. Peter and Colin longed for the other fellow to go too. Then perhaps they could escape. But he didn't go. He sat there, drumming on something with his fingers. It was plain that he felt nervous and scared.

There were sounds outside of a horse being put between the shafts. Then the man with the socks called up the steps.

'All set! Come on out and drive. See you later.'

The man got up and went out of the caravan. To the boys' intense dismay he locked the door! Then he went quietly round to the front of the van, and climbed up to the driving seat. He clicked to the horse and it ambled off over the field.

'Hey!' whispered Colin. 'This is awful! He locked that door! We're prisoners!'

'Yes. What a bit of bad luck,' said Peter, crawling out from his very uncomfortable hiding-place. 'And did you notice, Colin, that one of the men had those socks on! He's the thief. And he's the one we've left behind, worse luck.'

'We've learnt a lot,' said Colin, also crawling out. 'We know the pearls are somewhere in the circus. What did he mean about the lions?'

'Goodness knows,' said Peter. 'Unless he's put them into the lions' cage and hidden them somewhere there. Under one of the boards, I expect.'

'We'll have to escape somehow,' said Colin, desperately. 'Could we get out of a window, do you think?'

The boys peeped cautiously out of the window at the front, trying to see where they were. The caravan came to a bright street lamp at that moment – and Peter gave Colin a sharp nudge.

'Look!' he whispered, 'that man who's driving the caravan has got on the tweed coat that matches the old cap we found up in the tree. It must be the man we saw painting the outside of the lions' cage!'

'Yes. And probably the thief borrowed his cap to wear, seeing that they live in the same caravan,' said Colin. 'That makes *one* of the bits of jigsaw pieces fit into the picture, anyway.'

They tried the windows. They were tightly shut.

Colin made a noise trying to open the window and the driver looked back sharply into the van. He must have caught sight of the face of one of the boys by the light of a street lamp, for he at once stopped the horse, jumped down, and ran round to the back of the van.

'Now we're for it!' said Peter, in despair. 'He's heard us. Hide quickly, Colin! He's unlocking the door!'

CHAPTER SEVENTEEN

Back at the circus field

THE KEY turned in the lock and the door of the caravan was pushed open. A powerful torch was switched on, and the beam flashed round the inside of the van.

The boys were under the bunks and could not be seen. But the man was so certain that somebody was inside the van that he pulled aside the draperies that hung over the side of the bunk where Peter was hiding. At once he saw the boy.

He shouted angrily and dragged poor Peter out. He shook him so hard that the boy yelled. Out came Colin at once to his rescue!

'Ah – so there are two of you!' said the man. 'What are you doing here? How long have you been in this van?'

'Not long,' said Peter. 'We came in by mistake. We wanted to get into another van – but in the dark we missed our way.'

'A pretty poor sort of story!' said the man, angrily. 'Now I'm going to teach you a lesson – that will stop you getting into other people's caravans.'

215

He put down his torch on a shelf, so that its beam lit the whole caravan. He pushed back his coat sleeves and looked very alarming indeed.

Colin suddenly kicked up at the torch. It jerked into the air and fell to the floor with a crash. The bulb was broken and the light went out. The caravan was in darkness.

'Quick, Peter, go for his legs!' yelled Colin, and dived for the man's legs. But in the darkness he missed them, shot out of the door, and rolled down the steps, landing with a bump on the road below.

Peter got a slap on the side of his head and dodged in the darkness. He, too, dived to get hold of the man's legs and caught one of them. The man hit out again and then staggered and fell. Peter wriggled away, half fell down the steps and rolled into the hedge.

At the same moment the horse took fright and galloped off down the road with the caravan swinging from side to side behind it in a most alarming manner. The man inside must have been very, very surprised indeed!

'Colin! Where are you?' shouted Peter. 'Come on, quickly! The horse has bolted with the caravan and the man inside it. Now's our chance!'

Colin was hiding in the hedge, too. He stepped out to join Peter, and the two set off down the road as fast as they could, running at top speed, panting loudly.

216

'Every single thing in this adventure goes wrong,' said Colin at last, slowing down. 'We can't even get into the right caravan when we want to – we have to choose the wrong one.'

'Well, we learnt quite a bit,' said Peter. 'And we know the thief is wearing those socks now, even if we still don't know who he is. Funny thing is – I seem to know his voice.'

'Have you any idea at all where we are?' asked Colin. 'I mean – do you suppose we're running *towards* home, or away from it? As this is a most contrary adventure, I wouldn't be surprised if we're running in the wrong direction as fast as ever we can!'

'Well, we're not,' said Peter. 'I know where we are all right. In fact, we'll soon be back at the circus field. Hey – should we slip into the field again and just have a look round for the man who's wearing the socks? I feel as if I simply *must* find out who he is!'

Colin didn't want to. He had had enough adventure for one night. But he said he would wait for Peter outside the gate if he badly wanted to go into the field again.

So Peter slipped over the fence and made his way to where he saw many lights. The show was over, and the people had gone home. But the circus people were now having their supper, and the light from lanterns and fires looked very bright and cheerful.

218

Peter saw some children playing together. One of them appeared very tall indeed – and Peter saw that she was walking on stilts, just as the stilt-walkers did in the ring. It was the rude little girl who had told him there was no one-legged man in the circus. She came walking over to where he stood by a caravan, but she didn't see him. She was absorbed in keeping her balance on the stilts.

She came and went – and Peter stared at something showing on the ground. Where the child had walked, her stilts had left peculiar marks pitted in the ground – regular, round marks – just like the ones by the wall round Milton Manor! There they were, showing clearly in the damp ground, lit by the flickering light of a nearby lantern!

'Look at that!' said Peter to himself. 'We were *blind*! Those marks weren't made by a one-legged man – they were made by a stilt-walker! Why ever didn't we think of it before?'

CHAPTER EIGHTEEN

Peter tells his story

PETER GAZED down at the number of strange round marks. He looked over at the child who was stilt-walking – yes, everywhere she went, her stilts left those round marks on the ground. Now another bit of the jigsaw had fitted into place.

'The thief was a stilt-walker,' said Peter to himself. 'He took his stilts with him to help him get over the wall. I must find Colin and tell him!'

He ran over to where Colin was waiting for him. 'Colin, I've discovered something exciting!' he said. 'I know what makes those peculiar round marks – and they're nothing to do with a one-legged man!'

'What makes them then?' asked Colin, surprised.

'Stilts!' said Peter. 'The ends of stilts! The thief was on stilts – so that he could easily get over that high wall. What a very clever idea!'

'But how did he do it?' said Colin puzzled. 'Come on, let's go home, Peter. I shall get into an awful row, it's so late. I'm terribly tired, too.'

'So am I,' said Peter. 'Well, we won't discuss this exciting evening any more now – we'll think about it and have a meeting tomorrow morning. I'll send Janet round for the others first thing. As a matter of fact, I haven't *quite* worked out how the thief did climb over the wall with stilts.'

Colin yawned widely. He felt that he really could not try to think out anything. He was bruised from his fall out of the caravan, he had banged his head hard, and he felt rather dazed. All he wanted to do was to get into bed and go to sleep!

Janet was fast asleep when Peter got home, so he didn't wake her. He got into bed, meaning to think everything out carefully – but he didn't, because he fell sound asleep at once!

In the morning he wouldn't tell Janet a word about the night's adventures. He just sent her out to get the others to a meeting. They came, wondering what had happened. One by one they hissed the password – 'Adventure!' – and passed through the door. Colin was last of all. He said he had overslept!

'What happened last night? Did you find the pearls? Do you know who the thief is?' asked Pam, eagerly.

'We didn't find the pearls – but we know everything else!' said Peter, triumphantly.

'*Do we?*' said Colin, surprised. 'You may, Peter – but I don't. I still feel sleepy!'

'Peter, tell us,' said George. 'Don't keep us waiting. Tell us everything!'

'Come on up to Little Thicket and I'll show you exactly how the thief got over that wall,' said Peter, suddenly deciding that that would be a very interesting way of fitting all the bits of the jigsaw together.

'Oh – you *might* tell us now!' wailed Janet, bitterly disappointed.

'No. Come on up to Little Thicket,' said Peter. So they all went together to Little Thicket, and walked over to the big gates of Milton Manor. John the gardener was there again, working in the front beds of the drive.

'John! May we come in again?' shouted Peter. 'We won't do any harm.'

John opened the gates, grinning. 'Discovered anything yet?' he asked as the children crowded through.

'Yes, lots,' said Peter, and led the way to the place where the thief had climbed over the wall. 'Come along with us and I'll tell you what we've discovered, John!'

'Right – but I'll just let this car in at the gates first,' said John, as a big black car hooted outside.

The children soon came to the place where they had been before. 'Now look,' said Peter, 'this is what happened. The thief was a stilt-walker, so all he had to do was to come to the outside of this wall, get up on his stilts – walk to the wall, lean on the top, take his feet from the stilts and sit on the wall. He then draws his stilts over the wall and uses them on this soft ground. On the hard garden paths they don't mark, and he is safe to come to earth and hide his stilts along the box hedging of the border.'

'Go on!' said Janet in excitement.

'He gets into the house, takes the pearls, and comes back to the wall,' said Peter. 'Up he gets on his stilts again and walks to the wall – and he leaves more of these peculiar round stilt-marks behind in the earth, of course!'

'Goodness – *that's* what they were!' said Pam.

'Yes. And as he clambers on to the wall, his cap catches a high branch of a tree and is jerked off,' said Peter. 'He leaves it there because he doesn't want to waste time getting it back. He catches one of his socks on that little sharp piece of brick and leaves a bit of wool behind . . . then he's up on the top of the wall, and down he jumps on the other side!'

'Which I heard him do!' said Colin. 'But, Peter – he had no stilts when I saw him. *What did he do with his stilts?*'

CHAPTER NINETEEN

Where are the pearls?

'YOU WANT to know what he did with the stilts he used when he climbed up on the wall after he had stolen the pearls?' said Peter. 'Well – I don't really know – but if all my reasoning is right, he must have flung them into a thick bush, somewhere, to hide them!'

'Yes – of course,' said Pam. 'But which bush?'

They all looked round at the bushes and trees near by. 'A holly bush!' said Colin, pointing over the wall. 'That's always so green and thick, and people don't go messing about with holly because it's too prickly!'

'Yes – that would certainly be the best,' said Peter, 'Come on, everyone.' He led the rest out of the Manor grounds and round to the other side of the wall at top speed.

They were soon finding out what a very scratchy, prickly job bending back the branches of the thick holly tree could be. But what a reward they had! There, pushed right into the very thickest part, were two long stilts! Colin pulled out one and Peter pulled out the other.

'You were right, Peter!' said Janet. 'You *are* clever! We've explained simply everything now – the old cap high up on a branch – the bit of wool – the peculiar round marks – how the thief climbed an unclimbable wall. Really, I think the Secret Seven have been very, very clever!'

'And so do I!' shouted another voice. They all turned, and there, flushed and breathless, was their friend the inspector of police, with John the gardener still a good ten yards off.

'Hallo!' said Peter, surprised. 'Did you hear all that?'

'Yes,' said the inspector, beaming but breathless. 'John here opened the gate to my car, and told me he thought you had solved the mystery. We knew you must be hot on the scent of something when you chased out of the gate like that. Well, what's your explanation? You've certainly beaten the police this time!'

Peter laughed. 'Ah well, you see – we can go snooping about the circus without anyone suspecting us – but if you sent seven policemen to snoop round the circus field, you'd certainly be suspected of something!'

'No doubt we should,' agreed the inspector. He picked up the stilts and examined them. 'A very ingenious way of scaling an enormously high wall.

228

I suppose you can't also tell me who the thief is, can you?'

'Well – it's a stilt-walker, of course,' said Peter. 'And I *think* it's a fellow called Louis. If you go to the circus you'll probably find him wearing blue socks with a little red thread running down each side.'

'And he'll have black hair with a little round bare place at the crown,' said Colin. 'At least – the thief *I* saw had a bare place there.'

'Astonishing what a lot you know!' said the inspector, admiringly; 'you'll be telling me the colour of his pyjamas next! What about coming along to find him now? I've got a couple of men out in the car. We can all go.'

'Oooh,' said Pam, imagining the Secret Seven appearing on the circus field with three big policemen. 'Hey – won't the circus people be afraid when they see us?'

'Only those who have reason to be afraid,' said the inspector. 'Come along. I do want to see if this thief of yours has a bare place on the crown of his head. Now, *how* do you know that, I wonder? Most remarkable!'

They all arrived at the circus field at last. The police got there first, of course, as they went in their car, but they waited for the children to come. Through the gate they all went, much to the amazement of the circus people there.

'There's Louis,' said Peter, pointing out the sullen-
looking young fellow over by the lions' cage. 'Bother
– he's got no socks on again!'

'We'll look at the top of his head then,' said Colin.

'Louis stood up as they came near. His eyes looked uneasily at the tall inspector.

'Got any socks on?' inquired the inspector, much to Louis's astonishment. 'Pull up your trousers.'

But, as Peter had already seen, Louis was bare-legged. 'Tell him to bend over,' said Colin, which astonished Louis even more.

'Bend over,' said the inspector, and Louis obediently bent himself over as if he were bowing to everyone.

Colin gave a shout. 'Yes – that's him all right! See the bare round patch at the crown of his head? Just like I saw when I was up in the tree!'

'Ah – good,' said the inspector. He turned to Louis again. 'And now, young fellow, I have one more thing to say to you. Where are the pearls?'

CHAPTER TWENTY

The end of the adventure

LOUIS STARED at them all sullenly. 'You're mad!' he said. 'Asking me to pull up my trouser legs, and bend over – and now you start talking about pearls. What pearls? I don't know anything about pearls – never did.'

'Oh yes, you do,' said the inspector. 'We know all about you, Louis. You took your stilts to get over that high wall – didn't you? – the one that goes round Milton Manor. And you got the pearls, and came back to the wall. Up you got on to your stilts again, and there you were, nicely on top, ready to jump down the other side.'

'Don't know what you're talking about,' mumbled Louis sulkily, but he had gone very pale.

'I'll refresh your memory a little more then,' said the inspector. 'You left stilt marks behind you – and this cap on a high branch – and this bit of wool from one of your socks. You also left your stilts behind you, in the middle of a holly bush. Now, you didn't do all those things for nothing. Where are those pearls?'

'Find 'em yourself,' said Louis. 'Maybe my brother's gone off with them in the caravan. He's gone, anyway.'

'But he left the pearls here – he said so,' said Peter, suddenly. 'I was in the caravan when you were talking together!'

Louis gave Peter a startled and furious glance. He said nothing.

'And *you* said the pearls would be safe with the lions!' said Peter. 'Didn't you?'

Louis didn't answer. 'Well, well!' said the inspector, 'we'll make a few inquiries from the lions themselves!'

So accompanied by all the children, and the two policemen, and also by about thirty interested circus people and by the little bear who had somehow got free and was wandering about in delight, the inspector went over to the big lions' cage. He called for the lion-keeper.

He came, astonished and rather alarmed.

'What's your name?' asked the inspector.

'Riccardo,' replied the man. 'Why?'

'Well, Mr Riccardo, we have reason to believe that your lions are keeping a pearl necklace somewhere about their cage or their persons.'

Riccardo's eyes nearly fell out of his head. He stared at the inspector as if he couldn't believe his ears.

'Open the cage and go in and search,' said the inspector. 'Search for loose boards or anywhere that pearls could be hidden.'

Riccardo unlocked the cage, still looking too astonished for words. The lions watched him come in, and one of them suddenly purred like a cat, but much more loudly.

Riccardo sounded the boards. None was loose. He turned, puzzled, to the watching people. 'Sir,' he said, 'you can see that this cage is bare except for the lions – and they could not hide pearls, not even in their manes – they would scratch them out.'

Peter was watching Louis's face. Louis was looking at the big water-trough very anxiously indeed. Peter nudged the inspector.

'Tell him to examine the water-trough!' he said.

Riccardo went over to it. He picked it up and emptied out the water. 'Turn it upside down,' called the inspector. Riccardo did so – and then he gave an exclamation.

'It has a false bottom soldered to it!' he cried. 'See, sir – this should not be here!'

He showed everyone the underneath of the water-trough. Sure enough, someone had soldered on an extra piece, that made a most ingenious false bottom. Riccardo took a tool from his belt and levered off the extra bottom.

Something fell out to the floor of the cage. 'The pearls!' shouted all the children at once, and the lions looked up in alarm at the noise. Riccardo passed the pearls through the bars of the cage, and then turned to calm his lions. The little bear, who was now by Janet, grunted in fear when he heard the lions snarling. Janet tried to lift him up, but she couldn't.

'Very satisfactory,' said the inspector, putting the magnificent necklace into his pocket. The children heard a slight noise, and turned to see Louis being marched firmly away by the two policemen. He passed a clothes-line – and there again were the blue

socks, that had helped to give him away, flapping in the wind!

'Come along,' said the inspector, shooing the seven children in front of him. 'We'll all go and see Lady Lucy Thomas – and *you* shall tell her the story of your latest adventure from beginning to end. She'll want to reward you – so I hope you'll have some good ideas! What do *you* want, Janet?'

'I suppose,' said Janet, looking down at the little bear still trotting beside her, 'I suppose she wouldn't give me a little bear, would she? One like this, but smaller so that I could lift him up? Pam would like one, too, I know.'

The inspector roared with laughter. 'Well, Secret

Seven, ask for bears or anything you like – a whole circus if you want it. You deserve it. I really don't know what I should do without the help of the S.S.S! You'll help me again in the future, won't you?'

'You bet!' said the Seven at once. And you may be sure they will!

WELL DONE, SECRET SEVEN

CONTENTS

CHAPTER ONE

The Secret Seven meet

'WHERE'S MY badge? Where's my badge?' said Janet. 'I know I put it into this drawer.' And out of the drawer came handkerchiefs, socks, and ribbons, flying in the air.

'Janet!' said Mummy, crossly. 'Do look what you are doing – I only tidied that drawer this morning. What is it you want – your Secret Seven Badge?'

'Yes! There's a meeting this morning, and I can't go without my badge,' said Janet. 'Peter wouldn't let me into the shed, I know he wouldn't. He's awfully strict about badges.' And away went another shower of handkerchiefs into the air.

'Well, you certainly won't find it in the drawer now,' said Mummy, and she bent and picked up a little round badge with the letters S.S. worked neatly on it. 'You have thrown it out of the drawer with your hankies, silly!'

'Oh, give it to me, Mummy, give it to me!' cried Janet. But Mummy wouldn't.

'No. You pick up all those things first and tidy them in the drawer,' she said.

'But the Secret Seven meet in five minutes!' cried Janet. 'Peter's down in our shed already.'

'Then you can be late,' said Mummy, and walked out of the room with the little badge! Janet groaned. She picked up everything and stuffed it back into the drawer as tidily as she could in a hurry. Then she tore downstairs.

'I've done it, Mummy, and I *promise* I'll do it better when the meeting is over.'

Mummy laughed. She held out the little badge to Janet. 'Here you are. You and your Secret Seven meetings! How you can bear to meet in that stuffy little shed in this hot weather I don't know! *Must* you keep the door *and* the window shut all the time?'

'We have to,' said Janet, pinning on the badge proudly. 'It's a *very* Secret Society, and we can't have anyone listening to our meetings. Not that much has happened lately. We really need something to liven us up – an adventure like the last one.'

'Take the biscuit-tin down with you,' said Mummy. 'And you can have a bottle of orangeade. Here's Scamper come to find you!'

The lovely golden spaniel came trotting into the room. 'Woof,' he said to Janet. 'Woof!'

'Yes, yes – I know I'm late,' said Janet, giving him a pat. 'I suppose Peter sent you to fetch me. Come along. Thanks for the biscuits and orangeade, Mummy.'

She went down the garden-path, hugging the biscuit-tin and the bottle of orangeade. As she came near the shed, she heard voices. It sounded as if all the other six were there!

Janet banged on the door, and Scamper flung himself against it too.

'Password!' yelled six voices.

'Adventure!' yelled back Janet, giving the password for that week. No one could go to a meeting without saying the password.

The door flew open, and Peter, Janet's brother, stood there, frowning. 'Any need to yell out the password like that?' he said.

'Sorry,' said Janet. 'You all yelled out at me, and I just yelled back. Anyway, there's no one to hear. Look, I've brought the biscuit-tin and some orangeade.'

Peter looked to see if she had on her badge. He had seen his sister hunting madly for it ten minutes back, and he had made up his mind he wouldn't allow her in if she hadn't found it. But there it was, pinned to her dress.

Janet went into the shed. Peter shut the door and bolted it. The window was shut too. The hot summer sun streamed in at the one window, and Janet blew out her cheeks.

'My goodness – it's boiling hot in here! Honestly, I shall melt.'

'We're *all* melting,' said Pam. 'I think this is a silly place to have our weekly meetings when it's so hot. Why can't we have them out in the woods some-where, in the shade of a tree?'

'No,' said Jack at once. 'My sister Susie would always be hanging around – we wouldn't be a Secret Society any more.'

'Well, couldn't we think of somewhere cool and hidden, where nobody would find us?' said Colin. 'For instance, I've got a hiding place in my garden where nobody can find me at all, and it's as cool and as hidden as can be.'

'Where is it?' asked Jack.

'Up a tree,' said Colin. 'We've a big tree with some broad branches half-way up, and I've got a couple of cushions up there, and a box to keep things in. It's cool and breezy, and the branches swing about in the wind. And I've got a really good view all round too. I can always see if anyone is coming!'

They all listened to this speech in silence. Then they looked at one another, their eyes shining.

'Marvellous idea!' Peter said. 'We'll do it ourselves! A house up a tree where we could meet and nobody know! We'll do it!'

CHAPTER TWO

A wonderful idea

THE SECRET SEVEN discussed the new idea. They all thought it very good indeed. Colin felt very proud to think he had given them such a fine idea.

'If we could find a big enough tree, and flat enough branches, we could make a very fine meeting-place there,' said Peter. 'We could take up boards and boxes and cushions, and make a little store-place for biscuits and drinks and books and things.'

'It would be super,' said Janet. 'Nobody would *ever* guess we were there, and nobody could possibly hear what we say.'

'Let's get out of this hot shed and go and find somewhere now,' said Colin. 'I know exactly what an ice-cream feels like when it begins to melt. As for poor old Scamper, he's panting as if he's run a race.'

So he was. His pink tongue hung out, long and wavy, and he panted loudly. Peter got up.

'Come on, old boy. You can have a drink at the stream when we go past.'

They took the biscuit-tin with them, but they all had a drink of the orangeade before they left.

Scamper rushed on to the stream as soon as he knew they were going that way.

'Hey! – don't drink *all* the stream!' called Peter. Scamper lapped and lapped. They went on their way and left him still lapping.

'We'll go to Windy Woods,' said Colin. 'There are some enormous trees there, easy to climb too.'

They came to Windy Woods. It was cool and shady there. 'Now let's look carefully and see if we can spot a good tree,' said Jack. 'Big enough to hold all the Secret Seven!'

'What about Scamper?' said Janet, suddenly. 'He can't climb a tree. He won't be able to come to the meetings.'

'We could make him a sort of harness, and pull him up,' said George.

'He'd hate that,' said Peter. 'Anyway he's not really a member. He needn't come. Or he could sit at the bottom of the tree and guard us.'

'Oh yes! He could bark if anyone came near,' said Barbara. 'He would be a fine gate-keeper.'

'Tree-keeper!' said Pam. 'Look, what about *this* tree? It's enormous.'

'No good,' said Peter, looking up at the great beech. 'No low-down branches to climb up on. We must have a tree that's easy to climb, or we'll spend all our time getting up and down.'

They separated, and began to look for likely trees. There didn't seem to be so many after all. George found one that he thought was just right, but when he climbed up a little way he soon saw that it was impossible to have any kind of house up there.

'No good!' he called down. 'The branches criss-cross too much and are far too thick.'

Down he came, and then Jack shouted out. 'Come here, all of you. What about *this* tree?'

They ran up and looked at Jack's tree. 'Yes,' said Colin, 'that really does look a likely one. One low branch waist-high to climb on – places to put your feet up the trunk after that – another branch there to cling to – and what looks like a nice lot of flattish branches half-way up. I'll shin up and see.'

'No, I'll go,' said Jack. 'I found it. You come after.'

He stood on the low branch and then made his way up, putting his feet on to jutting-out pieces of the trunk that really seemed made for foot-holds! Boughs spread out in just the right places to hold on to, and then Jack came to the place where branches grew out level from the great tree trunk.

'It's fine!' he called down. 'There are about six branches here, all on the same level, more or less, and there's a hole in the trunk too. It would make a fine cupboard. Come on up! There's room for everyone!'

The others climbed up in excitement. Peter came last of all, in case anyone got stuck and wanted help. But it was such an easy tree to climb that nobody wanted any help at all.

'It's the biggest tree in the wood, I should think,' said Peter, when they were all sitting on the platform of branches. 'What luck to have so many broad

branches all about the same level. Where's the hole you told us about, Jack?'

'Here,' said Jack, and moved away from the part of the trunk he was leaning against. The others saw a very large hole. Jack thrust his hand in and felt round it.

'It goes down about two feet,' he said. 'It would make a good store-place for us, just what we want.

Well, shall we make this our Secret Seven Tree, our new meeting-place?'

'Oh *yes*,' said everyone at once, and they began to talk about what they would do to make it a proper tree-house.

Peter took out a note-book. 'Now,' he said, 'suggestions and ideas one at a time please. I'll write them all down.'

CHAPTER THREE

The big tree

EVERYONE WAS full of ideas. 'We could bring some small boards to put across the branches and make a proper little platform,' said Colin. 'We've got some in our shed at home.'

'And rope to tie them on with,' said Jack.

'Yes, and cushions to sit on,' said Pam. 'Only we'd have to stuff them in the hole in the tree whenever we left, in case it rained.'

'Can't do that. The hole's not big enough,' said Jack.

'Well, I could bring an old waterproof sheet – a rubber one – to cover up any of our things when we leave,' said Barbara. 'Then they would be quite all right.'

'Good idea,' said Peter, scribbling fast in his note-book. 'Any more ideas?'

'Stores for the cubby-hole in the tree,' said Janet. 'Unbreakable mugs and things like that. I'll bring those. Mummy always lets us have them when we want them, so long as we take them back some-time.'

'This is fine,' said Peter, scribbling quickly. 'Boards to make a platform. You can bring those, Colin.'

'Rope to tie them with,' said Jack. 'I'll bring that.'

'Cushions for me,' said Pam.

'Rubber sheet for me,' said Barbara.

'Mugs for me,' said Janet. 'What about you, George?'

'I'll bring some food for the cubby-hole,' said George.

'Great!' said Peter. 'And I'll bring the drinks. Gosh, we're going to have a glorious time. It will be a wonderful meeting-place. Don't you go and tell that awful sister of yours, Jack.'

'As if I'd tell Susie!' said Jack, indignantly. 'When shall we begin to make the tree-house?'

'Why not tomorrow?' said Peter. 'Nobody is going away to the sea just yet. It shouldn't take us long to put everything together up here. This place is just *made* for a tree-house!'

A loud and mournful howl rose up from the foot of the tree. Then there came a scrabbling noise.

'Oh, poor Scamper!' said Janet. 'He's been as good as anything waiting for us. I guess he wishes he could climb like our cat. He'd be up beside us in half a jiffy!'

'We're coming, Scamper,' called Peter. He took one last look round the tree. 'It really couldn't be better,' he said. 'And there's only one more thing to hope for.'

'What's that?' asked Jack, beginning to climb down.

'Something for the Secret Seven to *do*,' said Peter. 'We haven't had any adventure or mystery or excitement for ages.'

'I'm glad you said that,' said Pam. 'When you say things never happen – they always do!'

'I hope you're right,' said Peter. He parted the leaves of the tree behind him. 'What a long way we can see!' he said. 'Right over the wood, and across to the hill. I can see the road winding up the hill too, and cars on it.'

'Come on,' called Jack, who was half-way down the

tree now. 'It's getting late. I shall get into a row, I know I shall. My mother says our meetings always last an hour too long!'

'Well, this was a really good one anyhow,' said Colin, slithering down much too fast. 'Gosh, now I've torn my shorts.'

'I should think so, going down the tree as if it was a slippery-slip!' said Barbara.

Scamper gave them a tremendous welcome. He leapt on one after another as the Secret Seven jumped down to the ground, barking and licking with all his might. Peter laughed.

'Poor old Scamper – you won't like our new meeting-place, will you? Hey – look – what about giving Scamper that hole over there as a kind of kennel when we are up the tree?'

He pointed to what looked almost like a small cave in a nearby tree. It was old and rotten, and a hole had appeared at the foot of its trunk. It would just about fit Scamper.

'We could put one of his rugs in there, and a bone, so that he would know it was his place,' said Peter. 'And we could say, "On guard, Scamper!" to him, so that he would stay there till we came down.'

'Oh *yes* – he would be our sentinel,' said George. 'He'd make an awfully good one. He would bark as soon as anyone came near.'

They all felt happy now that they had made a good plan for Scamper. He wouldn't be able to come up the tree and join their meetings as he did in the shed – but at least he would be doing *something* for them and feeling important because he was on guard.

'Woof,' said Scamper, exactly as if he understood every word, and agreed thoroughly. He wagged his tail and ran in front of them. *He* knew it was dinner-time, if they didn't!

CHAPTER FOUR

Making the tree-house

THE NEXT DAY was really very exciting. If anyone had been in Windy Woods he or she would have been most astonished to see the file of children going down the path, each carrying some kind of load.

They had all met at Peter's house with their goods. Janet, his sister, had mugs and plates and spoons. Colin had a set of boards, which Jack had to help him with. Jack had coiled yards and yards of rope round his waist and looked really most peculiar.

Barbara was carrying a big rubber sheet carefully folded, and she was helping Pam with a set of old cushions.

'They're a bit dirty and flattened out,' said Pam, 'but I didn't think that would matter. I got them out of the garden-shed, they've been there ages. I could only find six, so we'll have to get another somewhere.'

Janet ran to get one from her garden-shed, where the Secret Seven usually held their meetings. That made seven cushions, one for everyone.

George had some chocolate, and also a great big tin of mixed biscuits. 'Mother gave me them,' he said. 'She says your mother keeps supplying our Society with food, and it's her turn now.'

'Wonderful,' said Peter, with much approval. 'What a smashing tin!' He had taken some money from his money-box and had bought a bottle of lemonade and one of orangeade, and he also had two bottles full of water to use with the drinks.

Even Scamper had to carry something! He had one of his little rugs rolled up tightly and tied with string. He was carrying it in his mouth, feeling most important. He loved it when the children really let him take part in everything they were doing.

'Woooooooof-woof,' he said, with his mouth full of rug.

'He says he likes to be carrying something like everyone else,' said Janet. 'That's right, isn't it, Scamper?'

Scamper wagged his tail, and almost dropped his rug in his longing to bark properly. 'Ooooof,' he said.

The Seven set off down the path, came to Windy Woods, and made their way to their tree.

'We ought to carve S.S. on the trunk, for Secret Seven,' said Pam.

'Well, we can't,' said Peter. 'My father says that scribbling on walls and pavements and carving on trees is only done by idiots. And if anyone in the Secret Seven wants to be an idiot he can jolly well get out.'

'I only said we *ought* to carve S.S.,' said Pam, quite hurt. 'I didn't mean that we should. You know I'm not a hooligan.'

'Yes. I do know,' said Peter. 'I was only just

telling you what my father said. Let's make Scamper his little sentry-box place before we go up the tree.'

It was fun showing Scamper his 'sentry-box'. He sniffed all round, and then sat down at the entrance, his mouth open as if he were smiling.

'He's pleased. He's smiling,' said Janet. 'Come out, Scamper and we'll put your rug in. Then you'll know this is your own place – your sentry-box. And you're the sentinel on guard. ON GUARD, Scamper. You know what that means, don't you?'

'Woof,' said Scamper, and looked suddenly serious. He ran out.

Peter stuffed his rug into the hole. Then he dropped a bone there for Scamper, and then he put an old cap of his in the hole too.

'On guard, Scamper,' he said, pointing. 'On guard, old fellow. Very important. Guard my cap for me till I come back. On guard!'

Scamper went back into the hole, sniffed solemnly at the cap, then at the bone. He turned round and sat himself upright at the entrance to the hole again, looking important. Nothing would now make him leave his 'sentry-box' until Peter told him he might. He was a very, very good guard when he knew he had to be.

'Now we can get on with our own job without old Scamper leaping round us and barking and getting in the way all the time,' said Peter. 'Let's tie the boards and the rubber sheet to the ropes – then one of us can go up the tree with the rope-end, and pull the whole lot up at once.'

This seemed a very good idea, but wasn't. Peter didn't tie the ropes securely enough round the boards – and as Jack was hauling the package up the tree, a rope slipped and down came all the boards and the rubber sheet, bumping and slipping against the tree!

One board hit Colin on the shoulder, and the rubber sheet unfolded and fell neatly over Pam's head. The others squealed with laughter as Pam yelled and struck out, wondering what had happened to her.

'Oh dear – sorry!' said Peter, pulling the sheet off poor Pam. 'We'll tie the things more firmly this time.'

'You let *me* tie them,' said Colin, rubbing his shoulder. 'I'm not going to have a shower of heavy boards fall on me again!'

'This is *fun*,' said George. 'This is really *fun*! I bet nobody ever had such fun making a tree-house before!'

CHAPTER FIVE

Great fun

ALL THE Seven really enjoyed themselves making the tree-house. It took them the whole of the morning. Placing the boards and roping them firmly in place wasn't quite so easy as they had thought it would be.

The boards kept slipping about, and had a most annoying habit of falling down the tree and having to be fetched up again. Every time one fell, Scamper barked to tell them.

'He probably thinks we don't notice when a board falls down,' said Janet, with a giggle. 'Oh dear – whose turn is it to climb down after that one?'

'It seems to me that it's a question of too many cooks spoiling the broth,' said Jack. 'With all of us sitting about on the branches that we want to put the boards on it's really difficult. You girls get down to lower branches. Go on. Four of us up here are enough to rope down the boards.'

The girls climbed down a little, putting themselves the other side of the tree for safety. 'Bother!

271

There goes one of the cushions!' said Pam. 'Well, it can wait. There'll be another board falling down in a minute, and whoever gets that can get the cushion too.'

The boys had a fine old time putting the boards in place, and roping them firmly to make a kind of platform. At last they had done the job really well.

'Quite safe now,' said Jack, testing the platform

by walking over it slowly. 'Nobody is going to slip down between two boards, and no board is going to get out of place. We've done a really good job.'

The girls came up and admired the platform. The cushion was rescued from the ground below, and soon the wooden platform looked quite cosy, set out with seven rather dirty, flat cushions.

The mugs, plates, drinks, biscuit-tin and packets of chocolate were put into the convenient cubby-hole. The rubber sheet was neatly tied to a branch ready to be spread over the cushions and platform when the Seven left.

'There!' said Peter, pleased. 'Our new head-quarters, Meeting-Place of the Secret Seven Society. Sentinel on guard down below. Everything ready to tackle our next adventure, if only it comes!'

'I don't mind if it doesn't,' said Pam. 'This is enough adventure for me. Fancy having a treehouse like this! Ah – here comes the wind!'

A gust blew strongly, and the branches of the big tree rocked and shook. The platform rocked too.

'Lovely!' said Janet, as she felt the platform moving. 'I feel as if I'm on a ship now – that swaying feeling is just like being in a boat.'

'It's half-past twelve,' said Peter. 'Let's have a

biscuit and a drink, and go home. We can come back this afternoon. We'll bring books and a game and enjoy ourselves.'

'It's funny how grown-ups don't like us to eat just before we have a meal, in case we can't eat our dinner or tea afterwards,' said Janet, nibbling a biscuit. 'I could eat six of these super biscuits and still feel hungry for my lunch.'

'Well, one is all you're going to have,' said Peter, putting the lid on hastily. 'If we eat six at a time there soon won't be any left. A big tin like this ought to last us for ages!'

In the afternoon they all went back to the tree-house. Scamper took his place down below as sentinel again. He seemed quite to understand, and wagged his tail cheerily as one by one the Secret Seven went up the tree.

The wind was stronger in the afternoon, and it was very pleasant to feel the platform rocking. 'I almost expect to hear a splash of water,' said Janet. 'It's so like a boat. I love it!'

They sat or lay about on the platform on their cushions, reading or talking, nibbling at some of George's chocolate. It was nice to hear the wind rustling the leaves round them, and to feel the breeze in their hair.

And then suddenly Scamper began barking down

below. 'Wuff-wuff, woof, woof, WOOF! Wuff-wuff-woof-woof-WOOF!'

'What's up with Scamper?' said Peter, and he peered cautiously down the tree. He heard a voice.

'Now then – what's up with *you*! Don't you come near me or my kitten!'

'It's a boy,' whispered Peter to the others. 'A scruffy-looking boy. He's got a kitten cuddled into his neck. Scamper's leaping round him like anything.'

'He won't hurt him,' whispered back George. 'I expect he's stopping him climbing this tree! He may have thought the boy wanted to. Where's the kitten? Move over and let me see.'

Peter wouldn't move over, so George gave him a shove. Peter clutched at one of the ropes that held a board, and his board tipped up. He almost shot headlong down the tree, but just stopped himself in time by clutching at a branch.

Pam squealed in fright. Peter gave her a sharp nudge. 'Quiet!' he hissed. 'Do you want our hiding-place discovered on the very first day?'

The boy on the ground below looked round, startled by Pam's squeal. He couldn't think where it had come from. Then he looked up the tree.

'Hey!' he called. 'Anyone up there? Who is it?'

Nobody said a word. Pam held her breath until she thought she would burst. Peter glared at her.

'Is anyone up there?' shouted the boy. 'I'm coming up to see.'

Peter gave a low groan. Just what he had been afraid of!

But Scamper had other ideas. What! Let a strange boy climb up the tree he was guarding! What nonsense!

Scamper leapt at the boy, growling. He didn't mean

to bite him or even to snap – but the boy didn't know that. He had just put up an arm to get hold of the lowest branch of the tree. He put it down in a hurry and faced Scamper.

'What's the matter? What are you so excited about? Get down. If you're after my kitten you can think again. Get down I say!'

But not until the boy had walked right away from the tree did Scamper stop leaping and barking. As soon as he saw that the stranger no longer meant to climb, Scamper became his own friendly self again. He placed himself between the tree and the boy and wagged his tail.

'I don't know why you won't let me climb that tree, but if you don't want me to, I won't,' the Seven heard the boy say. 'I can always come back when you're not here if I want to, anyway! I'm going now. You've frightened my poor little kitten nearly to death!'

The Seven heard the crackling of twigs and pine-needles as the boy walked away. Scamper gave one bark of warning, and then went back to his 'sentry-box', very pleased with himself indeed. Aha! He was a fine sentinel. No one could climb that tree unless he let them.

The Seven said nothing until there was no further sound from down below. Pam spoke first. She looked as if she was going to cry.

'I'm sorry, I'm sorry! Don't tell me off! I thought you were going to fall down the tree, Peter, and I couldn't HELP squealing.'

'Well, next time you squeal you'll be turned out of the Secret Society,' said Peter. 'Giving away our marvellous tree-house the very first day we make it!'

Pam went very red. 'I promise I won't do it again,' she said, in a small voice. 'Anyway, the boy's gone, so no harm's done.'

'Thanks to Scamper,' said Peter, still annoyed. 'And how do you know the boy won't come back when we're gone?'

'He won't remember the tree,' said Pam. 'Don't make such a fuss, Peter. I feel bad enough about it anyway.'

'Have some more chocolate,' said George, anxious to change the subject. He didn't want anyone to remind him that it was because of his violent shove Peter had nearly fallen down the tree, and so made Pam squeal.

'Thanks,' said Peter, and took some chocolate. So did everyone, and immediately felt better. They nibbled and talked about how marvellous Scamper was as a guard.

'I bet he's gone back to his sentry-box and is sitting up there as alert as can be,' said Jack. 'I wish I had a dog like him. He's wonderful.'

'*I* don't think that boy will come back,' said Colin after a time. 'I think he was probably just having a walk through the woods – with his kitten! Funny thing to take a kitten about when you go for a walk.'

'Let's have a game of cards,' said Pam. 'I've brought some. And what about a drink? I'm awfully thirsty.'

It really was fun up in the tree-house. They drank orangeade, crunched up a chocolate biscuit each and played a rather tiresome game of cards. The wind would keep flipping the cards off the platform and blowing them down the tree.

'I feel that dominoes would be better,' said George at last. 'At least they wouldn't blow off so easily. Bother – there goes one of my cards again. I'll bring some dominoes tomorrow.'

At five o'clock it was time to go home. They put the cushions in a neat pile and tied the rubber sheet over them. They put everything else away into the tree-hole. A small grey squirrel suddenly ran up a bough and looked at them in amazement.

'Hello!' said Peter. 'How are you? And how's your family? Don't you dare rob our cubby-hole!'

The squirrel chattered a little, and then disappeared with a beautiful bound. Everyone laughed, and Scamper heard them from his post down below. He barked.

'All right, Scamper! We're coming!' called Peter. 'And we'll bring you a chocolate biscuit for being such a good guard. Here we come!'

CHAPTER SIX

Next morning

THE NEXT MORNING they all met at Peter's house again and went off to Windy Woods. Some of them had things to eat, and Peter had the drinks again. Janet had a big book with her. She had promised to lend it to Colin for the day.

'Here's Daddy's book that I told you about,' she said. 'It's all about ships – every single ship there is. I told you I'd bring it to show you. But Daddy says I've GOT to give it back to him in two or three days' time. So don't keep it too long.'

'Thanks awfully,' said Colin, and took it, very pleased. He loved ships, and this was really a wonderful book. He knew he must be very careful with it indeed.

Scamper trotted with them, as usual. They came to Windy Woods and made their way to their tree. Scamper at once put himself into his 'sentry-box' and sat there, serious and important.

'Woof,' he said, and Janet patted him.

'Yes, we know you'll be on guard,' she said. 'Good dog!'

They all climbed up. Peter undid the rubber sheet from the cushions and spread them out over the platform. Just as he had finished the girls gave a startled cry. 'Look! The lid of the biscuit-tin is off, and most of the biscuits are gone! We left quite a lot, but only a few are here. And some of the chocolate we left is gone too, and the lemonade bottle is empty. It was half-full.'

They all looked into the cubby-hole. Yes – the biscuits were certainly gone. The Secret Seven looked at one another. Then Janet spoke suddenly.

'Do you know what I think? I think it's that cheeky little squirrel! I bet he came here after we had gone, looked into our cubby-hole, and took our things. Squirrels are very clever!'

'But what about the lemonade?' asked Peter, doubtfully.

'Squirrels use their paws like monkeys,' said Janet. 'We've seen them holding nuts in their paws and chewing them. I'm sure that squirrel would be clever enough to take the cork out of the bottle. I expect it emptied some of the lemonade out. It wouldn't like the taste.'

'I can believe in a squirrel that takes a cork out of a bottle and even empties some of the lemonade out,' said Peter. 'But I can't somehow believe in a squirrel that puts the cork back again. I believe it's that boy!'

'So do I,' said George. But the others didn't. They were sure it was the squirrel.

'Anyway, don't let's worry,' said Jack. 'We've got plenty of food today. If the squirrel likes a few biscuits and a bit of chocolate, he can have them.'

They had been sensible that morning and had brought dominoes to play with. However, they could just as well have brought cards, because there was no wind. The sun was not to be seen, and the clouds were low.

'I hope it's not going to rain,' said Colin, looking up. 'I believe it is.'

'Well, we shan't feel it much, hidden away in the middle of a thick old tree,' said Pam. 'I don't expect we'll get a single drop on our platform.'

When it did begin to rain, and the drops pattered on the leaves, only one or two got through to their platform. But Colin was worried.

'I'd better put this ship book into the cubby-hole,' he said. 'Hadn't I, Janet? Your father might be cross if it got wet.'

'Well he would,' said Janet. 'He's very careful about books. Put it at the back of the cubby-hole, then it won't even get a drop.'

So the game was stopped while Colin tucked the big book away very carefully behind the little pile of food in the hole. The rain came down harder. It was rather fun to sit and listen to it pelting down on the leaves, and yet get hardly a drop on the platform.

By dinner-time the rain had stopped. 'We'd better make a dash for it now,' said Peter, trying to peer through the branches to see if there was any blue sky. 'Now what about our things? Do you suppose it's

safe to leave them, after some of the biscuits and chocolates have been taken?'

'Quite safe,' said Pam, horrified at the thought of dragging everything down the tree to take home. 'If the squirrel – or whoever the thief was – didn't take the cushions or the mugs and things yesterday it's not likely he will today. And we've only left a few biscuits.'

'Right,' said Peter. 'We'll just tie up the cushions in the rubber sheet and go. Scamper! We're coming!'

'Woof!' said Scamper, and they heard him leaping up at the tree-trunk. He had been very bored in his sentry-box all by himself.

They went down the tree carefully, because the rain had made parts of it rather slippery. Scamper gave them a most hilarious welcome.

They all went off to their homes, and alas, nobody noticed that Colin wasn't carrying the book of ships. He had forgotten all about it, and it was still tucked away in the cubby-hole half-way up the great big tree.

CHAPTER SEVEN

Windy Woods at night

IT WASN'T until Colin was undressing for bed that night that he suddenly remembered the book of ships. Where was it?

Then, with a shock, he knew. He had left it in the tree-house cubby-hole. How dreadful! Suppose that mischievous squirrel found it and tore the pages or nibbled at them! Suppose a storm came and blew rain into the hole and spoilt the book! How angry Janet's father would be!

Colin dressed hurriedly again. He must go and get the book. But he had reckoned without his family. They seemed to be continually moving about the house that night, running upstairs, standing in the hall, going in and out of the garden. It was maddening.

Colin sat by his window till half-past ten. Would his tiresome family never, never go to bed? Ah, that sounded like Granny coming upstairs.

It wasn't until eleven o'clock that Colin felt it was safe to slip out of the house. He got safely out into the garden and jumped when an owl hooted suddenly. He stopped.

Would he know the way to the tree in the dark? It was almost dark now, and in the wood it would be pitch-black. Colin felt a nasty little stab of fear. It wouldn't really be very nice in Windy Woods at night. Suppose he missed the way, didn't find the tree, and got lost? He really would feel an awful idiot, and his mother would be worried and cross.

He had to pass Peter's farm on the way. He wondered if Peter was awake. If he was, he would go with him, he was sure. He stepped into Peter's garden and made his way quietly to the farm-house. He knew where Peter's bedroom was.

The farm-house was in complete darkness. Everyone was in bed. Colin took up a few small pebbles and threw one carefully at Peter's window. It fell back again. Colin threw another, waiting for it to hit the window.

But it didn't. The window was open and the pebble flew inside and hit Peter neatly on the cheek, as he slept peacefully in bed.

He woke with a jump, sat up and stared crossly round the dark room. He rubbed his cheek, wondering what had happened. Another pebble came in at the window and hit the wall.

'Hallo! Someone's throwing stones!' said Peter to himself, and he went cautiously to the window. He made out someone standing below.

'Who is it?' whispered Peter as loudly as he could without making too much noise.

'It's me, Colin!' came a whisper from below. 'Peter, listen – I've left your father's book in the tree-house, in the cubby-hole. I must get it. Will you come with me?'

'Oooh yes,' said Peter, thrilled at the idea of going into Windy Woods at night and climbing up into the tree-house. It would be quite an adventure! Lovely!

He slipped on a jersey and a pair of shorts, and shinned down the tree that grew obligingly outside his

window. In a moment he and Colin were slipping down the path like shadows.

Colin felt perfectly brave the moment that Peter was with him. 'I was afraid I might not find the tree,' he whispered, as they padded along. 'You're so good at finding your way, and I thought you'd know it even in the dark.'

'Yes, I shall,' said Peter, 'But anyway I've brought a torch with me. This is fun, isn't it?'

They came to Windy Woods, which were quiet tonight. Very little wind was about, and the trees made hardly any noise. An owl hooted again and made both boys jump. 'I'm glad I'm not a mouse,' said Peter. 'I should be scared stiff of an owl's hoot!'

They came to their tree. Peter went up first, shining the torch down now and again for Colin, who found it difficult to climb in the dark. At last they came to the platform. It looked strange and desolate in the light of Peter's torch.

'Now to get the book,' said Colin, and he shone the torch in at the hole. He gave a sudden exclamation.

'Hey! Someone's been here again! Everything is upside down and muddled up as if someone's been hunting for something. Food probably.'

'Well, we didn't leave much,' said Peter. 'Bother! It can't be that squirrel. It must be someone who has discovered our tree-house. Is your book there?'

'Yes, thank goodness,' said Colin. 'Peter, *who* comes here? It's maddening!'

'Can't think,' said Peter. And then he heard a sound that astonished him. It was a very small sound indeed, and it came from somewhere in the tree.

'Did you hear that?' whispered Peter. 'It sounded like a tiny mew, but there can't be a cat up here!'

He swung his torch round and about to see if he could find a hidden cat, and then he suddenly clutched Colin and pointed silently.

In the light of his torch was a pair of bare feet! Someone – *someone*, was sitting silently on a branch above them, his feet showing in the torchlight. Who *could* he be?

CHAPTER EIGHT

Someone in the tree-house

PETER SUDDENLY made a grab for the two bare feet and caught hold of them. There was a yell, and the feet began to kick out. But Peter held them tightly.

'You come on down,' he said, angrily. 'Who are you? How dare you come to our tree-house and mess our things up. Come on down!'

'Let me go,' said a boy's voice, and then there came a mewing noise again, and to the two boys' surprise a small kitten leapt down to a nearby branch and stared at Peter and Colin with wide-open green eyes.

'A kitten!' said Colin. 'It must be that boy with the kitten! He did come back after all!'

'Don't pull me, don't pull me!' called the boy on the bough above. 'I'm slipping.'

Peter let go his feet. 'Come on down then, and don't play the fool, because we're two to one,' he said.

The feet came down lower, then the legs, and then a thin body. Then came the whole boy, looking scared and white-faced.

'Sit down,' ordered Peter. 'Don't move. Now you just tell us what you're doing in our tree.'

295

The boy sat down. He looked up at them
sulkily. He was thin and pale, and his hair wanted
cutting.

'I only came here to hide,' he said. 'I've not done
any harm, except to take a few biscuits last night. But
if you'd been as hungry as I was, you'd have taken
them too.'

'What are you hiding from?' asked Colin. 'Have
you run away from home or something?'

'I shan't tell you anything,' said the boy. 'You might tell the police.'

'We shan't,' said Colin. 'At least, not if we can help it. Why should we tell the police anyhow?'

The kitten crept quietly back to the boy and cuddled into his coat. Colin and Peter saw that it had a bleeding leg. The boy put up his hand and stroked it gently. It began to purr.

Both Colin and Peter suddenly felt certain that the boy couldn't be terribly bad because he so obviously loved the kitten – and the kitten trusted him. They stared at the sullen boy.

'Go on – tell us,' said Peter, keeping the light of his torch full on the boy. 'We might be able to help you.'

'Will you let me stay here at night?' asked the boy. 'In case they find me. They know I'm somewhere in Windy Woods.'

'Who?' asked Peter. 'Tell us everything. What's your name, to begin with?'

'Jeff,' said the boy, still stroking the kitten. 'It all began when my mother went to hospital. I lived with her. My dad's dead, so there's only us two. But when Mum was taken to hospital I was sent to my Uncle Harry and my Aunt Lizzy.'

'Well, go on,' said Peter. 'Why did you run away?'

'I stayed there a week,' said Jeff, 'and my mother didn't come out of hospital, and nobody would tell me anything. Suppose she never came out? What was I to do? All I had was my kitten.'

'Well, wouldn't your uncle and aunt have looked after you?' asked Peter.

'I didn't want them to,' said Jeff. 'They are bad. My mother always said so, and she knew. They've got bad friends, and they do bad things.'

'What do they do?' asked Peter.

'Oh – steal – and worse things,' said Jeff. 'They were all right to me, I mean they gave me food, and my aunt mended some of my clothes, but they were cruel to my kitten.'

Colin and Peter stared at Jeff in sympathy. Peter knew how he would have felt if someone had been unkind to Scamper. 'Did – did they hurt the kitten's leg where it's bleeding?' he asked.

Jeff nodded. 'Yes. Uncle kicked at it. It's not so bad now, but it was very bad at first. So that day I ran away, and took the kitten with me. I hid in an empty house, first, but they came after me. Then I came to this wood, and guessed you were up this tree, when your dog barked. So when you'd gone I climbed up.'

'I see,' said Peter. 'And ate our biscuits and chocolate. But why are your uncle and aunt bothering about you? They know you can go back when you want to.'

' 'Tisn't my aunt,' said Jeff. 'It's my uncle and his friend Mr Tizer. They're afraid I know too much.' .

'Too much about what?' asked Colin.

'I used to sleep in the sitting-room,' explained Jeff. 'And one night I heard them talking about some plan they were making. I just heard a few things – but I couldn't make head or tail of them. I turned over to get more comfortable, and my uncle jumped up and accused me of listening.'

'Ah, and now that you've run away they're afraid you will tell someone what you heard,' said Colin. 'Did you hear much?'

'No – nothing to make any sense,' said Jeff. 'But they don't believe that, and they're after me. I saw Mr Tizer in the woods today with his dog. They're hunting me, and I'm scared. That's why I came up to your tree-house. Can't I stay?'

'Yes – you stay here for the night,' said Peter. 'Get out the cushions. Make yourself comfortable. And tomorrow we'll all come and think what to do! Don't you worry – the Secret Seven will put things right!'

CHAPTER NINE

Another meeting

PETER AND COLIN helped the boy to get out the cushions from the rubber sheet. The kitten sat on a nearby branch, watching. It was a dear little thing, a fluffy tabby.

'You can have the rest of our biscuits, and a drink too, if you want to,' said Colin. 'Oh! – I nearly forgot that ship book! I *must* get it out of the cubbyhole!'

He pulled it out, and then the two boys began to climb down the tree again, feeling carefully for footholds. It wasn't nearly so easy to climb down in the dark as it was in the daylight!

'Good night,' called the boy, gratefully. 'And thanks for your help. Are you coming tomorrow? Could you bring me a spot of milk for my kitten, please?'

'Yes, of course – and a bit of fish if we can,' called back Peter. 'Don't fall out of the tree when you're asleep.'

'No, I shan't,' said the boy, sounding much more cheerful.

Colin and Peter made their way home, talking in low voices about the boy and his curious story.

'What do you suppose his uncle and that friend of his – Mr Tizer – were planning to do, and were afraid Jeff had overheard?' said Peter. 'If it was a robbery or something we ought to try and stop it.'

'Well – if we *can* find out anything from Jeff, I really do think we ought to tell someone,' said Colin. 'Your parents, for instance.'

'Yes. But it would be nice to see if the Secret Seven can do something about it first,' said Peter. 'We'll call a meeting tomorrow – up the tree, with Jeff there – and we'll see what we can get out of him. He must have heard *something* that was said!'

'Right,' said Colin, beginning to feel excited. 'This is great! Just when we thought nothing would ever happen, something does. Do you want me to go and tell everyone tomorrow morning that something is up, and we must meet at the tree?'

'Yes,' said Peter. 'Passwords and everything. I'll be at the bottom of the tree, and nobody must yell out the password – just whisper it. Badges must be worn too.'

'Good,' said Colin, pleased. 'Well, we'll say good night here – this is your gate, isn't it? Good thing I went back for this book tonight, wasn't it? We wouldn't have caught Jeff if I hadn't.'

The boys went their different ways, and Peter wondered whether or not to wake Janet and tell her about the boy in the tree-house, but he decided not to. It would keep till morning.

All the Secret Seven were excited next morning when they heard about the meeting to be held, and were told about Jeff.

'Can we take Scamper with us, do you think?' asked Pam. 'Do you suppose he would frighten the kitten?'

'No. He's nice with kittens,' said Peter. 'Anyway, he'll be on guard down below, and the kitten will be up the tree with Jeff. I must remember to take a bottle of milk, and a saucer, and some fish.'

'Good thing we had haddock for breakfast,' said Janet. 'I'll wrap a bit up in grease-proofpaper. Poor little kitten! Do you suppose its leg will be all right? Imagine anyone kicking a *kitten*!'

Promptly at ten o'clock the Secret Seven met at the foot of the tree. The password was whispered importantly to Peter.

'Adventure!'

'Adventure!'

'Adventure! Is that boy up there?'

'Yes. Got your badge on? Good. Are we all here now? Well, up we go. Scamper, on guard, please!'

Scamper looked at Peter, wagged his tail, and at once ran to his sentry-box in the nearby tree. He sat down on his bit of rug there, and looked quite stern as if to say, 'Strangers, beware! I'm on guard. Grrrrrrrrr!'

Peter went up the tree first, the bottle of milk in his pocket, and the little saucer between his teeth. The others followed. Peter saw Jeff peering down anxiously as he heard them climbing up.

'Hello, Jeff!' said Peter, clambering up on to the platform of boards. 'Had a good night? How's the kitten?'

'Its leg is much better,' said Jeff. 'And I slept all night except when the wind blew too hard. I say – nobody will give me away will they? How many of you are there?'

'Seven,' said Peter. 'Move up a bit, Jeff, and make room. We're a Secret Society – the Secret Seven. We have our password and badges, and we hold meetings. If anything turns up for us to do, we do it.'

Jeff sat at the back of the platform and looked at each member climbing up. Colin he knew from the night before. Barbara, Janet, Pam, George, Jack – they all climbed up and grinned kindly at him. The kitten mewed.

'Here's your milk, you tiny little thing!' said Peter, and he poured some out of the bottle into the saucer he had brought. 'Janet, where's the bit of fish?'

The meeting was forgotten as the Seven crowded together on the little platform to watch the hungry kitten lap the milk and pounce on the fish. Jeff watched too. He smiled round gratefully at the children.

'Thanks,' he said. 'Thanks a lot!'

CHAPTER TEN

Jeff tries to remember

PETER HAD also brought a jar of potted meat and a slab of cake for Jeff, and Colin had brought half a loaf and some butter. The boy took them hungrily, and didn't even wait to cut a slice of bread.

He tore at it with his teeth, and the others watched him, feeling shocked to see such hunger.

Janet gently took the bread from him, cut a large slice, buttered it and spread it thickly with potted meat. 'You'll like this better than mouthfuls of bread!' she said.

Jeff ate everything they had brought, except the biscuits they were keeping for mid-morning. He wiped his mouth on the sleeve of his jacket with a sigh.

'That was good,' he said. 'I can't tell you how good!'

The kitten had finished its meal now too, and was sitting beside Jeff, washing its face.

'It looks fatter already,' said Janet, stroking it. 'Poor little thing! Imagine kicking a baby like this! You wouldn't think there'd be anyone bad enough, would you?'

'Mr Tizer's *very* bad,' said Jeff. 'Worse than my uncle. He kicks me too.'

'We want you to tell us all you can,' said Peter, settling himself as comfortably as he could, with his back to the tree-trunk. 'We think we ought to try and find out what it was that Mr Tizer and your uncle were so afraid you had overheard. They must have been planning something wrong – something that ought to be stopped.'

Jeff stared at them. 'Stopped? Who's going to stop it? Not me. Nor you either. Nobody can stop Mr Tizer, not even the police. Anyway I don't know anything.'

'Jeff, you must try and think,' said Colin. 'You said you were asleep in the sitting-room on the sofa when your uncle and Mr Tizer were planning something. You said you woke up and turned over, and they were angry with you because they thought you'd heard what they were talking about. You *must* be able to remember *something*!'

'I can't,' said Jeff, looking sullen.

Peter felt sure he could if he really wanted to. 'You're afraid of Mr Tizer,' he said. 'That's why you won't try to remember. It's mean of you. We've been sorry for you and the kitten and helped you. Now you should help us. We'll see you don't come to any harm.'

Jeff stroked the kitten, and it purred loudly. 'Well – you've been really kind,' he said at last. 'And I'll try to remember what I overheard. But it doesn't make any sense to me, and it won't to you, either!'

'Never mind. Tell us,' said Colin.

Jeff frowned as he tried to remember. 'Let me see,' he began. 'I was asleep – and I woke up – and I heard their voices . . .'

'Yes. Go on,' said Peter.

'I don't know what they were talking about,' said Jeff. 'I was too sleepy to hear properly. I just heard a few things – things that don't make any sense.'

'What things?' asked Barbara, wishing she could jog Jeff and make him go faster in his story.

'Well – let's see – they talked about MKX,' said Jeff, frowning hard. 'Yes, I remember that clearly, MKX.'

'MKX?' said Jack. 'What in the world does that mean? Would it be a code-word for someone helping them in their plans?'

'I don't know,' said Jeff. 'But I do remember MKX. And I remember a date too – Thursday the 25th. They said that two or three times. That's next Thursday, isn't it?'

'Yes,' said Peter. 'It is. Perhaps that was the date of their next robbery or whatever they were planning to do! I say, this is exciting. Go on, Jeff. Remember something else!'

'Don't hurry me,' said Jeff. 'Else I shall remember wrong.'

There was a dead silence at once. No one wanted Jeff to 'remember wrong'!

'They spoke about someone too,' said Jeff, wrinkling his forehead. 'Let's see. Yes – Emma Lane. They kept on about Emma Lane, I do remember that.'

'Emma Lane? That's a good clue,' said Colin. 'We might be able to find out who she is. I've never heard of her.'

'Anything else?' asked Peter. 'You really are doing very well, Jeff. Think hard.'

Jeff was pleased. He thought again, going back in his memory to that night on the sofa, hearing the two men's voices again in his mind.

'Oh, yes!' he said suddenly, 'they said something about a red pillow. That puzzled me. A red pillow. I remember that.'

It puzzled the others too. A red pillow didn't seem to fit into anything. Who would have a red pillow, and what for?

'MKX. Thursday the 25th. Emma Lane. A red pillow,' said Peter. 'What a mix-up! I can't make head or tail of any plot with those four things in it. In fact, the only thing that is at all possible to follow up is the Emma Lane clue. Anything more, Jeff! Think, do think!'

'There was something about a grating,' said Jeff. 'Watching through a grating – yes, that was it! Does that help you at all?'

No, it didn't. It just added to all the mystery! How were the Secret Seven to tackle all that?

313

CHAPTER ELEVEN

Talking and planning

JEFF COULDN'T remember anything more at all. He began to look worried when the Seven pressed him. He went rather white, and Peter noticed it.

'All right. No more questions,' he said. 'We will discuss all this, and have a few biscuits to help us, and a drink of something. Like a biscuit, Jeff?'

Although it was only about an hour since he had eaten a huge meal, Jeff was quite ready to eat again. So was the kitten! It nibbled a biscuit that Janet held out to it, and was quite playful.

'It's feeling better,' said Jeff. 'Listen! Is that your dog barking?'

It was. Scamper barked a few little barks at first, and then burst into loud and angry ones. Peter peered down the tree. Jeff clutched Colin, looking frightened.

'Don't give me away if it's me they're after!' he said. 'Please, please don't!'

Two men were below the tree, walking past. Peter made Jeff look down. He shrank back at once, looking so scared that Peter knew immediately that

the men were Mr Tizer and Jeff's uncle. They were looking for him still, and were under the very tree that poor Jeff was in!

They didn't know that, of course. Scamper was taking all their attention. He capered round the men, pretending to snap and snarl. He didn't like them at all.

'Brute of a dog!' said one of the men, and picked up

a dead branch. He flung it at Scamper. Peter went red with rage. It didn't hit Scamper, but it sent him quite mad! He flew at the two men, and they took to their heels at once!

Scamper chased them about a quarter of a mile through the woods, and then came back, panting, very pleased with himself.

'Good dog!' called down Peter, and Scamper wagged his tail at once. 'On guard again, Scamper, on guard!'

Scamper went to his tree and sat down. No dog could have looked more pleased or important. The Secret Seven sat back with a sigh of relief. Poor Jeff was white and trembling, and the kitten had gone into hiding under his torn coat.

'Cheer up, Jeff,' said Peter. 'Scamper has chased them away. I wonder how they guessed you were here.'

'I think it's because of the kitten,' said Jeff. 'They've only got to ask if anyone has seen a boy with a kitten. Several people in the wood have seen me about, foresters and walkers and such. Mr Tizer and my uncle will get me in the end.'

'No, they won't,' said Peter. 'I must say I didn't like the look of them. Now – what are we going to do about this?'

The Seven talked and talked. MKX. Who or what

was that? Emma Lane. How could they possibly find out where she lived? The red pillow. Impossible clue! The 25th. That was a definite date, but what was going to happen on it, and where? The grating. Where was that – and why was someone going to watch through it?

'I don't think even that famous detective Sherlock Holmes could have made head or tail of this,' said Peter, at last. 'It doesn't seem any use to discuss it at all.'

'No. But it's fun and very exciting,' said Pam. 'I think we ought to tell someone. What about your parents, Peter?'

'Yes. We'd better tell them,' said Peter, not wanting to in the least. 'If we could find out something ourselves, we would have a shot at it. But I don't see how we can. Except that we could find out if there *is* an Emma Lane. That might lead us somewhere.'

'How could we?' asked Barbara.

'Ask at the post office,' said George, feeling rather bright. 'They know where everyone lives.'

'Yes. Good idea,' said Peter. 'You and Jack can ask on the way home. And if it leads to nothing we'll tell my father and mother.'

'I don't want you to,' said Jeff. 'I'll get into trouble if the police go into this.'

'Sorry Jeff,' said Peter. 'But this affair has got to be

sorted out. It's a pity it's beyond the power of the Secret Seven. We've never had a failure yet! Still – this really is too difficult for anything!'

'We'd better go,' said George. 'I keep getting into rows for being late. I bet you others do too.'

'Yes, we do!' said Janet. 'And you and Jack are going to call at the post office, aren't you? We really must go.'

'When will you be back here again?' asked Jeff anxiously.

'This afternoon probably. Or after tea,' said Peter. 'We'll decide as we go home. We'll bring you some more food. Anyway, you can eat the rest of the biscuits and the chocolate. That will keep you going. Now don't look so scared. You'll be quite all right! No one can possibly guess you are up here.'

Jeff looked very doubtful. He watched the Seven climb down one by one. He heard Scamper's excited welcome. The kitten shrank back in fright against him when she heard the loud barks.

If Mr Tizer hears those barks, he'll guess something's up, thought poor Jeff in a panic. I may be safe up in this tree, but I've no way of escape if Mr Tizer found out I was here and climbed up after me!

CHAPTER TWELVE

Emma Lane

GEORGE AND JACK called in at the post office as Peter had told them. They knew the post office girl, and she smiled at them.

'I hope it won't bother you to find out for us,' began George, very politely. 'But we want to know where someone called Emma Lane lives. It's rather important. Can you possibly tell us?'

'It will take me a few minutes,' said the girl taking down a big directory. 'I'll find out for you now.'

The boys waited patiently. The girl turned over page after page, running her finger down lists of names.

'Yes,' she said. 'There *is* an Emma Lane. Mrs Emma Lane, one, Church Street. That must be the one you want. It's the only Emma Lane there is. The others are Elizabeth and Elsie.'

'Oh *thanks*!' said George, delighted. 'One, Church Street. That's easy to remember!'

'We'll go and tell Peter after dinner,' said Jack. 'Then perhaps we could all go and find out exactly who Emma Lane is and what she does.'

So, after dinner, they went round to Peter's house

and he and Janet listened with great interest to their bit of news.

'We'll go straightaway to Emma Lane's and see if we can find out anything at all,' said Peter. 'She might know Mr Tizer, for instance.'

'Yes. She might tell us something about him, and that awful uncle of Jeff's,' said George. 'Shall we get the others and all go together?'

'No,' said Peter. 'It might look a bit peculiar, seven of us arriving to talk to Emma!'

They set off to Church Street. Number One was a dear little house, neat and pretty with a tiny well-kept front garden.

The four children stopped outside, and debated who was to go to the door and what to say.

'You go, Peter,' said George. 'We did our bit going to the post office. I wouldn't know *what* to say to Emma Lane!'

'All right. Janet and I will go,' said Peter, and he and his sister walked up the little path to the neat green front door. They rang the bell.

A small girl opened the door and stared at them. She didn't say a word.

'Er – could you tell me if Mrs Emma Lane is in?' asked Peter, politely.

'Who's she?' asked the little girl. 'I've never heard of any Emma Lane.'

This was most surprising. Peter was puzzled. 'But
the post office said she lived here,' he said. 'Isn't there
an Emma Lane here? What about your mother?'

'My mother's called Mary Margaret Harris,' said
the small girl. 'And I'm Lucy Ann Harris.'

A voice called up the hall passage. 'Who's that,
Lucy?'

'I don't know,' called back Lucy. 'It's just two children asking for someone who doesn't live here.'

A lady came up the passage, her hands covered in flour. She smiled at Peter and Janet. 'I'm making cakes,' she said. 'Now, who is it you want?'

'They want an Emma Lane,' said the little girl, laughing. 'But she doesn't live here, does she, Mother?'

'Emma Lane? Why, she's your grandmother, you silly child!' said the lady. Lucy stared at her mother in surprise.

'I never knew Granny's name was Emma,' she said. 'I never heard anyone call her Emma Lane. You call her Mother and I call her Granny.'

'Well, she's got a name, all the same,' said the lady. She turned to Peter and Janet. 'The old lady doesn't live here now,' she said. 'She went away three months ago to the seaside, and we've got her house instead. Did you want to speak to her?'

'No – well, yes – but it doesn't matter,' said Peter, feeling rather muddled. 'Thank you very much. I'm sorry to have bothered you in the middle of making cakes.'

He and Janet went down the path. 'What a silly girl not to know her grandmother's name,' said Janet.

'Well, do *you* know the names of our two grannies?' said Peter. 'We know their surnames, but I don't know the Christian name of either of our grannies! I've never heard anyone call them by name, except that *we* call them Granny, and Mummy and Daddy call them Mother.'

'Do you suppose that little girl's granny has anything to do with Mr Tizer's plans?' asked Janet. Peter shook his head.

'No, she's an old lady, and she must be nice if she lived in that lovely little house, and anyway she's not there. She's not the Emma Lane we want, and yet she was the only one the post office knew!'

They walked on in silence. Peter sighed. 'We had better tell Mummy and Daddy, Janet. It's all too muddled and difficult this time. There's not even anything we can do to unravel the muddle. A red pillow! MKX! It's just silly.'

CHAPTER THIRTEEN

A nasty shock

DADDY WAS in for tea. Peter broke the news to him while he was spreading slices of bread and butter with honey.

'Daddy! The Secret Seven are in the middle of something again!'

Daddy and Mummy both looked up at once. 'You and your Secret Seven! What's up this time?' said Daddy. 'Nothing serious, I hope.'

'We don't know,' said Peter. 'But as two of the people in it are supposed to be really bad – and I think they are – then it might be serious. But although we know quite a lot, it's all so silly and muddled and difficult that we can't make head or tail of it. So we thought we'd better tell *you*!'

'Fire ahead,' said Daddy. 'I can hardly wait to hear!'

'You're not to laugh, Daddy,' said Janet. 'The Secret Seven is a *proper* Society, and you know it's already done quite a lot of things.'

'I'm not really laughing,' said Daddy. 'Nor is Mummy. Tell us all about it.'

So Peter and Janet told the tale of their tree-house and Jeff and the kitten, and his wicked uncle and Mr Tizer, and all the curious collection of things that Jeff had remembered.

Daddy ate his tea all the time. He listened, asking a few questions now and again. Mummy listened too, exclaiming once or twice that she thought the tree-house sounded very dangerous. At last the tale came to an end.

'It certainly wants looking into,' said Daddy. 'But if you want my opinion, I think that boy Jeff has made most of it up. He's feeling miserable because his mother has gone into hospital, he doesn't like his uncle and aunt, he got into trouble with them, and ran away. And you were very kind to him, so he's made up a nice little tale!'

'Oh *no*, Daddy,' said Janet at once. 'He *didn't* make it up. He really didn't. And the kitten *was* hurt. Somebody *had* kicked it!'

'Well, look here, go and fetch that boy Jeff and bring him here to me,' said Daddy. 'If there's anything in his story I'll soon find out, and if there *is* any funny business going on we'll find that out too. He can tell us the address of his uncle, and the police can go and see if there's anything in his tale.'

'He doesn't want the police to be told,' said Peter.

'Of course he doesn't, if he's made up the tale!' said Daddy. 'Now you go and fetch him. Tell him I shan't bite his head off. As for all the things he says he remembers hearing when he was half-asleep, well, *I* think he dreamt them! Don't look so upset, both of you. When you get a bit older you'll learn not to believe all the tales people tell you!'

'But Daddy, he was speaking the truth, I'm sure he was,' said Janet, almost in tears.

'Right. Then we'll certainly do something to help him,' said Daddy. 'Go and get him now. I'll finish what I'm working on and be ready as soon as you get back.'

Peter and Janet set off rather gloomily to the tree-house. It was very, very damping to have Daddy and Mummy so certain that Jeff was a fraud. *They* didn't think he was. Well, now Jeff would have to go with them and tell Daddy everything. He would probably be so scared that he wouldn't say a word!

'I hope Jeff *will* come back with us,' said Peter,

suddenly thinking that it might be very, very difficult to get him to climb down the tree if he didn't want to. They said no more till they got to the tree.

Peter called up. 'Jeff! Come on down! We've got something to tell you.'

Nobody answered. Peter called again. 'JEFF! It's me, Peter. Come on down. There's nobody here but me and Janet. It's important.'

There was no reply. But wait – yes, there was! A tiny little mew sounded from up above. The kitten!

'The kitten's there,' said Peter. 'So Jeff must be there too. I wonder if he's all right? I'll go up and see.'

Up he went. He climbed up on to the platform which was still strewn with cushions. The kitten ran to him, mewing.

There wasn't a sign of Jeff! Peter called again and peered upwards, thinking the boy might have climbed higher. No – he wasn't there either! Then he caught sight of a piece of paper stuck into a crevice of the tree-trunk. Peter took it and read it.

'They've found me,' said the note. 'They say they'll come up and throw the kitten down the tree if I don't climb down to them. They would too. Take care of the kitten – and thanks for everything. Jeff.'

Peter slithered down the tree so quickly that he grazed his hands and knees. He held out the paper to Janet. 'Look at that! They've found him. They must have come back again, guessing he might be up here, with Scamper barking round like that. Poor Jeff!'

Janet looked upset and alarmed. 'Oh dear – *now* what are we to do? We don't even know where Jeff lives. We can't find out anything, or help him. Oh look, that poor little kitten is coming down the tree all by itself!'

Peter lifted it down. It mewed. 'We'll look after you all right,' he said. 'Where has your master gone to? That's what *we'd* like to know!'

CHAPTER FOURTEEN

George gets an idea

PETER AND JANET went home, the kitten cuddled against Peter. Daddy was waiting for them.

'Well – where's the boy Jeff?' he said.

'He's gone,' said Peter, and showed his father the note.

'You won't hear of *him* again,' said Daddy. 'I tell you, it was just a made-up tale. Forget it! Ask your mother if you can keep the kitten, though we don't really want another cat. I don't think much of the boy, deserting the kitten like that!'

'He didn't, Daddy,' said Janet, trying not to cry. 'He *had* to leave it. Those men were cruel.'

Daddy went back to his work. Peter and Janet looked at one another. Daddy was so often right about things. Perhaps he was right about this too. Perhaps Jeff *had* been a fraud, and made up a tale to tell them.

'What are we going to do?' asked Janet, wiping her eyes. Peter considered.

'We'll have to give it up,' he said. 'We can't very well go against what Daddy says, and we *know* we can't do anything ourselves, because we don't understand what any of the things Jeff remembered can possibly mean. And now Jeff is gone, and we don't know where, we can't even get him to tell his tale to anyone!'

'We'll have to call a meeting and tell the others,' said Janet, gloomily. 'They won't like it. It sounded so exciting at first, now it's just a silly make-up. And I liked Jeff, too.'

'So did I,' said Peter. 'Let's write notes and slip them into the letter-boxes to tell the others there will be a meeting tomorrow. Down in the shed, I think, for a change.'

The notes were written and delivered. At ten o'clock the next morning the Seven collected together in the shed. The password 'Adventure' seemed most disappointing to Janet and Peter now that there *was* no adventure.

'I've got gloomy news,' said Peter. 'We told Daddy everything, and he didn't believe it. He told us to fetch Jeff, and promised to listen to his story – but Jeff was gone!'

Everyone was startled. 'Gone!' said Jack. 'Where?'

Peter produced the note and everyone read it solemnly. 'We've got the kitten,' said Peter. 'And that's all that's left of Jeff and his peculiar tale.'

'So we can't go on with anything,' said George, in dismay. 'I was just getting all worked up about it, thinking we were in for another excitement.'

'I know. But we were wrong,' said Peter. 'This affair is closed. We can't go any further or find out anything more. It's our first failure.'

It was a very gloomy meeting indeed. Everyone felt very flat. They wondered where Jeff was. Had he *really* cheated them and told them a made-up tale? It was very difficult to believe.

'We saw Mr Tizer and Jeff's uncle, you know,' said Colin, suddenly. '*They* couldn't have been made up.'

'We've only got Jeff's word for it that they were his uncle and Mr Tizer,' Peter reminded him. 'He certainly said they were, but for all we know they might have been two foresters, or even poachers. They looked pretty nasty, anyway.'

There was a silence. 'All right,' said George at last. 'It's finished. We don't do anything more. Are we going to the tree-house today?'

'I don't feel like it somehow, this morning,' said Janet. 'Does anyone? I feel disappointed and rather cross.'

Everyone laughed. Janet was hardly ever cross. Colin patted her on the back. 'Cheer up! We'll soon get over it. And anyway, finished or not, I'm still going to keep my eyes open! Who knows – I might meet Emma Lane walking down the street, carrying a red pillow embroidered with the letters MKX!'

That made everyone roar with laughter. They said goodbye and went off feeling more cheerful. 'What's the date?' said George to Colin, as they went down the lane together. 'Wednesday the 24th, isn't it? Well, it's tomorrow that things were supposed to happen, according to Jeff.'

'He probably made up the date,' said Colin. 'What are we going to do this morning? We've plenty of time left.'

'Let's go down to the canal,' said George. 'We may

see some barges going along. I like the canal, it's so long and straight and quiet.'

'I like it too,' said Colin. 'I'll go and get my boat. You get yours too. Meet me in that road that goes under the railway bridge, down by the canal.'

'What road?' asked George, but Colin had already gone. George raised his voice. 'Colin! What road do you mean? I don't want to miss you!'

'You know the road, idiot,' yelled back Colin. 'It's EMBER LANE!'

Colin was so far away by this time that it was difficult to catch what he said. It sounded like 'EMMA LANE'. George stood rooted to the spot. Ember Lane. *Emma Lane.* Jeff might have misheard what his uncle had said – it was probably Ember Lane he meant, not Emma Lane! They sounded so much the same. EMBER LANE!

'It might be that. It might be,' said George to himself in excitement. 'We'll have a really good look round Ember Lane – just *in case*!'

CHAPTER FIFTEEN

The red pillow

WITH THEIR boats the two boys met at the beginning of Ember Lane. George began to tell Colin excitedly what he thought.

'When you called out Ember Lane it sounded exactly like *Emma* Lane,' he said. 'Suppose that's what Jeff meant? He might have heard wrong, he was half-asleep. Ember Lane. I'm sure that was what it was.'

'And you think something was to happen in Ember Lane on the 25th?' said Colin, looking very thrilled. 'Gosh, you may be right. But what could happen here?'

They looked round Ember Lane. Although it was called a lane, it was nothing of the sort, though it might have been years ago.

It was a rather wide, dirty street, with great warehouses on either side. It led down to the canal. There were a good many people about, taking parcels from the warehouses, and running messages. It was difficult to imagine any robbery or anything out of the way taking place here.

Colin and George examined the street very carefully.
They came to one warehouse that had a grating let
into the bottom of the wall. They peered down.
People were in an underground room below, busy
packing up parcels. The grating gave them a little
light and air, though it also let in the dust.

'Well, there's a *grating*!' said George, standing up after peering through for some time. 'I suppose someone could stand here and watch through it, as Jeff said, but what would be the point?'

'Someone might watch from the *other* side of the grating,' said Colin. 'If he stood on that table down there, look, he could peer into the street through the grating. If the place was in darkness, he wouldn't be seen peering out. It would be quite a good place to watch from.'

'It might,' said George. 'Yes, it might. A grating to watch through in Ember Lane. This is rather good! Are we on the track of anything, do you think?'

'Probably not!' said Colin. 'If we are we shall probably spot a red pillow on a sofa somewhere, or hear someone hissing, "MKX, you're wanted"!'

They went to sail their boats on the canal till dinner-time. Then they went home, peeping through the grating at the foot of the warehouse in Ember Lane as they went. The underground room below was empty now. The workers had gone to lunch.

'We'd better tell Peter,' said Colin as they parted. 'Let's go along this afternoon and tell him. He ought to know, I think, even though there may be nothing in it.'

Peter was most interested. 'That's bright of you,' he said. 'Emma Lane. Ember Lane. Anyone could mishear that quite easily. But I don't think so much of the grating. There are gratings everywhere.'

'Not in Ember Lane,' said Colin. 'We looked, and that's the only one.'

'Janet and I will go along and have a look at Ember Lane this afternoon,' said Peter. 'And the grating.'

They went. Ember Lane looked gloomy and dirty. Janet and Peter examined the grating with interest. Colin was right. There *was* only one in Ember Lane.

'Well, it doesn't tell us much,' said Peter. 'Even if we decided that this was the grating through which Mr Tizer or someone was going to watch, *why* should they want to watch? And what? It's no crime to peer through a grating.'

'They might want to watch unseen for something or someone, so that they could signal his coming to somebody waiting to pounce,' said Janet. Peter stared at her, most impressed.

'Yes. That's exactly what they *might* do!' he said. 'But what could they see from there? Let's stand with our backs to the grating and see if we can spot what would be within their sight.'

They stood and looked hard, their eyes ranging over the warehouse opposite, the pavement, and a lamp-post.

'Well, all that could be seen from behind that grating is the warehouse opposite, though not all of it,' said Janet. 'And the lamp-post, and the pavement near it, and that red pillar-box. Yes, I'm sure that red pillar-box could be seen too.'

Janet suddenly stopped. She caught her breath and looked round at Peter, her eyes shining. 'Peter,' she said, 'Peter! The red pillow!'

'The red pillow? Where?' said Peter, puzzled. 'Oh, Janet – JANET! I see what you mean! It wasn't a red *pillow* that Jeff heard, it was red *pillar-box*. And there it is!'

The two stared at the red pillar-box, thinking hard. A girl went up to it and posted some letters. Peter and Janet felt absolutely certain that 'red pillow' meant 'red pillar-box'. And it could be watched from behind the only grating in Ember Lane.

'We're getting somewhere,' said Peter, suddenly feeling quite out of breath. 'Jeff *did* hear something. His tale wasn't made up – but because he was half-asleep when he heard the men talking, he didn't hear properly.'

'If only we could find what MKX was,' said Janet. 'But we can't. I expect all the men in Mr Tizer's gang have numbers or letters. But we're certainly putting a few of the jigsaw pieces together, Peter. Let's go and tell the others!'

CHAPTER SIXTEEN

And now MKX

EVERY MEMBER of the Secret Seven felt excited when they heard the latest news. They thought that Janet had been very clever in realising that the red pillow was a mistake for red pillar-box.

Barbara thought for a moment and then said that she wondered if the man watching behind the grating might be waiting to signal to someone when the postman came to empty the box.

'Someone might be waiting to steal the letters from him,' she said.

'That's an idea,' said Peter. 'But there isn't much point in stealing ordinary letters. They're not worth anything!'

'That's true,' said Jack. 'It's sacks of registered parcels and letters that are usually stolen. They're worth something. But not ordinary letters. I don't somehow think the watcher is watching the pillar-box, he's probably watching for someone waiting there, or passing it.'

'Is it worth telling Daddy all this, Janet, do you suppose?' said Peter, after the Seven had discussed everything thoroughly. 'After all – it's tomorrow *something* has been planned to happen. We haven't much time left.'

'Well – we might tell him this evening,' said Janet. 'Let's wait till then. We might think of something else important. I don't think Daddy will change his mind about things just because we've discovered that a red pillar-box can be watched through a grating in Ember Lane.'

'It does sound rather silly put like that,' said Peter. 'Well – we'll wait till this evening. Good-bye till then.'

But before they could tell their father of their latest ideas, Pam came dashing into the garden to find Peter and Janet. Barbara was just behind.

They found Peter and Janet watering their gardens. Pam flung herself on them.

'Peter! Janet! What do you think? We've seen MKX!'

Janet dropped her watering-can, startled. Peter stared in excitement.

'Who is he? Where did you see him?'

'It isn't a he. It's a van!' said Barbara. 'Pam and I were going home together, when we saw a post-office van standing near a pillar-box – you know, a mail-van, painted red.'

'And its letters were MKX!' cried Pam. 'MKX 102. What do you think of that? We couldn't believe our eyes when we saw it was MKX. I'm sure that's what Jeff meant – the mail-van, MKX.'

'But – but there must be plenty of cars with the letters MKX,' said Peter. 'Plenty.'

'Not in one place,' said Pam. 'I don't ever remember seeing MKX in our town before. I notice car numbers, because I want to see if I can spot a Z something someday. I haven't yet. Peter! That van *must* be the MKX those men spoke about when Jeff was half-asleep.'

Peter sat down on a garden-seat. 'I think you're right,' he said. 'Yes – I think you must be right. It's all beginning to fit in. Wait now, let's work it out.'

He sat up and thought, frowning hard. 'Yes, perhaps a mail van goes into Ember Lane, with a few sacks of registered parcels inside. The postman gets out of his van to go across to the red pillar-box to collect the letters.'

'Yes! YES!' cried Pam. 'And someone is watching through the grating to see when he is unlocking the pillar-box, with his back to the van, and signals to the others who are waiting out of sight somewhere. . . .'

'And at once they see the signal, rush to the van, and drive it off before the postman can get back to it!' cried Janet, taking the words out of Pam's mouth.

They all sat and looked at one another, their eyes

347

shining. They felt breathless. Had they solved every-thing, or was it just too clever to be true?

'Well, I shall certainly tell Daddy now,' said Peter, thrilled. 'What a bit of luck you noticed the letters on that mail-van, Pam and Barbara. Good work! We're a really great Secret Society, I think. Successes every time!'

'And we thought this one was a failure!' said Janet. 'Look, there's Daddy. Come and tell him now.'

So Peter's father was soon surrounded by four excited children, determined to make him believe that what they had discovered REALLY MATTERED!

He listened carefully. He pursed up his mouth and gave his head a little scratch, looking with twinkling eyes at the children. 'Well, well, this is rather a different tale this time. Most ingenious! Yes, I'll do something about it.'

He went inside and rang up the Inspector of Police, and asked him to come along. 'I've a curious tale to tell you,' he said. 'You may or may not believe it, but I think you ought to hear it.'

And before ten minutes had passed the kind-faced Inspector was sitting in the garden, listening solemnly to the children's tale.

He glanced at Peter's father when they had finished. 'This is important,' he said. 'There have been too many mail-van robberies lately. We'll catch the ring-leaders this time, thanks to the valiant Secret Seven!'

CHAPTER SEVENTEEN

Top Secret

HE GOT up to go. The children pressed round him. 'Tell us what you are going to do! Do, do tell us!'

'I'm going to discuss the whole matter with other people,' said the Inspector, smiling down at the four children. 'You've not given me much time to make preparations, you know! According to you, it's all fixed for tomorrow!'

'How shall we know what's going to happen?' asked Pam. 'It's *our* affair this – can't we see what's going to happen?'

'I'll let you know tomorrow, at ten o'clock,' said the big Inspector, twinkling at them. 'Call a meeting of your Secret Society down in the shed, and I'll be there to report to you!'

There was such excitement that evening among the Secret Seven that their parents thought they would never get them to bed. Colin, George, and Jack were all told by the other four, and spent a wonderful time thinking how clever they had been.

'Well, we'll meet down in the shed at ten tomorrow,' said Colin. 'Passwords, and everything, and you all

realise, of course, that not one single word of what the Inspector tells us is to be told to ANYONE ELSE.'

'Of course,' said everyone.

At five to ten they had all arrived at the shed except the Inspector. He came promptly at ten o'clock.

'Have to let him in without the password,' said Peter. But Janet called out loudly. 'Password, please!'

The Inspector grinned to himself outside the shed. 'Well,' he said, 'I don't know it, but there's one word that seems to me to be a very good password for you at the moment, and that is – ADVENTURE!'

'Right!' shouted everyone in delight, and the door opened. In went the Inspector and was given a large box to sit on. He beamed round at them all.

'This is SECRET,' he said. 'Top secret. We've made inquiries, and we think it is possible that a robbery may be planned this evening when the postman drives up in his mail-van to make the seven-thirty collection of letters from the red pillar-box in Ember Lane. At that time of the evening he has on board his van some sacks of registered letters.'

'Oooooh!' said Pam. 'Just what we thought!'

'Now what we are going to do is this,' said the Inspector. 'A postman will drive up as usual with the mail-van. He will park it in the usual place. He will go across to the pillar-box and unlock it, with his back to the van.'

'Yes,' said everyone, hanging on to the Inspector's words. 'What next?'

'Well, the watcher behind the grating will probably signal to others waiting opposite in hiding,' said the Inspector. 'They will rush to the van, jump into the driver's seat, two of them probably, and drive it away.'

'But, will you let them do that?' said Pam. 'With all the sacks inside!'

'The sacks won't be inside, my dear,' said the Inspector. 'But six fine policemen will, and WHAT a shock for the two men when they park the mail-van somewhere lonely and go to unlock the van door.'

'Oh!' cried the Seven, and gazed at the Inspector in delight.

'And the man signalling behind the grating will find two policemen waiting for him in the passage outside the underground room,' said the big Inspector. 'Very interesting; don't you think so?'

'Please – PLEASE can we be somewhere and watch?' asked Peter. 'After all, if it hadn't been for us you wouldn't have known anything about this.'

'Well now, you listen,' said the Inspector, dropping his voice low and making everything sound twice as exciting. 'There's a warehouse called Mark Donnal's in Ember Lane, and it's got a back entrance in the road behind, Petton Road. Nobody will say anything if seven children go in one by one, and make their way to a window overlooking Ember Lane at the front of the warehouse. In fact, I wouldn't be surprised if there isn't someone there to show you the very room you want!'

Every single one of the Secret Seven wanted to hug the big Inspector, but as he got up at that moment, they couldn't. They beamed in delight at him.

'Thank you! It's marvellous of you! We'll be there, if our parents let us.'

'I think you'll find that will be all right,' said the Inspector, and off he went.

'WELL!' said Peter, looking round. 'This is wonderful. Seats in the very front row.'

'Yes. But we shan't be able to see the best bit of all, when the men open the van, and out come the police-men!' said Jack.

'Never mind, we'll see plenty!' said Peter. 'I wonder where Jeff is. I suppose that awful Mr Tizer took him away and locked him up somewhere till the raid was over. I wonder what will happen to poor old Jeff.'

'Mew,' said the kitten, who was on Janet's knee. Its leg was healed now, and it was a fat, amusing little thing. Janet hugged it.

'I expect poor Jeff misses you,' she said. 'Never mind, maybe we'll be able to do something for Jeff if he's found, and you can go back to him.'

'I wish tonight was here,' said George, getting up. 'It'll never come!'

But it did come, and it brought a most exciting evening with it!

CHAPTER EIGHTEEN

An exciting finish

THE SEVEN spent the rest of the morning up in the tree-house, talking over everything. Scamper put himself on guard as usual, but no one came by. The afternoon dragged on, and tea-time came. Then the children began to feel intensely excited.

At half-past six they went one by one down to Ember Lane. They thought they had better not go in a bunch in case they attracted attention. They found the back entrance of Mark Donnal's warehouse in Petton Road, and went up the steps to it. The door swung open silently as they reached the top step. Most mysterious!

But behind it, keeping guard, was one of the village policemen! He grinned at each child as he or she walked in, and took them up the stairs, along dusty passages, to a little room at the front.

'We've got a marvellous view of the red pillarbox,' said Janet to Peter. 'We shall see everything. I wonder if the signaller is down behind the grating yet.'

They asked the policeman. He nodded. 'Yes, he's there all right. We've watched him go into the under-

359

ground room, complete with white handkerchief for signalling. There are now two policemen in a cupboard outside the door, waiting!'

It was too exciting to be borne! The children simply couldn't sit still. The time went by slowly. Seven o'clock – ten-past – twenty-past – twenty-five-past . . .

A clock on a nearby church tower suddenly chimed the half hour. Half-past seven! Now was the time!

Everything happened very suddenly and quickly. There came the roar of a car-engine, and round a corner came the red mail-van, MKX 102. It stopped

and the driver jumped out. He took a sack and ran across to the red pillar-box. He unlocked it, his back to his van.

And then two men suddenly came from a small alley-way and sprinted at top speed to the van. There was no one in Ember Lane except the postman, all the workers had gone home long ago.

But many watchers saw the two men. The seven children stared breathlessly, so did the policeman with them, so did the signaller behind the grating.

And so did many hidden eyes belonging to watchful police, including the Inspector himself!

The men leapt into the front of the van. One got into the driving-seat, the other next to him. There was a roar of the engine, and the van drove off at top speed, vanishing round the corner.

The postman straightened up. He didn't seem surprised. He was in the secret too! The children rocked to and fro on their seats in excitement. A few policemen appeared from odd places and spoke to one another. Then there came a noise from down below!

'That's the signaller being caught!' said Peter. 'I bet it is!'

It was, of course. He had walked out of the underground room straight into the arms of the waiting policemen. And, lo and behold, it was Mr Tizer!

But the evening's excitement wasn't yet finished! Before half an hour had gone, the mail-van was back again, but this time it was driven by a uniformed policeman, with another beside him. Inside were the two men. As the children watched, the van doors were opened, and four policemen got out with the two men held firmly by the arms.

'Got them nicely,' said the policeman who was in the room with the children. 'They must have parked quite nearby, opened the van, and got the surprise of their lives, and here they are, back again to talk to the Chief!'

It was maddening to have to go home after that. What an excitement! How wonderful to be in at the finish, but how dull afterwards!

The Seven went to Peter's house to supper, talking all at once. Nobody could possibly hear what anyone else said. And waiting at the house for them was – Jeff! The kitten was back in his arms, and he looked scared but happy.

'Hallo,' he said, 'the police know all about everything now, don't they? They came to my uncle's house and found me. Uncle had locked me up in an attic. I haven't got to go back to him any more.'

'What's going to happen to you then?' asked Peter.

'They're trying to find out about my mother,' said Jeff, hugging the kitten. 'I told you I didn't even know what hospital she'd gone to. I'm to stay here till they know. Your mother said I could.'

Jeff looked clean and his hair was brushed. Peter's mother had felt sorry for him and had done what she could when the police brought him to her. Now he was to have supper with the Seven. He was very happy.

The telephone rang, and Peter's mother went to answer it. She came back, smiling. 'It's about your mother, Jeff,' she said. 'She's better! She's leaving hospital tomorrow and going back home, and you're to be there to greet her!'

Jeff stood with tears in his eyes. He couldn't say a word. He held the kitten so tightly that it mewed. He turned to the Seven, finding his tongue at last.

'It's you that have done all this!' he said, stammering in his joy. 'It's all because of you. I'm glad I found your tree-house. I'm glad I met you. You're a wonderful Secret Society, the best in all the world!'

'Well, we do feel rather pleased with ourselves tonight,' said Peter, grinning at Jeff. 'Don't we, Scamper, old boy? Do *you* agree that we're a good Secret Society? Do you agree that we must go on and do lots more exciting things?'

'Woof,' said Scamper and thumped his tail on the floor. 'WOOF!'

Well done, Secret Seven! Do let's hear your next adventure soon.

SECRET SEVEN ON THE TRAIL

CONTENTS

CHAPTER ONE

The Secret Seven meet

'MUMMY, HAVE you got anything we could have to drink?' asked Janet. 'And to eat too?'

'But you've only *just* finished your breakfast!' said Mummy in surprise. 'And you each had two sausages. You can't possibly want anything more yet.'

'Well, we're having the very last meeting of the Secret Seven this morning,' said Janet. 'Down in the shed. We don't think it's worth while meeting when we all go back to school, nothing exciting ever happens then.'

'We're going to meet again when the Christmas holidays come,' said Peter. 'Aren't we, Scamper, old boy?'

The golden spaniel wagged his tail hard, and gave a small bark.

'He says, he hopes he can come to the last meeting too,' said Janet. 'Of course you can, Scamper.'

'He didn't say that,' said Peter, grinning. 'He said that if there were going to be snacks of any kind at this meeting, he'd like to join in!'

371

'Woof,' agreed Scamper, and put his paw up on Peter's knee.

'I'll give you lemons, and some sugar, and you can make your own lemonade,' said Mummy. 'You like doing that, don't you? And you can go and see if there are any rock-buns left in the tin in the larder. They'll be stale, but I know you don't mind that!'

'Oh, thanks, Mummy,' said Janet. 'Come on Peter. We'd better get the things now, because the others will be here soon!'

They ran off to the larder, Scamper panting behind. Rock-buns! Stale or not, Scamper liked those as much as the children did.

Janet took some lemons, and went to get the sugar from her mother. Peter emptied the stale rock-buns on to a plate, and the two of them, followed by Scamper, went down to the shed. Janet had the lemon-squeezer and a big jug of water. It was fun to make lemonade.

They pushed open the shed door. On it were the letters S.S. in green – S.S. for the Secret Seven!

'Our Secret Society has been going for some time now,' said Janet, beginning to squeeze a lemon. 'I'm not a bit tired of it, are you, Peter?'

'Of course not!' said Peter. 'Just think of all the

adventures we've had, and the exciting things we've done! But I do think it's sensible not to bother about the Secret Seven meetings till the hols. For one thing, in this Christmas term the days get dark very quickly, and we have to be indoors.'

'Yes, and nothing much happens then,' said Janet. 'Oh, Scamper – you won't like that squeezed out lemon-skin, you silly dog! Drop it!'

Scamper dropped it. He certainly didn't like it! He sat with his tongue hanging out, looking most disgusted. Peter glanced at his watch.

'Nearly time for the others to come,' he said. 'I hope they'll agree to this being the last meeting till Christmas. We'd better collect all the badges from them, and put them in a safe place. If we don't, someone is bound to lose one.'

'Or that silly sister of Jack's will take it and wear it herself,' said Janet. 'What's her name – Susie? Aren't you glad I'm not annoying to you, like Susie is to Jack, Peter?'

'Well, you're pretty annoying sometimes,' said Peter, and immediately got a squirt of lemon-juice in his eye from an angry Janet! 'Oh, don't do that. Don't you know that lemon-juice stings like anything? Stop it, Janet!'

Janet stopped it. 'I'd better not waste the juice,' she said. 'Ah, here comes someone.'

Scamper barked as somebody walked up the path and knocked on the door.

'Password!' called Peter, who never opened the door to anyone until the correct password was called.

'Pickled onions!' said a voice, and giggled.

That was the latest password of the Secret Seven, suggested by Colin, whose mother had been pickling onions on the day of the last meeting they had had. It was such a silly password that everyone had laughed, and Peter had said they would have it till they thought of a better one.

'Got your badge?' said Peter, opening the door.

Outside stood Barbara. She displayed her badge proudly. 'It's a new one,' she said. 'My old one's got so dirty, so I made this.'

'Very good,' said Peter. 'Come in. Look, here come three others.'

He shut the door again, and Barbara sat down on a box beside Janet, and watched her stirring the lemonade. Rat-a-tat! Scamper barked as knocking came at the door again.

'Password!' called out Peter, Janet and Barbara together.

'Pickled onions!' yelled back everyone. Peter flung open the door and scowled.

'How MANY times am I to tell you not to yell out

374

the password!' he said. 'Now everyone in hearing distance has heard it.'

'Well, you all yelled out PASSWORD at the tops of your voices,' said Jack. 'Anyway, we can easily choose a new one.' He looked slyly at George, who had come in with him. 'George thought it was pickled cabbage, and we had to tell him it wasn't.'

'Well, of all the – ' began Peter, but just then another knock came on the door and Scamper growled.

'Password!' called Peter.

'Pickled onions!' came his mother's voice, and she laughed. 'If that *is* a password! I've brought you some home-made peppermints, just to help the last meeting along.'

'Oh. Thanks, Mummy,' said Janet, and opened the door. She took the peppermints and gave them to Peter. Peter frowned round, when his mother had gone.

'There you are, you see,' he said. 'It just happened to be my mother who heard the password, but it might have been anybody. Now who's still missing?'

'There's me here, and you, George, Jack, Barbara and Pam,' said Janet. 'Colin's missing. Oh, here he comes.'

Rat-tat! Scamper gave a little welcoming bark. He knew every S.S. member quite well. Colin gave the password and was admitted. Now the Secret Seven were complete.

'Good,' said Peter. 'Sit down, Colin. We'll get down to business as soon as Janet pours out the lemonade. Hurry up, Janet!'

CHAPTER TWO

No more meetings till Christmas!

JANET POURED out mugs of the lemonade, and Peter handed round the rock-buns.

'A bit stale,' he said, 'but nice and curranty. Two each and one for old Scamper. Sorry, Scamper; but, after all, you're not a *real* member of the Secret Seven, or you could have two.'

'He couldn't,' said Jack. 'There are only fifteen buns. And anyway, I *always* count him in as a real member.'

'You can't. We're the Secret *Seven*, and Scamper makes eight,' said Peter. 'But he can always come with us. Now listen, this is to be the last meeting, and – '

There were surprised cries at once.

'The *last* meeting! Why, what's happening?'

'The *last* one! Surely you're not going to stop the Secret Seven?'

'Oh but, Peter – surely you're not meaning –'

'Just let me *speak*,' said Peter. 'It's to be the last meeting till the holidays come again. Tomorrow all of us boys go back to school, and the girls go to

379

their school the day after. Nothing ever happens in term-time, and anyway we're too busy to look for adventure, so –'

'But something *might* happen,' said Colin. 'You just never know. I think it's a silly idea to stop the Secret Seven for the term-time. I really do.'

'So do I,' said Pam. 'I like belonging to it, and wearing my badge, and remembering the password.'

'Well, you can still wear your badges if you like,' said Peter, 'though I *had* thought of collecting them today, as we're all wearing them, and keeping them till our meeting next hols.'

'I'm not giving *mine* up,' said Jack, firmly. 'And you needn't be afraid I'll let my sister Susie get it, either, because I've got a perfectly good hiding place for it.'

'And suppose, just *suppose*, something turned up in term-time,' said Colin, earnestly. 'Suppose one of us discovered something strange, something that ought to be looked into. What would we do if the Secret Seven was disbanded till Christmas?'

'Nothing ever turns up in term-time,' repeated Peter, who liked getting his own way. 'And anyway I've got to work hard this term. My father wasn't at all pleased with my last report.'

'All right. You work hard, and keep out of the Society till Christmas,' said Jack. 'I'll run it with Janet. It can be the Secret Six till then. S.S. will stand for that as much as for Secret Seven.'

That didn't please Peter at all. He frowned. 'No,' he said. 'I'm the head. But seeing that you all seem to disagree with me, I'll say this. We won't have any *regular* meetings, like we have been having, but only call one if anything *does* happen to turn up. And you'll see I'm right. Nothing will happen!'

'We keep our badges, then, and have a password,' said Colin. 'We're still a very live Society, even if nothing happens. And we'll call a meeting at once if something does?'

'Yes,' said everyone, looking at Peter. They loved being the Secret Seven. It made them feel important, even if, as Colin said, nothing happened for them to look into.

NO MORE MEETINGS TILL CHRISTMAS!

'All right,' said Peter. 'What about a new password?'

Everyone thought hard. Jack looked at Scamper, who seemed to be thinking too. 'What about Scamper's name?' he said. '"Scamper" would be a good password.'

'It wouldn't,' said Janet. 'Every time anyone gave the password Scamper would think he was being called!'

'Let's have *my* dog's name – Rover,' said Pam.

'No, have my aunt's dog's name,' said Jack. 'Cheeky Charlie. That's a good password.'

'Yes! Cheeky Charlie! We'll have that,' said Peter. 'Nobody would ever think of that for a password. Right – Cheeky Charlie it is!'

The rock-buns were passed round for the second time. Scamper eyed them longingly. He had had his. Pam took pity on him and gave him half hers, and Barbara did the same.

Scamper then fixed his eyes mournfully on Jack, who quickly gave him a large piece of his bun too.

'Well!' said Peter. 'Scamper's had more than any real member of the Secret Seven! He'll be thinking he can run the whole Society soon!'

'Wuff,' said Scamper, thumping his tail on the ground, and looking at Peter's bun.

The lemonade was finished. The last crumb of cake had been licked up by Scamper. The sun came out and shone down through the shed window.

'Come on, let's go out and play,' said Peter, getting up. 'School tomorrow! Well, these have been such good hols. Now, Secret Seven, you all know the password, don't you? You probably won't have to use it till the Christmas holidays, so just make up your minds to remember it.'

CHAPTER THREE

The Famous Five

SCHOOL BEGAN for the boys next day, and they all trooped off with their satchels and bags. The girls went off the day after. All the Secret Seven wore their little badges with S.S. embroidered on the button. It was fun to see the other children looking enviously at them, wishing they could have one too.

'No, you can't,' said Janet, when the other girls asked her if they could join. 'It's a *Secret* Society. I'm not supposed even to talk about it.'

'Well, I don't see why you can't make it a bit bigger and let *us* come in,' said the others.

'You can't have more than seven in our Society,' said Janet. 'And we've got seven. You go and make Secret Societies of your own!'

That was an unfortunate thing to say! Kate and Susie, who was Jack's tiresome sister, immediately went off to make a Society of their own! How very annoying!

They got Harry, Jeff and Sam as well as themselves. Five of them. And then, to the intense annoyance of the Secret Seven, these five appeared at school with badges of their own!

On the buttons they wore were embroidered two letters, not S.S., of course, but F.F. Everyone crowded round to ask what F.F. meant.

'It means "Famous Five",' said Susie. 'We've named ourselves after the Famous Five in the "Five" books! *Much* better idea than "Secret Seven".'

Susie was very irritating to poor Jack. 'You haven't got nearly such a good Society as *we* have,' she said. 'Our badges are bigger, we've got a splendid password, which I wouldn't *dream* of telling you, and we have a secret sign, too. *You* haven't got that!'

'What's your secret sign?' said Jack, crossly. '*I've* never seen you make it.'

'Of course not. I tell you it's a *secret* one!' said Susie. 'And we're meeting every single Saturday morning. And, what's more, we've got an adventure going already!'

'I don't believe you,' said Jack. 'Anyway, you're just a copy-cat. It was *our* idea! You're mean.'

'Well, you wouldn't let me belong to your silly Secret Seven,' said Susie, annoyingly. 'Now I belong to the Famous Five, and I tell you, we've got an adventure already!'

Jack didn't know whether to believe her or not. He thought Susie must be the most tiresome sister in the world. He wished he had one like Janet. He went gloomily to Peter and told him all that Susie had said.

'Don't take any notice of her,' said Peter. 'Famous Five indeed! They'll soon get tired of meeting and playing about.'

The Famous Five Society was very annoying to the Secret Seven that term. The members wore their big badges every single day. Kate and Susie huddled together in corners at break each morning and talked in excited whispers, as if something really *was* happening.

Harry, Jeff and Sam did the same at their school, which annoyed Peter, Colin, Jack and George very much.

They met in the summer-house in Jack's garden, and Susie actually ordered Jack to keep out of the garden when the 'Famous Five' held their meetings in the summer-house!

'As if I shall keep out of my own garden!' said Jack, indignantly, to Peter. 'But you know Peter, I believe they really *have* got hold of something. I think something *is* up. Wouldn't it be awful if *they* had an adventure and we didn't? Susie would crow like anything.'

Peter thought about this. 'It's up to you to find out about it,' he said, at last. 'After all, they've stolen our idea, and they're doing it to annoy us. You try and find out what's up, Jack. We'll soon put a stop to it!'

So Jack went to hide in a bush at the back of the summer-house when he heard that Susie had planned another meeting there for that Saturday morning. But unfortunately Susie was looking out of the bedroom window just then, and saw him squeezing into the laurel bush!

She gazed down in rage, and then suddenly she smiled. She sped downstairs to meet the other four at the front gate, instead of waiting for them to go down to the summer-house.

They all came together, and Susie began to whisper excitedly.

'Jack's going to try and find out what we're doing! He's hidden himself in the laurel bush at the back of the summer-house to listen to all we say!'

'I'll go and pull him out,' said Harry at once.

'No, don't,' said Susie. 'I've got a better idea. Let's go down to the summer-house, whisper the password so that he can't hear it, and then begin to talk as if we really *had* found an adventure!'

'But why?' said Kate.

'You're silly! Don't you see that Jack will believe it all, and if we mention places such as that old house up on the hill, Tigger's Barn, he'll tell the Secret Seven, and – '

'And they'll all go and investigate it and find there's nothing there!' said Kate, giggling. 'What fun!'

'Yes. And we can mention names too. We'll talk about Stumpy Dick, and – Twisty Tom, and make Jack think we're right in the very middle of something,' said Susie.

'And we could go to Tigger's Barn ourselves and wait till the Secret Seven come, and have a good laugh at them!' said Jeff, grinning. 'Come on, let's go down to the summer-house now, Susie. Jack will be wondering why we are so late.'

'No giggling, anybody!' Susie warned them, 'and just back me up in all I say. And be as solemn as you can. I'll go down first, and you can all come one by one, and don't forget to *whisper* the password, because he mustn't hear *that*.'

She sped down the garden and into the summer-house. Out of the corner of her eye she saw the laurel bush where poor Jack had hidden himself very uncomfortably. Susie grinned to herself. Aha! She was going to have a fine revenge on Jack for keeping her out of *his* Secret Society!

One by one the others came to the summer-house. They whispered the password, much to Jack's annoyance. He would dearly have loved to pass it on to the Secret Seven! But he couldn't hear a word.

However, he heard plenty when the meeting really began. He couldn't help it, of course, because the Famous Five talked so loudly. Jack didn't guess that it was done on purpose, so that he might hear every word.

He was simply amazed at what the Famous Five said. Why, they seemed to be in the very middle of a Most Exciting Adventure!

CHAPTER FOUR

Susie tells a tale

SUSIE LED the talking. She was a good talker, and was determined to puzzle Jack as much as she could.

'I've found out where those crooks are meeting,' she said. 'It's an important piece of news, so please listen. I've tracked them down at last!'

Jack could hardly believe his ears. He listened hard.

'Tell us, Susie,' said Harry, playing up well.

'It's at Tigger's Barn,' said Susie, enjoying herself. 'That old, deserted house up on the hill. A tumble-down old place, just right for crooks to meet in. Far away from anywhere.'

'Oh yes. I know it,' said Jeff.

'Well, Stumpy Dick and Twisty Tom will both be there,' said Susie.

There were 'oooohs' and 'ahs' from her listeners, and Jack very nearly said 'Ooooh' too. Stumpy Dick and Twisty Tom – good gracious! What *had* the Famous Five got on to?

'They're planning something we must find out about,' said Susie, raising her voice a little, to make sure that Jack could hear. 'And we've simply *got* to do something. So one or two of us must go to Tigger's Barn at the right time and hide ourselves.'

'I'll go with you, Susie,' said Jeff at once.

Jack felt surprised when he heard that. Jeff was a very timid boy, and not at all likely to go and hide in a deserted place like Tigger's Barn. He listened hard.

'All right. You and I will go together,' said Susie. 'It will be dangerous, but what do we care about that? We are the Famous Five!'

'Hurrah!' said Kate and Sam.

'When do we go?' said Jeff.

'Well,' said Susie, 'I *think* they will meet there on Tuesday night. Can you come with me then, Jeff?'

'Certainly,' said Jeff, who would never have *dreamed* of going to Tigger's Barn at night if Susie's tale had been true.

Jack, out in the bush, felt more and more surprised. He also felt a great respect for the Famous Five. My word! They were as good as the Secret Seven! Fancy their getting on to an adventure like this! What a good thing he had managed to hide and hear about it!

He longed to go to Peter and tell him all he had heard. He wondered how his sister Susie knew anything about this affair. Bother Susie! It was just like her to make a Secret Society and then find an adventure for it.

'Suppose Stumpy Dick discovers you?' said Kate.

'I shall knock him to the ground,' said Jeff in a very valiant voice.

This was going a bit too far. Not even the Famous Five could imagine Jeff facing up to anyone. Kate gave a sudden giggle.

That set Sam off, and he gave one of his extraordinary snorts. Susie frowned. If the meeting began to giggle and snort like this, Jack would certainly know it wasn't serious. That would never do.

She frowned heavily at the others. 'Shut up!' she whispered. 'If we begin to giggle Jack won't believe a word.'

'I c-c-can't help it,' said Kate, who never could stop giggling once she began. 'Oh, Sam, please don't snort again!'

'Sh!' said Susie, angrily. 'Don't spoil it all.' Then she raised her voice again so that Jack could hear. 'Well, Famous Five, that's all for today. Meet again when you get your orders, and remember, don't say a word to ANYONE about Tigger's Barn. This is OUR adventure!'

'I bet the Secret Seven wish they could hear about this,' said Jeff, in a loud voice. 'It makes me laugh to think they don't know anything.'

He laughed, and that was the signal for everyone to let themselves go. Kate giggled again, Sam snorted, Susie roared, and so did Harry. They all thought of Jack out in the laurel bush, drinking in every word of their ridiculous story, and then they laughed all the more. Jack listened crossly. How dare they laugh at the Secret Seven like that?

'Come on,' said Susie, at last. 'This meeting is over. Let's go and get a ball and have a game. I wonder where Jack is? He might like to play too.'

As they all knew quite well where Jack was, this made them laugh again, and they went up the garden path in a very good temper. What a joke to play on a member of the Secret Seven! Would he rush off at once and call a meeting? Would the Secret Seven go to Tigger's Barn on Tuesday night in the dark?

'Susie, you don't *really* mean to go up to Tigger's Barn on Tuesday night, do you?' said Jeff, as they went up the path.

'Well, I did think of it at first,' said Susie. 'But it would be silly to. It's a long way, and it's dark at night now, and anyway, the Secret Seven might not go, and it would be awfully silly for any of us to go and hide there for nothing!'

'Yes, it would,' said Jeff, much relieved. 'But you'll be able to see if Jack does, won't you, Susie? If he slips off somewhere on Tuesday night, won't we have a laugh!'

'We certainly will!' said Susie. 'Oh, I *do* hope he does! I'll tell him it was all a trick, when he comes back, and won't he be FURIOUS!'

CHAPTER FIVE

Jack tells the news

JACK CREPT carefully out of the laurel bush as soon as he felt sure that the others were safely out of the way. He dusted himself down and looked round. Nobody was in sight.

He debated with himself what to do. Was it important enough to call a meeting of the Secret Seven? No – he would go and find Peter and tell him first. Peter could decide whether to have a meeting or not.

On the way to Peter's house Jack met George. 'Hello!' said George, 'you look very solemn! What's up? Have you had a row at home or something?'

'No,' said Jack. 'But I've just found out that the Famous Five are in the middle of something. I heard Susie telling them, down in our summerhouse. I was in the laurel bush outside.'

'Is it important?' asked George. 'I mean, your sister Susie's a bit of a nuisance, isn't she? You don't want to pay too much attention to her. She's conceited enough already.'

'Yes, I know,' said Jack. 'But she's clever, you

know. And after all, *we* managed to get into quite a few adventures, didn't we? And there's really no reason why the Famous Five shouldn't, too, if they keep their eyes and ears open. Listen, and I'll tell you what I heard.'

He told George, and George was most impressed. 'Tigger's Barn!' he said. 'Well, that *would* be a good meeting-place for crooks who wanted to meet without being seen. But how did Susie get hold of the names of the men? Oh Jack, it would be absolutely *maddening* if the Famous Five hit on something important before we did!'

'That's what *I* think,' said Jack. 'Especially as Susie's the ring-leader. She's always trying to boss me, and she would be worse than ever if her silly Society discovered some gang or plot. Let's find Peter, shall we? I was on the way to him when I met you.'

'I'll go with you, then,' said George. 'I'm sure Peter will think it's important. Come on!'

So two solemn boys walked up the path to Peter's house, and went round the back to find him. He was chopping up firewood, one of his Saturday morning jobs. He was very pleased to see Jack and George.

'Oh, hallo,' he said, putting down his axe. 'Now I can knock off for a bit. Chopping wood is fine for about five minutes, but an awful bore after that. My mother doesn't like me to do it, because she thinks I'll chop my fingers off, but Dad's hard-hearted and makes me do it each Saturday.'

'Peter,' said Jack, 'I've got some news.'

'Oh, what?' asked Peter. 'Tell me.'

So Jack told him about how he had hidden in the laurel bush and overheard a meeting of the Famous Five. 'They've got a password, of course,' he said, 'but I couldn't hear it. However, they forgot to whisper once they had said the password, and I heard every word.'

He told Peter what he had heard, but Peter didn't take it seriously. He was most annoying.

He listened to the end, and then he threw back his head and laughed. 'Oh Jack! Surely you didn't fall for all that nonsense? Susie must have been pretending. I expect that's what they do at their silly meetings – pretend they are in the middle of an adventure, and kid themselves they're clever.'

'But it all sounded absolutely serious,' said Jack, beginning to feel annoyed. 'I mean, they had no idea I was listening, they all seemed quite serious. And Jeff was ready to go and investigate on Tuesday evening!'

'What, *Jeff*! Can you imagine that little coward going to look for a *mouse*, let alone Stumpy Dick and the other fellow, whatever his name is!' said Peter, laughing again. 'He'd run a mile before he'd go to Tigger's Barn at night. That sister of yours was just making up a story, Jack, silly kid's stuff, like pretending to play at Red Indians or something, that's all.'

'Then you don't think it's worth while calling a meeting of the Secret Seven and asking some of us to go to Tigger's Barn on Tuesday night?' said Jack, in a hurt voice.

'No, I don't,' said Peter. 'I'm not so stupid as to believe in Susie's fairy-tales.'

'But suppose the Famous Five go, and discover something *we* ought to discover?' said George.

'Well, if Jack sees Susie and Jeff creeping off somewhere on Tuesday evening, he can follow them,' said Peter, still grinning. 'But they won't go! You'll see I'm right. It's all make-believe!'

'All right,' said Jack, getting up. 'If that's what you think there's no use in talking about it any longer. But you'll be sorry if you find you ought to have called a

meeting and didn't, Peter! Susie may be a nuisance, but she's jolly clever, *too* clever, and I wouldn't be a bit surprised if the Famous Five weren't beginning an adventure *we* ought to have!'

Peter began to chop wood again, still smiling in a most superior way. Jack marched off, his head in the air, very cross. George went with him. They said nothing for a little while, and then George looked doubtfully at Jack.

'Peter's very certain about it all, isn't he?' he said. 'Do you think he's right? After all, he's the chief of the Secret Seven. We ought to obey.'

'Look here, George. I'm going to wait and see what Susie does on Tuesday evening,' said Jack. 'If she stays at home, I'll know Peter's right, and it's all make-believe on her part. But if she goes off by herself, or Jeff comes to call for her, I'll know there's something up, and I'll follow them!'

'That's a good idea,' said George. 'I'll come with you, if you like.'

'I don't know what time they'll go, though, if they *do* go,' said Jack. 'I know, you come to tea with me on Tuesday, George. Then we can follow Susie and Jeff at once, if they slip off. And if they don't go out, then we'll know it's nonsense and I'll apologise to Peter the next morning for being so stupid.'

'Right,' said George, pleased. 'I'll come to tea on

Tuesday, then, and we'll keep a close watch on Susie. I'm glad I haven't got a sister like that! You never know what she's up to!'

When Jack got home, he went straight to his mother. 'Mother,' he said, 'may I have George to tea on Tuesday, please?'

Susie was there, reading in a corner. She pricked up her ears at once, and grinned in delight. She guessed that Jack and George meant to follow her and Jeff – if they went! All right, she would take the joke a little farther.

'Oh, that reminds me, Mother,' she said. 'Could I have *Jeff* to tea on Tuesday too? It's rather important! I can? Thank you very much!'

CHAPTER SIX

Susie's little trick

JACK WAS pleased when he heard Susie asking for Jeff to come to tea on Tuesday.

'That just proves it!' he said to himself. 'They will slip off to Tigger's Barn together. Peter was quite wrong! Let me see. Tuesday is the evening Mother goes to a Committee Meeting, so Susie and Jeff can go off without anyone bothering. And so can I! Aha! George and I will be on their track all right.'

Jack told George, who agreed that it did look as if there really was something in all that had been said at the meeting of the Famous Five.

'We'll keep a sharp eye on Susie and Jeff, and follow them at once,' said George. 'They'll be most annoyed to find we are with them in Tigger's Barn! We'd better take a torch, Jack. It will be dark.'

'Not awfully dark,' said Jack. 'There will be a moon. But it might be cloudy so we certainly will take a torch.'

Susie told Jeff, with many giggles, that Jack had asked George to tea on Tuesday. 'So I've asked for you to come too,' she said. 'And after tea, Jeff, you and I will slip out secretly, and make Jack and George think we are off to Tigger's Barn, but really and truly we will only be hiding somewhere, and we'll go back and play as soon as we are certain Jack and George have gone off to try and follow us to Tigger's Barn! Oh, dear, they'll go all the way there, and won't find a thing, except a horrid old tumble-down house!'

'It will serve them right!' said Jeff. 'All I can say is that I'm very glad *I'm* not going off to that lonely place at night.'

Tuesday afternoon came, and with it came Jeff and George after school, on their way to tea with Jack and Susie. The two boys walked with Jack, who pretended to be astonished that Jeff should go to tea with Susie.

'Going to play with her dolls?' he asked. 'Or perhaps you're going to spring-clean the dolls' house?'

Jeff went red. 'Don't be stupid,' he said. 'I've got my new railway set with me. We're going to play with that.'

'But it takes ages to set out on the floor,' said Jack, surprised.

'Well, what of it?' said Jeff, scowling. Then he remembered that Jack and George thought that he and Susie were going off to Tigger's Barn, and would naturally imagine that he wouldn't have time to play such a lengthy game as trains. He grinned to himself. Let Jack be puzzled! It would do him good!

They all had a very good tea, and then went to the playroom upstairs. Jeff began to set out his railway lines. Jack and George would have liked to help, but they were afraid that Susie might point out that Jeff was *her* guest, not theirs. Susie had a very sharp tongue when she liked!

So they contented themselves with trying to make a rather complicated model aeroplane, keeping a sharp eye on Susie and Jeff all the time.

Very soon Jack's mother put her head in at the door. 'Well, I'm off to my Committee Meeting,' she said. 'You must both go home at eight o'clock, Jeff and George – and Jack, if I'm not back in time for your supper, make yourselves something, and then go and have your baths.'

'Right, Mother,' said Jack. 'Come and say good-night to us when you get back.'

As soon as her mother had gone, Susie went all mysterious. She winked at Jeff, who winked back. Jack saw the winks, of course. They meant him to! He was on the alert at once. Ah, those two were probably going to slip out into the night!

'Jeff, come and see the new clock we've got down-stairs,' said Susie. 'It has a little man who comes out at the top and strikes a hammer on an anvil to mark every quarter of an hour. It is nearly a quarter past seven, let's go and watch him come out.'

'Right,' said Jeff, and the two went out, nudging each other, and laughing.

'There they go,' said George. 'Do we follow them straightaway?'

Jack went to the door. 'They've gone downstairs,' he said. 'They will get their coats out of the hall cupboard. We'll give them a minute to put them on, then we'll get ours. We shall hear the front door bang,

I expect. It won't take us a minute to follow them.'

In about a minute they heard the front door being opened, and then it shut rather quietly, as if it was not really meant to be heard.

'Did you hear that?' asked Jack. 'They shut it very quietly. Come on, we'll pull on our coats and follow. We don't want to track them too closely, or they'll see us. We will certainly surprise them when they get to Tigger's Barn, though!'

They put on their coats, and opened the front door. It was fairly light outside because of the rising moon. They took a torch with them, in case the clouds became thick.

There was no sign of Jeff and Susie.

'They have gone at top speed, I should think!' said Jack, closing the door behind him. 'Come on, we know the way to Tigger's Barn, even if we don't spot Jeff and Susie in front of us.'

They went down the garden path. They did not hear the giggles that followed them! Jeff and Susie were hiding behind the big hall curtains, and were now watching Jack and George going down the path. They clutched one another as they laughed. What a fine joke they had played on the two boys!

CHAPTER SEVEN

At Tigger's Barn

JACK AND GEORGE had no idea at all that they had left Jeff and Susie behind them in the hall. They imagined that the two were well in front of them, hurrying to Tigger's Barn! They hurried too, but, rather to their surprise, they did not see any children in front, however much they strained their eyes in the moonlit night.

'Well, all I can say is they must have taken bicycles,' said George, at last. 'They *couldn't* have gone so quickly. Has Susie a bike, Jack?'

'Oh yes, and I bet she's lent Jeff mine,' said Jack, crossly. 'They'll be at Tigger's Barn ages before us. I hope the meeting of those men isn't over before we get there. I don't want Susie and Jeff to hear everything without us hearing it too!'

Tigger's Barn was about a mile away. It was up on a lonely hill, hemmed in by trees. Once it had been part of a farmhouse, which had been burnt down one night. Tigger's Barn was now only a tumbledown shell of a house, used by tramps who needed shelter, by jackdaws who nested in the one remaining enormous chimney, and by a big tawny owl who used it to sleep in during the daytime.

Children had played in it until they had been forbidden to in case the old walls gave way. Jack and George had once explored it with Peter, but an old tramp had risen up from a corner and shouted at them so loudly that they had fled away.

The two boys trudged on. They came to the hill and walked up the narrow lane that led to Tigger's Barn. Still there was no sign of Jeff or Susie. Well, if they had taken bicycles, they would certainly be at Tigger's Barn by now!

They came to the old building at last. It stood there in the rather dim moonlight, looking forlorn and bony, with part of its roof missing, and its one great chimney sticking up into the night sky.

'Here we are,' whispered Jack. 'Walk quietly, because we don't want to let Jeff and Susie know we're here, or those men either, if they've come already! But everything is very quiet. I don't think the men are here.'

They kept in the shadow of a great yew hedge, and made their way on tiptoe to the back of the house. There was a front door and a back door, and both were locked, but as no window had glass in, it was easy enough for anyone to get inside the tumbledown place if they wanted to.

Jack clambered in through a downstairs window. A scuttling noise startled him, and he clutched George and made him jump.

'Don't grab me like that,' complained George, in a whisper. 'It was only a rat hurrying away. You nearly made me yell when you grabbed me so suddenly.'

'Sh!' said Jack. 'What's that?'

They listened. Something was moving high up in the great chimney that towered from the hearth in the broken-down room they were in.

'Maybe it's the owl,' said George, at last. 'Yes, listen to it hooting.'

A quavering hoot came to their ears. But it didn't really sound as if it came from the chimney. It seemed to come from outside the house, in the overgrown garden. Then an answering hoot came, but it didn't sound at all like an owl.

'Jack,' whispered George, his mouth close to Jack's ear, 'that's not an owl. It's men signalling to one another. They *are* meeting here! But where are Susie and Jeff?'

'I don't know. Hidden safely somewhere, I expect,' said Jack, suddenly feeling a bit shaky at the knees. 'We'd better hide too. Those men will be here in half a minute.'

'There's a good hiding-place over there in the

hearth,' whispered George. 'We can stand there in the darkness, right under the big chimney. Come on, quick. I'm sure I can hear footsteps outside.'

The two boys ran silently to the hearth. Tramps had made fires there from time to time, and a heap of ashes half-filled the hearth. The boys stood ankle-deep in them, hardly daring to breathe.

Then a torch suddenly shone out, and raked the room with its beam. Jack and George pressed close together, hoping they did not show in the great hearth.

They heard the sound of someone climbing in through the same window they had come in by. Then a voice spoke to someone outside.

'Come on in. Nobody's here. Larry hasn't come yet. Give him the signal, Zeb, in case he's waiting about for it now.'

Somebody gave a quavering hoot again. 'Oooooo-oo-oo! Ooooo, ooo-oo-oo!'

An answering call came from some way away, and after about half a minute another man climbed in. Now there were three.

The two boys held their breath. Good gracious! They were right in the middle of something very strange! Why were these men meeting at this tumble-down place? Who were they and what were they doing?

Where were Susie and Jeff, too? Were they listening and watching as well?

'Come into the next room,' said the man who had first spoken. 'There are boxes there to sit on, and a light won't shine out there as much as it does from this room. Come on, Larry – here, Zeb, shine your torch in front.'

417

CHAPTER EIGHT

An uncomfortable time

THE TWO boys were half-glad, half-sorry that the men had gone into another room. Glad because they were no longer afraid of being found, but sorry because it was now impossible to hear clearly what the men were saying.

They could hear a murmur from the next room.

Jack nudged George. 'I'm going to creep across the floor and go to the door. Perhaps I can hear what they are saying then,' he whispered.

'No, don't,' said George, in alarm. 'We'll be discovered. You're sure to make a noise!'

'I've got rubber-soled shoes on. I shan't make a sound,' whispered back Jack. 'You stay here, George. I DO wonder where Susie and Jeff are. I hope I don't bump into them anywhere.'

Jack made his way very quietly to the doorway that led to the next room. There was a broken door still hanging there, and he could peep through the crack. He saw the three men in the room beyond, sitting on old boxes, intently studying a map of some kind, and talking in low voices.

If only he could hear what they said! He tried to see what the men were like, but it was too dark. He could only hear their voices, one a polished voice speaking clearly and firmly, and the other two rough and unpleasant.

Jack hadn't the slightest idea what they were talking about. Loading and unloading. Six-two or maybe seven-ten. Points, points, points. There mustn't be a moon. Darkness, fog, mist. Points. Fog. Six-two, but it might go as long as seven-twenty. And again, points points, points.

What in the world could they be discussing? It was maddening to hear odd words like this that made no sense. Jack strained his ears to try and make out more, but it was no use, he couldn't. He decided to edge a little nearer.

He leaned against something that gave way behind him. It was a cupboard door! Before he could stop himself Jack fell inside, landing with a soft thud. The door closed on him with a little click. He sat there, alarmed and astonished, not daring to move.

'What was that?' said one of the men.

They all listened, and at that moment a big rat ran silently round the room, keeping to the wall. One of the men picked it out in the light of his torch.

'Rats,' he said. 'This place is alive with them. That's what we heard.'

AN UNCOMFORTABLE TIME

'I'm not sure,' said the man with the clear voice. 'Switch off that light, Zeb. Sit quietly for a bit and listen.'

The light was switched off. The men sat in utter silence, listening. Another rat scuttered over the floor.

Jack sat absolutely still in the cupboard, fearful that the men might come to find out who had made a noise. George stood in the hearth of the next room, wondering what had happened. There was such dead silence now, and darkness too!

The owl awoke in the chimney above him, and stirred once more. Night-time! It must go hunting. It gave one soft hoot and dropped down the chimney to make its way out through the bare window.

It was as startled to find George standing at the bottom of the chimney as George was startled to feel the owl brushing his cheek. It flew silently out of the window, a big moving shadow in the dimness.

George couldn't bear it. He must get out of this chimneyplace, he must! Something else might fall down on him and touch his face softly. Where was Jack? How mean of him to go off and leave him with things that lived in chimneys! And Jack had the torch with him too. George would have given anything to flick on the light of a torch.

He crept out of the hearth, and stood in the middle of the floor, wondering what to do. What *was* Jack

421

doing? He had said he was going to the doorway that led to the next room, to see if he could hear what the men said. But were the men there now? There wasn't a sound to be heard.

Perhaps they have slipped out of another window and gone, thought poor George. If so why doesn't Jack come back? It's horrid of him. I can't bear this much longer.

He moved over to the doorway, putting out his hands to feel if Jack was there. No, he wasn't. The next room was in black darkness, and he couldn't see a thing there. There was also complete silence. Where *was* everyone?

George felt his legs giving way at the knees. This horrible old tumbledown place! Why ever had he listened to Jack and come here with him? He was sure that Jeff and Susie hadn't been stupid enough to come here at night.

He didn't dare to call out. Perhaps Jack was somewhere nearby, scared too. What about the Secret Seven password? What was it now? Cheeky Charlie!

If I whisper Cheeky Charlie, Jack will know it's me, he thought. It's our password. He'll know it's me, and he'll answer.

So he stood at the doorway and whispered: 'Cheeky Charlie! Cheeky Charlie!'

No answer. He tried again, a little louder this time, 'Cheeky Charlie!'

And then a torch snapped on, and caught him directly in its beam. A voice spoke to him harshly.

'What's all this? What do you know about Charlie? Come right into the room, boy, and answer my question.'

CHAPTER NINE

Very peculiar

GEORGE WAS extremely astonished. Why, the men were still there! Then where was Jack? What had happened to him? He stood there in the beam of the torch, gaping.

'Come on in,' said the voice, impatiently. 'We heard you saying "Cheeky Charlie". Have you got a message from him?'

George gaped still more. A message from him? From Cheeky Charlie? Why, that was only a pass-word! Just the name of a dog! What did the man mean?

'*Will* you come into the room?' said the man, again. 'What's the matter with you, boy? Are you scared? We shan't eat a messenger from Charlie.'

George went slowly into the room, his mind suddenly working at top speed. A messenger from Charlie. Could there be someone called Charlie, Cheeky Charlie? Did these men think he had come from him? How very extraordinary!

'There won't be no message from Charlie,' said the man called Zeb. 'Why should there be? He's waiting

425

for news from *us*, isn't he? Here, boy – did Charlie send you to ask for news?'

George could do nothing but nod his head. He didn't want to have to explain anything at all. These men appeared to think he had come to find them to get news for someone called Charlie. Perhaps if he let them give him the message, they would let him go without any further questions.

'Can't think why Charlie uses such a dumb kid to send out,' grumbled Zeb. 'Got a pencil, Larry? I'll scribble a message.'

'A kid that can't open his mouth and speak a word is just the right messenger for us,' said the man with the clear voice. 'Tell Charlie what we've decided, Zeb. Don't forget that he's to mark the tarpaulin with white lines at one corner.'

Zeb scribbled something in a note-book by the light of a torch. He tore out the page and folded it over. 'Here you are,' he said to George. 'Take this to Charlie, and don't you go calling him Cheeky Charlie, see? Little boys that are rude get their ears boxed! His friends can call him what they like, but not you.'

'Oh, leave the kid alone,' said Larry. 'Where's Charlie now, kid? At Dalling's or at Hammond's?'

George didn't know what to answer. 'Dalling's,' he said at last, not knowing in the least what it meant.

Larry tossed him fifty pence. 'Clear off!' he said. 'You're scared stiff of this place, aren't you? Want me to take you down the hill?'

This was the last thing that poor George wanted. He shook his head.

The men got up. 'Well, if you want company, we're all going now. If not, buzz off.'

George buzzed off, but not very far. He went back again into the other room, thankful to see that the moon had come out again, and had lit it enough for him to make his way quickly to the window. He clambered out awkwardly, because his legs were shaking and were not easy to manage.

He made for a thick bush and flung himself into the middle. If those men really were going, he could wait till they were gone. Then he could go back and find Jack. WHAT had happened to Jack? He seemed to have disappeared completely.

The men went cautiously out of Tigger's Barn, keeping their voices low. The owl flew over their heads, giving a sudden hoot that startled them. Then George heard them laugh. Their footsteps went quietly down the hill.

He heaved a sigh of relief. Then he scrambled out of the bush and went back into the house. He stood debating what to do. Should he try the password again? It had had surprising results last time, so perhaps this time it would be better just to call Jack's name.

But before he could do so, a voice came out of the doorway that led to the further room.

'Cheeky Charlie!' it said, in a piercing whisper.

George stood stock still, and didn't answer. Was it Jack saying that password? Or was it somebody else who knew the real Cheeky Charlie, whoever he might be?

428

Then a light flashed on and caught him in its beam. But this time, thank goodness, it was Jack's torch, and Jack himself gave an exclamation of relief.

'It *is* you, George! Why in the world didn't you answer when I said the password? You must have known it was me.'

'Oh, Jack! Where were you? I've had an awful time!' said George. 'You shouldn't have gone off and left me like that. Where have you been?'

'I was listening to those men, and fell into this cupboard,' said Jack. 'It shut on me, and I couldn't hear another word. I didn't dare to move in case those men came to look for me. But at last I opened the door, and when I couldn't hear anything, I wondered where *you* were! So I whispered the password.'

'Oh, I see,' said George, thankfully. 'So you didn't hear what happened to *me*? The men discovered me – and – '

'*Discovered* you! What did they do?' said Jack, in the greatest astonishment.

'It's really very peculiar,' said George. 'You see, *I* whispered the password too, hoping *you* would hear it. But the *men* heard me whispering "Cheeky Charlie", and they called me in and asked me if I was a messenger from him.'

Jack didn't follow this, and it took George a little time to explain to him that the three men seemed really to think that someone they knew, who actually *was* called Cheeky Charlie, was using George as a messenger!

'And they gave *me* a message for him,' said George. 'In a note. I've got it in my pocket.'

'No! Have you really!' said Jack, suddenly excited. 'Gosh, this is thrilling. We might be in the middle of an adventure again. Let's see the note.'

'No. Let's go home and then read it,' said George. 'I want to get out of this tumbledown old place, I don't like it a bit. Something came down the chimney on me, and I nearly had a fit. Come on, Jack, I want to go.'

'Yes, but wait,' said Jack, suddenly remembering. 'What about Susie and Jeff? They must be somewhere here too. We ought to look for them.'

'We'll have to find out how they knew there was to be a meeting here tonight,' said George. 'Let's call them, Jack. Honestly, there's nobody else here now. *I'm* going to call them anyway!'

So he shouted loudly: 'JEFF! SUSIE! COME ON OUT, WHEREVER YOU ARE!'

His voice echoed through the old house, but nobody stirred, nobody answered.

'I'll go through the place with the torch,' said Jack, and the two boys went bravely into each broken-down, bare room, flashing the light all round.

There was no one to be seen. Jack suddenly felt anxious. Susie was his sister. What had happened to her?

'George, we must go back home as quickly as we can, and tell Mother that Susie's disappeared,' he said. 'And Jeff has too. Come on quick! Something may have happened to them.'

They went back to Jack's house as quickly as they could. As they ran to the front gate, Jack saw his mother coming back from her meeting. He rushed to her.

'Mother! Susie's missing! She's gone! Oh, Mother, she went to Tigger's Barn, and now she isn't there!'

His mother looked at him in alarm. She opened the front door quickly and went in, followed by the two boys.

'Now tell me quickly,' she said. 'What do you mean? Why did Susie go out? When – '

A door was flung open upstairs and a merry voice called out: 'Hallo, Mother! Is that you? Come and see Jeff's railway going! And don't scold us because it's so late; we've been waiting for Jack and George to come back.'

'Why, that's Susie,' said her mother, in surprise. 'What did you mean, Jack, about Susie disappearing. What a silly joke!'

Sure enough, there were Susie and Jeff upstairs, with the whole floor laid out with railway lines!

Jack stared at Susie in surprise and indignation. Hadn't she gone out, then? She grinned at him wickedly.

'Serves you right!' she said rudely. 'Who came spying on our Famous Five meeting? Who heard all sorts of things and believed them? Who's been all the way to Tigger's Barn in the dark? Who's a silly-billy, who's a – '

Jack rushed at her in a rage. She dodged behind her mother, laughing.

'Now, Jack, now!' said his mother. 'Stop that, please. What has been happening? Susie, go to bed. Jeff, clear up your lines. It's time for you to go. Your mother will be telephoning to ask why you are not home. JACK! Did you hear what I said? Leave Susie alone.'

Jeff went to take up his lines, and George helped him. Both boys were scared of Jack's mother when she was cross. Susie ran to her room and slammed the door.

'She's a wicked girl,' raged Jack, 'she – she – she – '

'Go and turn on the bath-water,' said his mother, sharply. 'You can both go without your supper now. I WILL NOT have this behaviour.'

George and Jeff disappeared out of the house as quickly as they could, carrying the boxes of railway things. George completely forgot what he had in his pocket – a pencilled note to someone called Cheeky Charlie, which he hadn't even read! Well, well, well!

CHAPTER TEN

Call a meeting!

GEORGE WENT quickly along the road with Jeff. Jeff chuckled.

'I say, you and Jack fell for our little trick beautifully, didn't you? Susie's clever, she laid her plan well. We all talked at the tops of our voices so that Jack would be sure to hear. We knew he was hiding in the laurel bush.'

George said nothing. He was angry that Susie and the Famous Five should have played a trick like that on the Secret Seven – angry that Jack had been so easily taken in – but, dear me, what curious results that trick had had!

Susie had mentioned Tigger's Barn just to make Jack and the Secret Seven think that the Famous Five had got hold of something that was going on there, and had talked about a make-believe Stumpy Dick and Twisty Tom. And lo and behold, something *was* going on there, not between Stumpy Dick and Twisty Tom, but between three mysterious fellows called Zeb, Larry, and had he heard the other man's name? No, he hadn't.

435

'You're quiet, George,' said Jeff, chuckling again. 'How did you enjoy your visit to Tigger's Barn? I bet it was a bit frightening!'

'It was,' said George, truthfully, and said no more. He wanted to think about everything carefully, to sort out all he had heard, to try and piece together what had happened. It was all jumbled up in his mind.

One thing's certain, he thought, suddenly. We'll have to call a meeting of the Secret Seven. How strange that the Famous Five should have played a silly joke on us and led us to Something Big – another adventure, I'm sure. Susie's an idiot, but she's done the Secret Seven a very good turn!

As soon as George got home he felt in his pocket for the note that Zeb had given him. He felt round anxiously. It would have been dreadful if he had lost it!

But he hadn't. His fingers closed over the folded piece of paper. He took it out, his hand trembling with excitement. He opened it, and read it by the light of his bedroom lamp.

Dear Charlie,

Everything's ready and going O.K. Can't see that anything can go wrong, but a fog would be very welcome as you can guess! Larry's looking after the points, we've arranged that. Don't forget the lorry, and get the tarpaulin truck cover marked with white at one corner. That'll save time in looking for the right load. It's clever of you to send out this load by truck, and collect it by lorry!

All the best,
Zeb

George couldn't make head or tail of this. What in the world was it all about? There was a plot of some kind, that was clear, but what did everything else mean?

George went to the telephone. Perhaps Peter wouldn't yet be in bed. He really MUST get on to him and tell him something important had happened.

Peter was just going to bed. He came to the telephone in surprise, when his mother called him to it.

'Hallo! What's up?'

'Peter, I can't stop to tell you everything now, but we went to Tigger's Barn, Jack and I, and there *is* something going on. We had quite an adventure, and – '

'You don't mean to tell me that that tale of Susie's was true!' said Peter, disbelievingly.

'No. At least, it was all made-up on her part, as you said, but all the same, something *is* going on at Tigger's Barn, Peter, something Susie didn't know about, of course, because she only mentioned the place in fun. But it's serious, Peter. You must call a meeting of the Secret Seven tomorrow evening after tea.'

There was a pause.

'Right,' said Peter, at last. 'I will. This is most odd, George. Don't tell me anything more over the phone, because I don't want Mother asking me too many questions. I'll tell Janet to tell Pam and Barbara there's a meeting tomorrow evening at five o'clock in our shed, and we'll tell Colin and Jack. Gosh! This sounds pretty mysterious.'

'You just wait till you hear the whole story!' said George. 'You'll be amazed.'

He put down the receiver, and got ready for bed, quite forgetting that he had had no supper. He couldn't stop thinking about the happenings of the evening. How odd that the password of the Secret Seven should be Cheeky Charlie, and there should be a real man called by that name!

And how extraordinary that Susie's bit of make-believe should suddenly have come true without her knowing it! Something *was* going on at Tigger's Barn!

He got into bed and lay awake for a long time. Jack was also lying awake thinking. He was excited. He wished he hadn't been shut up in that silly cupboard, when he might have been listening all the time. Still, George seemed to have got quite a lot of information.

The Secret Seven were very thrilled the next day. It was difficult not to let the Famous Five see that they had something exciting on hand, but Peter had strictly forbidden anyone to talk about the matter at school, just in *case* that tiresome Susie, with her long ears, got to hear of it.

'We don't want the Famous Five trailing us

around,' said Peter. 'Just wait till this evening, all of you, and then we'll really get going!'

At five o'clock every single member of the Secret Seven was in the shed in Peter's garden. All of them had raced home quickly after afternoon school, gobbled their teas, and come rushing to the meeting.

The password was whispered quickly, as one after another passed into the shed, each wearing the badge with S.S. on. 'Cheeky Charlie, Cheeky Charlie, Cheeky Charlie.'

Jack and George had had little time to exchange more than a few words with one another. They were bursting to tell their strange story!

'Now, we're all here,' said Peter. 'Scamper, sit by the door and keep guard. Bark if you hear anything at all. This is a most important meeting.'

Scamper got up and went solemnly to the door. He sat down by it, listening, looking very serious.

'Oh, do hurry up, Peter,' said Pam. 'I can't wait a minute more to hear what it's all about!'

'All right, all right,' said Peter. 'You know that we weren't going to call another meeting till the Christmas hols, unless something urgent happened. Well, it's happened. Jack, you start off with the story, please.'

Jack was only too ready to tell it. He described how he had hidden in the laurel bush to overhear what the

Famous Five said at their meeting in the summer-house. He repeated the ridiculous story that Susie had invented to deceive the Secret Seven, and to send them off on a wild-goose chase just to make fun of them.

He told them how Peter had laughed at the story and said it *was* just in Susie's imagination, but how he and George had decided to go to Tigger's Barn just in case it wasn't.

'But I was right,' interrupted Peter. 'It *was* a story, but just by chance there was some truth in it, too, though Susie didn't know.'

George took up the tale. He told the others how he and Jack had gone to Tigger's Barn, thinking that Susie and Jeff were in front of them. And then came the thrilling part of their adventure in the old tumble-down house!

Everyone listened intently, and held their breath when George came to the bit where the three men arrived.

Then Jack told how he went to the doorway to listen, and fell into the cupboard, and George told how he had gone to look for Jack, and had said the password, Cheeky Charlie, which had had such surprising results.

'Do you mean to say, there actually *is* a man called Cheeky Charlie?' asked Barbara, in amazement. 'Our

password is only the name of a dog. Imagine there being a *man* called that, too! My goodness!'

'Don't interrupt,' said Peter. 'Go on, both of you.'

Everyone sat up with wide eyes when George told how the men had thought he was a messenger from Cheeky Charlie, and when he told them about the note they had given him, and produced it from his pocket, the Secret Seven were speechless with excitement!

The note was passed from hand to hand. Peter rapped on a box at last.

'We've all seen the note now,' he said. 'And we've heard Jack and George tell what happened last night. It's quite clear that we've hit on something strange again. Do the Secret Seven think we should try and solve this new mystery?'

Everyone yelled and banged on boxes, and

Scamper barked in excitement too.

'Right,' said Peter. 'I agree too. But we have got to be very, very careful this time, or else the Famous Five will try and interfere, and they might spoil everything. Nobody – NOBODY – must say a single word about this to anyone in the world. Is that agreed?'

It was. Scamper came up and laid a big paw on Peter's knee, as if he thoroughly agreed too.

'Go back to the door, Scamper,' said Peter. 'We depend on you to give us warning if any of those tiresome Famous Five come snooping round. On guard, Scamper.'

Scamper trotted back to his place by the door obediently. The Seven crowded more closely together, and began a grand discussion.

'First, let's sort out all the things that Jack and George heard,' said Peter. 'Then we'll try and make out what they mean. At the moment I'm in a muddle about everything and haven't the slightest idea what the men are going to do.'

'Right,' said Jack. 'Well, as I told you, I heard the men talking, but their voices were very low, and I could only catch words now and again.'

'What words were they?' asked Peter. 'Tell us carefully.'

'Well, they kept saying something about "loading

and unloading",' said Jack. 'And they kept on and on mentioning "points".'

'What sort of points?' asked Peter.

Jack shook his head, completely at a loss.

'I've no idea. They mentioned figures too. They said "six-two" quite a lot of times, and then they said "maybe seven-ten". And they said there mustn't be a moon, and I heard them talk about darkness, fog, and mist. Honestly, I couldn't make head or tail of it. I only know they must have been discussing some plan.'

'What else did you hear?' asked Janet.

'Nothing,' answered Jack. 'I fell into the cupboard then, and when the door shut on me I couldn't hear another word.'

'And all *I* can add is that the men asked me if Cheeky Charlie was at Dalling's or Hammond's,' said George. 'But goodness knows what *that* meant.'

'Perhaps they are the name of a workshop or works of some kind,' suggested Colin. 'We could find out.'

'Yes. We might be able to trace those,' said Peter. 'Now, this note. Whatever can it mean? It's got the word "points" here again. And they talk about trucks and lorries. It's plain that there's some robbery planned, I think. But what kind? They want fog, too. Well, that's understandable, I suppose.'

'Shall we take the note to the police?' said Barbara, suddenly gripped by a bright idea.

'Oh no! Not yet!' said George. 'It's *my* note and I'd like to see if we can't do something about it ourselves before we tell any grown-ups. After all, we've managed lots of adventures very well so far. I don't see why we shouldn't be able to do something about this one too.'

'I'm all for trying,' said Peter. 'It's so exciting. And we've got quite a lot to go on, really. We know the names of three of the four men – Zeb, which is probably short for Zebedee, a most unusual name; and Larry, probably short for Laurence; and Cheeky Charlie, who is perhaps the boss.'

'Yes, and we know he's at Dalling's or Hammond's,' said Jack. 'What do we do first, Peter?'

Scamper suddenly began to bark wildly and scrape at the door.

'Not another word!' said Peter, sharply. 'There's someone outside!'

CHAPTER ELEVEN

Any ideas?

PETER OPENED the door. Scamper tore out, barking. Then he stopped by a bush and wagged his tail. The Secret Seven ran to him.

A pair of feet showed at the bottom of the bush. Jack gave a shout of rage and pushed into the bush. He dragged someone out – Susie!

'How dare you!' he yelled. 'Coming here and listening! How dare you, Susie?'

'Let me go,' said Susie. 'I like you asking me how I dare! I'm only copying what *you* did on Saturday! Who hid in the laurel bush, and – '

'How did you know we were having a meeting?' demanded Jack, shaking Susie.

'I just followed you,' said Susie, grinning. 'But I didn't hear anything because I didn't dare to go near the door, in case Scamper barked. I did a sudden sneeze, though, and he must have heard me. What are you calling a meeting about?'

'As if we'd tell you!' said Peter, crossly. 'Go on home, Susie. Go on! Jack, take her home. The meeting is over.'

'Bother!' said Jack. 'All right. Come on, Susie. And if I have any nonsense from you, I'll pull your hair till you yell!'

Jack went off with Susie. Peter faced round to the others and spoke in a low voice.

'Listen. All of you think hard about what has been said, and give me or Janet any good ideas tomorrow. It's no good going on with this meeting. Somebody else belonging to the Famous Five might come snooping round too.'

'Right,' said the Secret Seven, and went home, excited and very much puzzled. *How* could they think of anything that would help to piece together the jumble of words they knew? Points. Six-two, seven-ten. Fog, mist, darkness. Dalling's. Hammond's.

Each of them tried to think of some good idea. Barbara could think of nothing at all. Pam tried asking her father about Dalling's or Hammond's. He didn't know either of them. Pam felt awkward when he asked her why she wanted to know, and didn't go on with the subject.

Colin decided that a robbery was going to be done one dark and foggy night, and that the goods were to be unloaded from a lorry somewhere. He couldn't imagine why they were to be sent in a truck. All the boys thought exactly the same thing, but, as Peter said, it wasn't much help because they didn't know what date, what place, or what lorry!

Then Jack had quite a good idea. He thought it would be helpful if they tried to find a man called Zebedee, because surely he must be the Zeb at Tigger's Barn. There couldn't be *many* Zebedees in the district!

'All right, Jack. It's a good *idea*,' said Peter. 'You can do the finding out for us. Produce this Zeb, and that may be the first step.'

'Yes, but how shall I find out?' said Jack. 'I can't go round asking every man I meet if he's called Zeb.'

'No. That's why I said it was a good *idea*,' said Peter, grinning. 'But that's about all it is. It's an impossible thing to do, you see; so that's why it will remain just a good idea and nothing else. Finding the only Zebedee in the district would be like looking for a needle in a haystack.'

'I shouldn't like to have to do *that*,' said Janet, who was with them. 'Peter and I have got about the only good idea, I think, Jack.'

'What's that?' asked Jack.

'Well, we looked in our telephone directory at home to see if any firm called Dalling or Hammond was there,' said Janet. 'But there wasn't, so we thought they must be somewhere farther off, not in our district at all. Our telephone book only gives the names of people in this area, you see.'

'And now we're going to the post-office to look in the big telephone directories there,' said Peter. 'They give the names of districts much farther away. Like to come with us?'

Jack went with them. They came to the post-office and went in. Peter took up two telephone books, one with the Ds in and one with the Hs.

'Now I'll look for Dalling,' he said, and thumbed through the Ds. The other two leaned over him, looking down the Ds too.

'Dale, Dale, Dale, Dales, Dalgleish, Daling, Dal-ish, Dallas, DALLING!' read Peter, his finger following down the list of names. 'Here it is – Dalling. Oh, there are three Dallings! Bother!'

'There's a Mrs A. Dalling, Rose Cottage, Hubley,' said Janet. 'And E.A. Dalling, of Manor House, Tallington, and Messrs. E. Dalling, Manufacturers of Lead Goods. Well – which would be the right Dalling? The manufacturers, I suppose.'

'Yes,' said Peter, sounding excited. 'Now for the Hs. Where are they? In the other book. Here we are – Hall, Hall – goodness, what a lot of people are called Hall! Hallet, Ham, Hamm, Hammers, Hamming, Ham-mond, Hammond, Hammond, Hammond – oh, LOOK!'

They all looked. Peter was pointing to the fourth name of Hammond. 'Hammond and Co.' Ltd. Lead manufacturers, Petlington.'

450

'There you are,' said Peter, triumphantly. 'Two firms dealing in lead, one called Hammond, one called Dalling. Cheeky Charlie must be something to do with both.'

'Lead!' said Jack. 'It's very valuable nowadays, isn't it? I'm always reading about thieves going and stealing it off church roofs. I don't know why churches so often have lead roofs, but they seem to.'

'It looks as if Cheeky Charlie might be going to send a load of lead off somewhere in a truck, and Zeb and the others are going to stop it, and take the lead,' said Peter. 'As you say, it's very valuable, Jack.'

'Charlie must have quite a high position if he's in both firms,' said Janet. 'Oh, dear – I do wonder what his real name is! Cheeky Charlie! I wonder why they call him that?'

'Because he's bold and has got plenty of cheek, I expect,' said Peter. 'If only Hammond's and Dalling's weren't so far away! We could go and snoop round there and see if we could hear of anyone called Cheeky Charlie.'

'They're miles away,' said Jack, looking at the addresses. 'Well, we've been quite clever, but I don't see that we've got very much farther, really. We just know that Dalling's and Hammond's are firms that deal in lead, which is very valuable stuff, but that's all!'

'Yes. It doesn't take us very far,' said Peter, shutting up the directory. 'We'll have to think a bit harder. Come on, let's go and buy some sweets. Sucking a bit of toffee always seems to help my thinking!'

CHAPTER TWELVE

A game – and a brainwave!

ANOTHER DAY went by, and Saturday came. A meeting was called for that morning, but nobody had much to say. In fact, it was rather a dull meeting after the excitement of the last one. The Seven sat in the shed eating biscuits provided by Jack's mother, and Scamper was at the door, on guard as usual.

It was raining outside. The Seven looked out dismally.

'No good going for a walk, or having a game of football,' said Peter. 'Let's stay here in the shed and play a game.'

'Fetch your railway set, Peter,' said Janet. 'And I'll fetch the farm set. We could set out the lines here in the midst of the toy trees and farm buildings, looking as if they were real countryside. We've got heaps of farm stuff.'

'Oh yes. Let's do that,' said Pam. 'I love your farm set. It's the nicest and biggest I've ever seen. Do get it! We could set it out, and the boys could put up the railway.'

'It's a jolly good thing to do on a rainy morning like

this,' said Jack, pleased. 'I wanted to help Jeff with *his* fine railway the other day, when George came to tea with me, but he was Susie's guest, and she wouldn't have let us join in for anything. You know, she's very suspicious that we're working on something, Peter. She keeps on and on at me to tell her if anything happened at Tigger's Barn that night.'

'Well, just shut her up,' said Peter. 'Scamper, you needn't watch the door any more. You can come and join us, old fellow. The meeting's over.'

Scamper was pleased. He ran round everyone, wagging his tail. Peter fetched his railway set, and Janet and Pam went to get the big farm set. It had absolutely everything, from animals and farm men to trees, fences, troughs and sties!

They all began to put up the two sets – putting together the lines and setting out a proper little countryside, with trees, fences, animals and farm buildings. It really was fun.

Peter suddenly looked up at the window. He had noticed a movement there. He saw a face looking in, and leapt up with such a fierce yell that everyone jumped in alarm.

'It's Jeff,' he cried. 'I wonder if he's snooping round for the Famous Five. After him, Scamper!'

But Jeff had taken to his heels, and, even if Scamper had caught him, nothing would have happened, because the spaniel knew Jeff well and liked him.

'It doesn't really matter Jeff looking in,' said Janet. 'All he'd see would be us having a very peaceful game! Let him stand out in the rain and look in if he wants to!'

The railway lines were ready at last. The three beautiful clockwork engines were attached to their line of trucks. Two were passenger trains and one was a goods train.

'I'll manage one train, you can do another train, Colin, and you can have a third one, Jack,' said Peter. 'Janet, you do the signals. You're good at those. And, George, you work the points. We mustn't have an accident. You can always switch one of the trains on to another line, if two look like crashing.'

'Right. I'll manage the points,' said George, pleased. 'I like doing those. I love seeing a train being switched off a main-line into a siding.'

The engines were wound up and set going. They tore round the floor, and George switched them cleverly from one line to another when it seemed there might be an accident.

And, in the middle of all this, Janet suddenly sat up straight, and said in a loud voice: 'WELL, I NEVER!'

The others looked at her.

'What's the matter?' said Peter. 'Well, I never *what*? Why are you looking as if you are going to burst?'

'Points!' said Janet, excitedly. 'Points!' And she waved her hand to where George was sitting working the points, switching the trains from one line to another. 'Oh Peter, don't be so *stupid*! Don't you remember? Those men at Tigger's Barn talked about *points*. Jack said they kept *on* mentioning them. Well, I bet they were *points on some railway line*!'

There was a short silence. Then everyone spoke at

once. 'Yes! It could be! Why didn't we think of it before? Of course! Points on the railway!'

The game stopped at once and an eager discussion began.

'Why should they use the points? It must be because they want to switch a train on to another line.'

'Yes, a train that contains something they want to steal – lead, probably!'

'Then it's a goods train. One of the trucks must be carrying the lead they want to steal!'

'The tarpaulin! Would that be covering up the load? Don't you remember? It had to be marked with white at the corner, so that the men would know it.'

'Yes! They wouldn't have to waste time then looking into every truck to see which was the right one. Sometimes there are thirty or forty trucks on a goods train. The white marks on the tarpaulin would tell them at once they had the right truck!'

'Woof,' said Scamper, joining in the general excitement.

Peter turned to him. 'Hey, Scamper, on guard at the door again, old fellow!' he said, at once. 'The meeting's begun again! On guard!'

Scamper went on guard. The Secret Seven drew close together, suddenly very excited. To think that one simple word had set their brains working like this, and put them on the right track at once!

'You are really clever, Janet,' said Jack, and Janet beamed.

'Oh, anyone might have thought of it,' she said. 'It just rang a bell in my mind somehow, when you kept saying "points". Oh, Peter, where are these points, do you think?'

Peter was following out another idea in his mind. 'I've thought of something else,' he said, his eyes shining. 'Those figures the men kept saying. Six-two, seven-ten. Couldn't they be the times of trains?'

'Oh *yes*! Like when we say Daddy's going to catch the six-twenty home, or the seven-twelve!' cried Pam.

'Six-two – there must be a train that starts somewhere at six-two. Or arrives somewhere then.'

'And they want a foggy or misty, dark night, because then it would be easy to switch the train into some siding,' said Jack. 'A foggy night would be marvellous for them. The engine-driver couldn't possibly see that his train had been switched off on the wrong line. He'd go on till he came to some signal, and the men would be there ready to take the lead from the marked truck – '

'And they'd deal with the surprised engine-driver, and the guard too, I suppose,' said Colin.

There was a silence after this. It suddenly dawned on the Seven that there must be quite a big gang engaged in this particular robbery.

'I think we ought to tell somebody,' said Pam.

Peter shook his head. 'No. Let's find out more if we can. And I'm sure we can now! For instance, let's get a time-table and see if there's a train that arrives anywhere at two minutes past six – 6.2.'

'That's no good,' said Jack, at once. 'Goods trains aren't in the time-tables.'

'Oh no. I forgot that,' said Peter. 'Well, what about one or two of us going down to the station and asking a few questions about goods trains and what time they come in, and where from? We know where the firms of Dalling and Hammond are. Where was it now – Petlington, wasn't it?'

'Yes,' said Janet. 'That's a good idea of yours to go down to the station, Peter. It's stopped raining. Why don't you go now?'

'I will,' said Peter. 'You come with me, Colin. Jack and George have had plenty of excitement so far, but you haven't had very much. Come on down to the station with me.'

So off went the two boys, looking rather thrilled. They really were on the trail now!

Peter and Colin arrived at the station just as a train was coming in. They watched it. Two porters were on the platform, and a man stood with them in dirty blue overalls. He had been working on the line, and had hopped up on to the platform when the train came rumbling in.

The boys waited till the train had gone out. Then they went up to one of the porters.

'Are there any goods trains coming through?' asked Peter. 'We like watching them.'

'There's one in fifteen minutes' time,' said the porter.

'Is it a very long one?' said Colin. 'I once counted forty-seven trucks pulled by a goods engine.'

'The longest one comes in here in the evening,' said the porter. 'How many trucks do you reckon it has as a rule, Zeb?'

The man in dirty overalls rubbed a black hand over

his face, and pushed back his cap. 'Well, maybe thirty, maybe forty. It depends.'

The boys looked at one another. *Zeb*! The porter had called the linesman *Zeb*! Could it be – could it *possibly* be the same Zeb that had met the other two men at Tigger's Barn?

They looked at him. He wasn't much to look at, certainly, a thin, mean-faced little man, very dirty, and with hair much too long. Zeb! It was such an unusual name that the boys felt sure they must be face to face with the Zeb who had been up at the old tumbledown house.

'Er – what time does this goods train come in the evening?' asked Peter, finding his tongue again at last.

'It comes in about six o'clock twice a week,' said Zeb. 'Six-two, it's supposed to be here, but sometimes it's late.'

'Where does it come from?' asked Colin.

'Plenty of places!' said Zeb, 'Turleigh, Idlesston, Hayley, Garton, Petlington . . .'

'Petlington!' said Colin, before he could stop himself. That was the place where the firms of Dalling and Hammond were. Peter scowled at him, and Colin hurried to cover up his mistake in calling attention to the town they were so interested in.

'Petlington, yes, go on, where else?' said Colin.

The linesman gave him another string of names,

and the boys listened. But they had learnt already a good deal of what they wanted to know.

The 6.2 was a goods train, that came in twice a week, and Petlington was one of the places it came from, probably with a truck or two added there, full of lead goods from Hammond's and Dalling's! Lead pipes? Sheets of lead? The boys had no idea, and it didn't really matter. It was lead, anyway, valuable lead, they were sure of that! Lead sent off by Cheeky Charlie for his firms.

'We've been playing with my model railway this morning,' said Peter, suddenly thinking of a way to ask about points and switches. 'It's a fine one, it's got points to switch my trains from one line to another. Very good they are too, as good as real points!'

'Ah, you want to ask my mate about *them*,' said Zeb. 'He's got plenty to deal with. He uses them to switch the goods trains from one part of the line to another. They often have to go into sidings, you know.'

'Does he switch the 6.2 into a siding?' said Peter. 'Or does it go straight through on the main-line?'

'Straight through,' said Zeb. 'No, Larry only switches the goods trains that have to be unloaded near here. The 6.2 goes right on to Swindon. You'll see it this evening if you come down.'

Peter had given a quick look at Colin to see if he had noticed the name of Zeb's mate – Larry! Zeb and Larry – what an enormous piece of luck! Colin gave a quick wink at Peter. Yes, he had noticed all right! He began to look excited.

'I wish we could see Larry working the points,' said Peter. 'It must be fun. I expect the switches are quite different from the ones on my railway lines at home.'

Zeb laughed. 'You bet they are! Ours take some

moving! Look, would you like to walk along the line with me, and I'll show you some switches that send a train off into a siding? It's about a mile up the line.'

Peter took a look at his watch. He would be very late for his dinner, but this was really important. Why, he might see the very points that Larry was going to use one dark, foggy night!

'Look out the kids don't get knocked down by a train,' the porter warned Zeb, as the linesman took the two boys down on to the track with him.

The boys looked at him with scorn. As if they couldn't tell when a train was coming!

It seemed a very long way up the line. Zeb had a job of work not far from the points. He left his tools by the side of the line he was to repair, and took the boys to where a number of lines crossed one another. He explained how the points worked.

'You pull this lever for that line, see? Watch how the rails move so that they lead to that other line over there, instead of letting the train keep on this line.'

Colin and Peter did a little pulling of levers them-selves, and they found it exceptionally hard work.

'Does the 6.2 come on this line?' asked Peter, innocently.

'Yes. But it goes straight on; it doesn't get switched to one side,' said Zeb. 'It never has goods for this district; it goes on to Swindon. Now don't you ever mess about on the railway by yourselves, or the police will be after you straight away!'

'We won't,' promised the two boys.

'Well, I must get on with my job,' said Zeb, not sounding as if he wanted to at all. 'So long! Hope I've told you what you wanted to know.'

He certainly had, much, much more than he imagined. Colin and Peter could hardly believe their luck. They made their way to the side of the line, and stood there for a while.

A GAME – AND A BRAINWAVE!

'We ought really to go and explore the siding,' said Peter. 'But we're dreadfully late. Bother! We forgot to ask what evenings the goods train comes in from Petlington!'

'Let's get back, and come again this afternoon,' said Colin. 'I'm so hungry. We can find out the two days the goods train comes through when we're here this afternoon, and explore the siding too.'

They left the railway and went to the road. They were both so excited that they could hardly stop talking. 'Fancy bumping into Zeb! Zeb himself! And hearing about Larry in charge of the points! Why, everything's as plain as can be. What a good thing Janet had the brain-wave this morning about points! My goodness, we are in luck!'

'We'll be back this afternoon as soon as we can,' said Peter. 'I vote the whole lot of us go. Gosh, this *is* getting exciting!'

CHAPTER THIRTEEN

An exciting afternoon

BOTH PETER'S mother and Colin's were very angry when they arrived back so late for their dinner. Janet was so full of curiosity to know what had happened that she could hardly wait till Peter had finished. He kept frowning at her as he gobbled down his hot stew, afraid that she would ask some awkward questions.

He sent her round to collect the Secret Seven, and they all arrived in a very short time, though Colin was late because he had to finish his dinner.

Peter told them everything, and they listened, thrilled. Well, what a tale! To meet Zeb like that, and to have him telling them so much that they wanted to know!

'Little did he know why we asked him so many questions!' said Colin, with a grin. 'I must say he was quite nice to us, though he's a mean-looking man with shifty eyes.'

'This afternoon we will all go to the siding,' said Peter. 'We'll find out what days that goods train comes along, too.'

So off they went. First they went to the station and

found the porter again. He had nothing much to do and was pleased to talk to them. He told them tales of this, that and the other on the railway, and gradually Peter guided him to the subject of goods trains.

'Here comes one,' said the porter. 'It won't stop at the station, though – no passengers to get on or off, you see. Want to count the trucks? It's not a very long train.'

Most of the trucks were open ones, and they carried all kinds of things, coal, bricks, machinery, crates. The train rumbled by slowly, and the Seven counted thirty-two trucks.

'I'd rather like to see that goods train Zeb told us about,' said Peter to the porter. 'The one that comes from Petlington and beyond, the 6.2, I think he said. It's sometimes a very long one, isn't it?'

'Yes. Well, you'd have to come on Tuesday or Friday,' said the porter. 'But it's dark then, so you won't see much. Look, the guard of that last goods train is waving to you!'

They waved back. The goods train got smaller and smaller in the distance and at last disappeared.

'I wonder things aren't stolen out of those open trucks,' said Peter, innocently.

'Oh, they are,' said the porter. 'There's been a whole lot of stealing lately, yes, even a car taken out of one truck, though you mightn't believe it!

Some gang at work, they say. Beats me how they do it! Well, you kids, I must go and do a spot of work. So long!'

The Seven wandered off. They walked by the side of the track for about a mile until they came to where the points were that Zeb had explained that morning.

Peter pointed them out. 'That's where they plan to switch the goods train off to a side-line,' he said. 'I wish we knew which evening. I think it must be soon, though, because that note George got said that everything was ready and going O.K.'

They followed the side-line, walking by the side of the railway. The line meandered off all by itself and finally came into a little goods yard, which seemed to be completely deserted at that moment.

Big gates led into the goods yard. They were open to let in lorries that came to take the goods unloaded from trucks sent down the side-line. But only empty trucks stood on the little line now, and not a soul was about. It was plain that no goods train was expected for some time.

'This is a very lonely little place,' said Colin. 'If a goods train was diverted down here, nobody would hear it or see it, except those who would be waiting for it! I bet there will be a lorry creeping in here some evening, ready to take the lead sheets or pipes or whatever they are, from the truck whose tarpaulin is marked with white lines!'

'What about coming here on Tuesday evening, just in *case* that's the night they've arranged?' said Jack, suddenly. 'Then, if we saw anything happening, we could telephone the police. And before Zeb and Larry and the other two could finish their unloading we could get the police here. I say, wouldn't that be a thrill?'

'I don't know. I think really we ought to get in touch with that big Inspector we like,' said Peter. 'We know quite enough now to be sure of what we say. The only thing we *don't* know is whether it's this Tuesday or if it's to be later on.'

They stood together, arguing, and nobody saw a burly policeman sauntering in through the open gates. He stared when he saw the children, and stood watching them.

'I'd like to see those points,' said Colin, getting tired of the argument. 'Show me them, Peter. We'll look out for trains.'

Peter forgot that children were not allowed to trespass on the railway lines. He set off up the side-line with the others, walking in the middle of the lines on his way to the points.

A loud voice hailed them. 'Hey, you kids there! What do you think you're doing, trespassing like that? You come back here. I've got something to say to you.'

'Let's run!' said Pam, in a panic. 'Don't let him catch us.'

'No. We can't run,' said Peter. 'I forgot we ought not to walk on the lines like this. Come back and explain, and if we say we're sorry, we'll be all right!'

So he led all the Seven back into the goods yard. The policeman came up to them, frowning.

'Now you look here,' he said; 'there's been too much nonsense from children on the railways lately. I've a good mind to take all your names and addresses and make a complaint to your parents about you.'

'But we weren't doing a thing!' said Peter, indignantly. 'We're sorry we trespassed, but honestly we weren't doing a scrap of harm.'

'What are you doing in this here goods yard?' said the policeman. 'Up to some mischief, no doubt!'

'We're not,' said Peter.

'Well, what did you come here for, then,' said the policeman. 'Go on, tell me. You didn't come here for nothing.'

'Tell him,' said Barbara, frightened and almost crying.

The policeman became very suspicious at once when he heard that there was something to tell. 'Oho! So there *was* something you were after!' he said. 'Now you just tell me, or I'll take your names and addresses!'

Peter wasn't going to tell this bad-tempered man anything. For one thing, he wouldn't believe the extraordinary tale that the Secret Seven had to tell, and for another, Peter wasn't going to give all his secrets away! No, if he was going to tell anyone, he would tell his father, or the Inspector they all liked so much!

It ended in the big policeman losing his temper thoroughly and taking down all their names and addresses, one by one. It was really maddening. To think they had come there to help to catch a gang of clever thieves, and had had their names taken for trespassing!

'I'll get told off if my father hears about this,'

said Colin, dolefully. 'Oh, Peter, let's tell our nice Inspector everything, before that policeman goes round to our parents.'

But Peter was angry and obstinate. 'No!' he said. 'We'll settle this affair ourselves, and the police can come in at the last moment, when we've done everything, yes, that horrid man, too, who took our names. Think of his face if he has to come along to this goods yard one night to catch thieves *we've* tracked down, instead of him! I'll feel jolly pleased to crow over him!'

'I'd like to come, too, on that night,' said Janet.

'Well I think just a few of us should go. If things turn dangerous it'll be better if there's just four of us rather than seven!'

No one could argue with that, so they decided that Jack, Colin, George and Peter should go alone.

CHAPTER FOURTEEN

Tuesday evening at last!

THERE WAS a meeting the next morning to talk over everything and to make arrangements for Tuesday. It was a proper November day, and a mist hung everywhere.

'My father says there will be a fog before tomorrow,' announced Peter. 'If so those men are going to be lucky on Tuesday. I don't expect the driver of the engine will even guess his train's on the side-line when the points send him there! He won't be able to see a thing.'

'I wish Tuesday would buck up and come,' said Jack. 'Susie *knows* there's something up, and she and her Famous Five are just *longing* to know what it is! Won't she be wild when she knows that it was her silly trick that put us on to all this?'

'Yes. I guess that will be the end of the Famous Five,' said Colin. 'Hey, Peter, look here. I managed to get hold of a railway map. My father had one. It shows the lines from Petlington, and all the points and everything. Jack, do you think it could have been a map like this that Zeb and Larry and the other man were looking at in Tigger's Barn?'

'Yes. It may have been,' said Jack. 'I bet those men have played this kind of game before. They know the railway so well. Oh, I do wish Tuesday would come!'

Tuesday did come at last. Not one of the Secret Seven could do good work at school that day. They kept on and on thinking of the coming night. Peter looked out of the window a hundred times that morning!

'Dad was right,' he thought. 'The fog did come down, a real November fog. And tonight it will be so thick that there will be fog-signals on the railways. We shall hear them go off.'

The four boys had arranged to meet after tea, with Scamper. Peter thought it would be a good thing to take him with them in case anything went wrong.

They all had torches. Peter felt to see if he had any sweets in his pocket to share with his friends. He had! Jolly good! He shivered with excitement.

He nearly didn't go with the others, because his mother saw him putting his coat on, and was horrified to think that he was going out into the fog.

'You'll get lost,' she said. 'You mustn't go.'

'I'm meeting the others,' said Peter, desperately. 'I *must* go, Mummy.'

'I really can't let you,' said his mother. 'Well – not unless you take Scamper with you. He'll know the way home if you don't!'

TUESDAY EVENING AT LAST!

'Oh, I'm taking Scamper, of *course*,' said Peter thankfully, and escaped at once, Scamper at his heels. He met the others at his gate and they set off.

The thick fog swirled round them, and their torches could hardly pierce it. Then they heard the bang-bang of the fog-signals on the railway.

481

'I bet Zeb and the rest are pleased with this fog!' said Colin. 'Look, there's the fence that runs beside the railway. If we keep close to that we can't lose our way.'

They arrived at the goods yard about five minutes to six, and went cautiously in at the gates, which were open. All the boys had rubber-soled shoes on, and they carefully switched off their torches as they went quietly into the goods yard.

They heard the sound of a lorry's engine throbbing, and stopped. Voices came to them, low voices, and then they saw a lantern held by someone.

'The gang are here, and the lorry sent by Cheeky Charlie!' whispered Jack. 'You can just see it over there. I bet it's got the name of Hammond or Dalling on it!'

'It *was* this Tuesday,' said Colin, in relief. 'I did hope we hadn't come all the way here in this fog for nothing.'

Bang! Bang-bang!

More fog-signals went off and yet more. The boys knew when trains were running over the main-line some distance away because of the sudden explosions of the fog-signals, warning the drivers to look out for the real signals or to go slowly.

'What's the time?' whispered George.

'It's about half-past six now,' whispered back

Peter. 'The 6.2 is late because of the fog. It may be along any time now, or it may be very late, of course.'

BANG! Another fog-signal went off in the next few minutes. The boys wondered if it had gone off under the wheels of the late goods train.

It had. The driver put his head out of his train and looked for the signal. It shone green. He could go on. He went on slowly, not knowing he was on the wrong line! Larry was there at the points, well-hidden by the darkness and the fog, and he had switched the goods train carefully on to the little side-line!

The goods train left the main-line. It would not go through the station tonight, it would only go into the little goods yard, where silent men awaited it. Larry switched the levers again, so that the next train would go safely on to the main-line. He did not want half a dozen trains on the side-line together! Then he ran down the single-line after the slow-moving train.

'It's coming! I can hear it,' whispered Peter suddenly, and he caught hold of Jack's arm. 'Let's go over there by that shed. We can see everything without being seen. Come on!'

Rumble-rumble-rumble! The goods train came nearer. The red eye of a lamp gleamed in the fog. Now what was going to happen?

CHAPTER FIFTEEN

In the goods yard

A FOG-SIGNAL went off just where the gang wanted the train to stop. Bang!

The engine pulled up at once, and the trucks behind clang-clanged as they bumped into one another. A hurried talk had gone on between Zeb, Larry and four other men by the coach. The boys could hear every word.

'We'll tell him he's on the wrong line. We'll pretend to be surprised to see him there. Larry, you tell him he'd better stay on this side-line till the fog clears and he can get orders and go back. Take him off to that shed and hot up some tea or something. Keep him there while we do the job!'

The others nodded.

Peter whispered to Jack: 'They're going to tell the engine-driver that he's run off the main-line by mistake into this side-line, and then take him off out of the way, the guard too, I expect. There won't be any fighting, which is a good thing.'

'Sh!' said Jack. 'Look, the engine-driver is jumping down. He's lost, I expect! Doesn't know where he is!'

'Hey, there, engine-driver, you're on the side-line!' called Larry's voice, and he ran up to the engine, a lamp swaying in his hands. 'You ought to be on the main-line, running through the station.'

'Ay, I should be,' said the driver, puzzled. 'There must have been some mistake at the points. Am I safe here, mate?'

'Safe as can be!' called back Larry, cheerily. 'Don't you worry! You're in a goods yard, well out of the way of main-line traffic. Better not move till you get orders, this fog's terrible!'

'Good thing I got on to a side-line, that's all I can say,' said the driver. The guard came up at that moment from the last van, and joined in the conversation. He thought it peculiar.

'Someone making a mess of the points,' he grumbled. 'Now we'll be here for the night, and my missus is expecting me for supper.'

'Well, you may be home for breakfast if the fog clears,' said the driver, comfortingly.

The guard didn't think so. He was very gloomy.

'Well, mates, come along to this shed,' said Larry. 'There's an oil-stove there, and we'll light up and have a cup of something hot. Don't worry about telephoning for orders. I'll do all that.'

'Who are you?' asked the gloomy guard.

'Who, me? I'm in charge of this yard,' said Larry,

most untruthfully. 'Don't you worry now. It's a blessing you got on to this side-line. I bet your orders will be to stay here for the night. I'll have to find somewhere for you to settle down.'

They all disappeared into the shed. A glow soon came from the window. Peter daringly peeped in, and saw the three men round an oil stove, and a kettle on top to boil water for tea.

Then things moved remarkably quickly. Zeb disappeared down the side-line to look for the truck covered by the tarpaulin with white marks. It was the seventh one, as he informed the others when he came back.

'We'll start up the lorry, and take it to the truck,' he said. 'Fortunately it's just where the yard begins, so we shan't have to carry the stuff far. Good thing, too, because it's heavy.'

The lorry was started up, and ran cautiously up the yard to the far end. There it stopped, presumably by the seventh truck. The four boys went silently through the fog and watched what happened for a minute or two.

The men were untying the tarpaulin by the light of a railway lantern. Soon it was entirely off. Jack could see the white paint at one corner that had marked it for the men.

Then began a pulling and tugging and painting as

the men hauled up the goods inside. What were they? The boys couldn't see.

'Sheets of lead, I think,' whispered Colin. 'Peter, when are we going to telephone the police? Don't you think we'd better do that now?'

'Yes,' whispered back Peter. 'Come on. There's a telephone in that little brick building over there. I noticed telephone wires going to the chimney there this afternoon. One of the windows is a bit open. We'll get in there. Where's Scamper? Oh, there you are. Now, not a sound, old boy!'

Scamper had behaved perfectly. Not a bark, not a whine had come from him, though he was very puzzled by the evening's happenings. He trotted at Peter's heels as the four boys went to telephone.

They had to pass the lorry on the way. Peter stopped dead and listened. No one was in the lorry. The men were still unloading the truck.

To the astonishment of the other three, he left them, leapt up into the driving seat and down again.

'Whatever are you doing?' whispered Jack.

'I took the key that turns on the engine!' said Peter, excited. 'Now they can't drive the lorry away!'

'Gosh!' said the others, lost in admiration at Peter's quickness. 'You *are* smart, Peter!'

They went to the little stone building. The door was locked, but, as Peter said, a window was open just a little. It was easy to force it up. In went Peter and flashed his torch round quickly to find the telephone. Ah yes, there it was. Good!

He switched off his torch and picked up the receiver. He heard the operator's voice.

'Number, please?'

'Police station – quickly!' said Peter.

And in two seconds a voice came again. 'Police station here.'

'Is the Inspector there, please?' asked Peter, urgently. 'Please tell him it's Peter, and I want to speak to him quickly.'

This peculiar message was passed on to the Inspector, who happened to be in the room. He came to the telephone at once.

'Yes, yes? Peter who? Oh *you*, Peter! What's up?'

Peter told him. 'Sir, I can't tell you all the details now, but the 6.2 goods train has been switched off the main-line on to the side-line here, near Kepley, where there's a goods yard. And there is a gang of men unloading lead from one of the waggons into a lorry nearby. I think a man called Cheeky Charlie is in charge of things, sir.'

'Cheeky Charlie! Chee – How do *you* know anything about that fellow?' cried the Inspector, filled with amazement. 'All right, don't waste time telling me now. I'll send men out straight away. Look out for them, and look out for yourselves too. That gang is dangerous. Cheeky Charlie, well, my word!'

CHAPTER SIXTEEN

Hurrah for the Secret Seven!

IT SEEMED a long time before any police cars came. The four boys were so excited that they could not keep still. Peter felt as if he really must go and see how the gang was getting on.

He crept out into the yard, and made his way to the lorry. It was dark there, and quiet. He crept forward, and suddenly bumped into someone standing still beside it.

The someone gave a shout and caught him. 'Here, who's this? What are you doing?'

Then a light was flashed on him, and Zeb's voice said: 'You! The kid who was asking questions the other day! What are you up to?'

He shook Peter so roughly that the boy almost fell over. And then Scamper came flying up!

'Grrrrrrrr!' He flew at Zeb and nipped him sharply on the leg. Zeb gave a yell. Two of the other men came running up. 'What's the matter? What's up?'

'A boy – and a dog!' growled Zeb. 'We'd better get going. Is the unloading finished? That kid may give the alarm.'

'Where is he? Why didn't you hang on to him?' said one of the men, angrily.

'The dog bit me, and I had to let the boy go,' said Zeb, rubbing his leg. 'They've both disappeared into the fog. Come on, hurry, I've got the wind up now.'

Peter had shot back to the others, alarmed at being so nearly caught. He bent down and fondled Scamper. 'Good boy!' he whispered. 'Brave dog! Well done, Scamper!'

Scamper wagged his tail, pleased. He didn't understand in the least why Peter should have brought him to this peculiar place in a thick fog, but he was quite happy to be with him anywhere.

'When's that police car coming?' whispered Colin, shivering as much with excitement as with cold.

'Soon, I expect,' whispered back Peter. 'Ah, here it comes – no, two of them!'

The sound of cars coming down the road that led to the goods yards was plainly to be heard. They came slowly, because of the fog. They would have got there very much more quickly if the evening had been clear.

They came into the yard and stopped. Peter ran to the first one. It was driven by the Inspector, and had four policemen in it. The second car was close behind, and policemen in plain clothes tumbled swiftly out of it.

'Sir! You've come just in time!' said Peter. 'Their lorry is over there. They've loaded it now. You'll catch them just at the right moment!'

The police ran over to the dark shape in the fog, the big lorry. Zeb, Larry, Cheeky Charlie and the other men were all in it, with the load of lead behind, but try as Zeb would he could not find the starting-key of the lorry!

'Start her up quickly, you ninny!' said Cheeky Charlie. 'The police are here! Drive the lorry at them if they try to stop us!'

'The key's gone. It must have dropped down,' wailed Zeb, and flashed a torch on to the floor below the steering-wheel. But it was not a bit of good looking there, of course. It was safely in Peter's pocket!

The police closed round the silent lorry. 'Game's up, Charlie,' said the Inspector's stern voice. 'You coming quietly, or not? We've got you right on the spot!'

'You wouldn't have, if we could have got this lorry to move!' shouted Zeb, angrily. 'Who's got the key? That's what I want to know. Who's got it?'

'I have,' called Peter. 'I took it out myself so that you couldn't get away in the lorry!'

'Good boy! Smart lad!' said a nearby policeman, admiringly, and gave the delighted Peter a thump on the back.

The fog suddenly thinned, and the scene became clearer in the light of many torches and lamps. The engine-driver and the guard came out of the shed in amazement, wondering what was happening. They had been left comfortably there by Zeb, drinking tea and playing cards.

The gang made no fuss. It wasn't worth it, with so many strong men around! They were bundled into the police cars, which drove away at a faster speed than they had come, thanks to the thinning of the fog!

'I'll walk back with you,' said the Inspector's cheerful voice. 'There's no room in the cars for me now. There's a bit of a squash there at the moment!'

He told the engine-driver to report what had happened to his headquarters by telephone, and left the astonished man, and the equally astonished fireman and guard, to look after themselves and their train.

Then he and the four boys trudged back to Peter's house. How amazed his mother was when she opened the door and found four of them with the big Inspector!

'Oh dear, what have they been up to now?' she said.

'A policeman has just been round complaining about Peter trespassing on the railway the other day, with his friends. Oh, don't say he's done anything terribly wrong!'

'Well, he's certainly been trespassing on the railway again,' said the Inspector, with a broad smile, 'but what he's done this time is terribly right, not terribly wrong. Let me come in and tell you.'

So, with a very excited Janet listening, the tale of that evening was told.

'And, you see,' finished the Inspector, 'we've got our hands on Cheeky Charlie at last. He's the boss of this gang that robs the goods trucks all over the place. A clever fellow but not *quite* so clever as the Secret Seven!'

The Inspector left at last, beaming, full of admiration once more for the Secret Seven. Peter turned to the others.

'Tomorrow,' he said solemnly, but with his face glowing – 'tomorrow we call a meeting of the Secret Seven – and we ask the Famous Five to come along too!'

'But why?' said Janet, surprised.

'Just so that we can tell them how the Secret Seven manage their affairs!' said Peter. 'And to thank them for putting us on the track of this most exciting adventure!'

'Ha! Susie won't like that!' said Jack.

'She certainly won't,' said Janet. 'Famous Five indeed! This will be the end of *them*!'

'Up with the Secret Seven!' said Jack, grinning. 'Hurrah for us – hip-hip-hurrah!'